DIAMONDS
ARE
TRUMPS

DIAMONDS
ARE
TRUMPS

by
Marty Slattery

St. Lukes Press
Memphis

St. Lukes Press
A Wimmer Company

Library of Congress Cataloging-in-Publication Data

Slattery, Martin J., 1938-
Diamonds Are Trumps / by Martin J. Slattery.
p. cm.
ISBN 0-918518-78-4
I. Title.
PS3569.L33D5   1990   89-48370
813'   .54--dc20   CIP

This book is a work of fiction, but like most works
of fiction, it is based on some real events
and real people. The names and details
have been changed in most instances
to protect the privacy and reputation
of those on whom this work is based.

For information address:
St. Lukes Press
4210 B.F. Goodrich Boulevard
Memphis, Tennessee 38118

" 'What matters it how far we go?' his scaly
  friend replied,
'There is another shore, you know, upon
  the other side.
The further off from England the nearer is
  to France—
Then turn not pale, beloved snail, but
  come and join the dance.
Will you, won't you, will you, won't you,
  will you join the dance?
Will you, won't you, will you, won't you,
  won't you join the dance?' "

"The Lobster-Quadrille"
ALICE'S ADVENTURES IN WONDERLAND

Pooh said, "Oh!" and "I didn't know,"
and thought how wonderful it would be
to have a Real Brain which could tell you
things.

THE HOUSE AT POOH CORNER

To:

Jo, the sweetest Murffle a
poor Bear could ask for.

and

To:

The Stockbroker and the Doctor
who made it all possible.

DIAMONDS
ARE
TRUMPS

The sign outside the ball park was blue and white;

LAWRENCE STADIUM
HOME OF THE
LODI DODGERS

Only the middle of May and it was already hot—ninety-some degrees.

Bill Mahoney stood behind the pitcher's mound, glove tucked under his arm, rubbing up a new baseball. The one in play a few moments earlier was last seen leaving Lawrence Stadium down the left-field line in a high graceful arc, foul by only a few feet. It went out just left of the sign on the outfield fence advertising Jameson Plumbing:

24 Hour Service
We'd Be Plumb Happy To Serve You

"Foo-o-o-o-oul ba-a-a-alll," intoned the umpire.

The public address announcer repeated it. Priscilla Penwick, the aging organist, pumped out several bars of "The Impossible Dream."

Bill glanced at the scoreboard. Top of the seventh. Two out. Giants 3. Dodgers 2. Count on the batter: 1 strike, 0 balls. No balls, he mused, still massaging the baseball, each hand rotating with an opposing motion as if he were trying to unscrew it. He scanned the stands near the announcer's booth. The old man wearing the white Panama hat seemed to be shaking his head. From the dugout came the raspy voice of manager John Christianson.

"Nuttin' but a long strike, kid," said J.C. "T'row smoke out dere."

Bill slipped the glove on and stepped back up on the mound.

He let his right arm hang loose and shook it. .... Come on, Arm, ... he said. .... Throw the goddam ball. .... His elbow hurt. It always hurt. All the way up to his ear. He examined the ball.

RAWLINGS
Cushioned Cork Center
5 oz.   9 in.

Two hundred sixteen raised red cotton stitches on the fat figure-eight cowhide cover. He knew because he had counted them.

"That's a *base*ball, Mahoney," yelled someone in the stands. A ripple of laughter flowed easily through the several hundred fans in attendance. That would be Harry, a bald, Buddha-like baseball buff often critical of play on the field. A transplanted New Yorker who had seen the Yankees play during their glory years, he seemed to view California League Class A baseball as a personal affront to his stature as a fan. Bill knew that Dean, Harry's equally vocal counterpart, would soon be entering the fray with some choice comments of his own.

He leaned forward, hands on his knees, and looked in to get the sign. A drop of sweat trickled off the end of his nose. The catcher, Dan "Loony" Lanoski, squatting stoically behind the plate like some prehistoric armadillo, flipped his index finger down out of a closed fist. The batter, six-feet, six-inches of strong young farmboy, stood ready at the plate.

Bill shook off the one finger that Loony displayed on the inside of his thick white thigh. Christ, Loony, he said to himself, not the fastball. This guy just hit the fastball downtown somewhere. Loony flashed the one finger again. Bill shook his head no. Up into the fist went the single digit—and down it came again. Bill straightened up and shook his head. Loony called time and trotted stiffly out to the mound, his knee movement restricted by shin guard straps.

"Go *tell* 'im, Lanoski," Dean yelled from the stands. "One's for the fastball, two's the curve ..."

"This guy can't hit the fastball," said Loony, his voice muffled through the face mask.

Both of them faced the center-field fence, ignoring the batter grooving his swing at the plate.

"You happen to see the last one leavin' the ball park?" said Bill.

"Luck," said Loony.

"That was a fastball," said Bill.

"Luck," said Loony. "J.C. says the book on this guy is hard stuff. Inside. On the hands ... in and tight."

Bill looked between the horizontal bars of the catcher's mask into the bright young eyes of Daniel Lanoski. Nineteen, maybe twenty, he thought. Nice kid. Good catcher. Prided himself on knowing the hitters.

"Hard stuff inside, eh?" said Bill.

"Yeh. In and tight. Show 'im the heater, Pops."

Pops ... Loony called him Pops. Some of the others too. J.C. called him Kid. But then J.C. was seventy-one years old. Loony was nineteen or twenty. And Bill ... well, for all they knew he was thirty-two. That's what he told them when he went to tryout camp that spring.

> Thirty-two, eh? Where you been playin'?
>
> Well, I been outta baseball for a few years.
>
> Yeh? Where'd you play when you *was* playin'?
>
> Oh ... Eastern League mostly. West Haven ... Glenn Falls. Played for Jim Davis.
>
> Jim Davis, eh?
>
> Yeh ... Up with the White Sox for a couple a years. Utility man ... good glove.
>
> Jim Davis ... Negro fella?
>
> No ... white.
>
> Hmmmm ... Can't say as I recall ...
>
> Helluva guy ... Came up in the late fifties.

What happened?

Well, like I said, good glove, no stick.

No, I mean to *you*?

Oh ... arm trouble.

Yeh?

Bone chips.

Bill displayed the ugly half-moon scar on the inside of his right elbow.

*   *   *   *   *

Bone chips. The Grinder. Makin' little ones outta big ones. The operation had been performed after his junior year in high school. That was the year that Clinton High captured the City 4A title and brought joy to the hearts of the Clinton Cougar alumni. None was more joyful than Coach Ernie Ballmeyer, unaffectionately known as "Ballbreaker" around the school. Ernie had labored in the darkness of Senior Civics and American History for the better part of his thirty-year tenure, attempting each spring to squeeze from young men of limited ability the cherished goal of a City Championship. It became an obsession; it was all he lived for. But arch rival Hamilton High spoiled even the best of his seasons.

Enter Bill Mahoney. A scrawny kid, tall for a freshman, though he never grew much more. He yearned to reach six feet, but never made it. Not much of a prospect if you just saw him slouching across the grim blacktop campus. Gawky. Awkward. But on a baseball diamond. On the mound. The hill. On that portion of the infield raised ten inches above the surrounding terrain. Put a baseball in his hand and place him on that blister of dirt and Bill Mahoney was King ... The fractured dread of those perilous days disappeared when he had a baseball in his hand. His body (not yet fully coherent) appeared to be grappling with forces of gravity unknown to others. Feet of incredible size stepped forward off the mound; arms and legs unfolded in random sections and a stick of a right arm came flailing madly from the top of that juvenile junk heap. Then the release; the final flick of the wrist that was almost disdainful. And the ball .... The ball came hurtling toward the plate at speeds impossible for young men to imagine. It literally exploded from those bony fingers. It became the size of a small, lethal gumdrop. To the frightened eye it looked as if it had a tail, like Halley's Comet. The sound that a slightly scuffed baseball makes moving toward home plate at speeds in excess of ninety miles an hour is a strange hissing sound. The first few tenths of a second after the ball is released there is a faint, impersonal *hissssss*. Then, as fear sharpens every sense, there is a quick shrill crescendo before the incongruous bass *thup!* in the catcher's glove, a sound that dampens itself quickly in the thick shroud of leather, a sound that is almost a non-sound, as if something were disappearing, being eaten. Less than half a second from hand to glove.

Steeeeeeeeerike!

And a sigh of relief from the batter. At least the ball hadn't hit him. With any luck the next two pitches would be strikes and he could repair to the safety of the dugout, only his pride slightly impaired. But alive. At least alive. Eight more guys before he'd have to hit again. Game might be over by then. Anything could happen.

Ballmeyer spotted him the first day. He remembered another Mahoney who had played for him a few years earlier. Not a great athlete, but a pleasant kid who knew his way around center field and hit for a respectable average. A check of the school records indicated that this scrawny kid was the younger brother. Eyes that had grown jaded watching pimply teen-agers stumble erratically from Masturbation to Music Appreciation to Executing the Sacrifice Bunt glowed with anticipatory fervor when they fell upon Bill Mahoney throwing a baseball. There would be no frosh or junior varsity seasons for young Mahoney. He was plucked from the faceless rabble and placed upon the Clinton Cougar varsity. The first year, Bill was plagued by inordinate wildness, often walking three or four batters in a row. And then striking out the side. Ballmeyer, his paunchy frame ill-suited to a baseball uniform, looking like a jumbo Boy Scout as he stood at the corner of the dugout, gnashed his teeth as Bill walked batter after batter.

> Throw strikes now, Billy. Hum it right
> in there. Right down the old pipe,
> Billy boy.

Under his muggy breath there were invectives and threats.

> Why can't the goddam kid throw
> *strikes*? ... *Jes*us! ...

Bill's control improved during his sophomore year and he was an All-League selection with an 8-1 record, his only loss coming on a one-hitter when Mike Faran booted an easy ground ball at third base and allowed the winning run to score. Ballmeyer raged about getting the glove *down* and getting in *front* of the goddam ball. But just the night before, Mike had managed to wrest from Prissy Darden her most prized possession: the pliable cloak of her virginity. It had taken some months, and it was not an easy matter to consummate that union in the cramped front seat of a 1939 Ford coupe, but in one night Mike learned something that Ernie Ballmeyer would never know: there were other things in life besides winning baseball games.

The arm trouble started in his junior year. Only a slight twinge at first. The elbow. A little swelling and pain after he pitched. He mentioned it to Ballmeyer.

> S'nothin', Billy, said the Coach. *Ev*erybody
> has a little arm trouble. *Ev*erybody ...
> Goes with the territory. Just growin' pains.
> Rest it for a few days. ...

They played every Tuesday and Friday and Ballmeyer continued to have him pitch every game. But the Coach secretly began to watch, checking to see if Bill was losing anything off the fastball. In the bargaining pews of his stained glass church, he pleaded with Eternal Forces for the proper maintenance of Bill Mahoney's strong right arm. It was the least he could do.

> Rest it on the weekends, said the
> Coach in answer to Bill's question
> about when he should rest his arm.

Chapter 1

We'll have it looked at this summer ...
after the season's over ...

Bill was the toast of the baseball establishment that year, and a terror to opposing batters. Everyone was talking about the Kid from Clinton. To complement his blazing fastball, he had developed a fair curveball and a devastating change. Looking for the Heater, the Smoke, when they came to the plate, batters found themselves foolishly lunging forward long before the delicate change-up drifted slowly by.

So Bill Mahoney played his junior year with strange sounds in his elbow, crunching noises as the bone chips got smaller and smaller each time the strong right arm whipped forward and the ball spun away, the red cotton stitches biting the air until near the end of its flight the ball began to rise, to hop, to do things that had major league scouts making coded notations in small black books. He pushed himself through the pain that tore at his arm.

The championship game with Hamilton was hardly a contest; they were cruelly overmatched. Bill struck out seventeen, walked one and allowed only two scratch hits, one a dribbler down the third-base line that Mike Faran, had he not been out feverishly banging the sweet secular form of Miss Prissy Darden until 3 A.M. the night before, probably could have handled with ease.

The man in the white Panama hat was seen to nod his approval. Ernie Ballmeyer was completely graceless in victory, pompous and condescending (after all, he still had Mahoney for another year), saying for publication that Hamilton had been outplayed *and* outcoached by the victorious Cougars.

True to his word, Ballmeyer got someone to look at Bill's arm after the season was over—a Doctor Highlen, who clucked his orthopedic tongue and devoutly took x-rays of The Arm like a tourist in Rome. The operation was performed in June and pronounced a success. Bill dutifully followed his rehabilitative regimen through the winter months and threw a baseball without pain on the first day of February. Ballmeyer hovered nearby, anxious as a nesting grouse.

How's it feel, Billy? Eh?
Okay, Coach. Feels good ... Good as
new. Good as *new,* Billy boy. A few
weeks and *whamo,* the old heater'll
be back. Just like the old days, eh
Billy? ... Zip zip *zip,* you're *out* ...

And he gave thanks at his stained glass church.

The pain came back later, near the end of the season. He pitched anyway. He used the change and the curve more often. No one seemed to notice.

He was five-feet eleven in his senior year (though when asked he would always say six feet), still thin, his boyish awkwardness replaced by an athlete's fluid grace. Girls began to hang around the ball field to watch him practice. Prissy Darden was among them, a stylish senior, pouty lips caked with Revlon Mantrap. Having lost Mike Faran to the fleshier fields of college coeds, she was in search of another trophy.

Bill's experience with women had been limited to several brief encounters. It was Mopsy Parker, the plumber's daughter, who initiated him into the inner circle one night in the back seat of Bongo Morrison's prewar Plymouth, numbing his genitals with a plumber's grip, playfully leaping on his outstretched lap. There was a disappointing tryst with Darlene Stentz who received the thrust of his lust on the tartan front of her new skirt. It never worked out. And there was the fair Louella Larkin with the cavernous eyes, scribbling poetry in the gloom of her attic, her spindly thighs welded together, sealed against sunlight and air. She kissed chastely and rarely, always smelling as if she had just eaten a hard-boiled egg. She had him read Pound and Dickinson. He wrote a poem called "Demon in My Eyes," but she didn't like it.

It was Prissy who invited him to the Spring Dance, accompanied him to the shrouded security of Lookout Mountain, moaned deliciously as he sprinted from foreplay to completion in less than four minutes. Well, she mused, nobody's perfect. Arm-in-arm they appeared on campus, the Jock and Maid

Prissy, she with his letterman sweater down to her knees, he with a Cheshire-cat grin. Ballmeyer tried to counsel him about sports and sex, but the latter subject was so alien to the Coach that he had trouble making his point.

> You know, Billy, that for an athlete,
> for a guy like yourself who has a real
> *fut*ure in sports, girls are ... not always
> the best thing ...
> Oh?
> Well, I mean girls are all *right*. Where
> would we be without girls, eh? Girls
> grow up to be *mot*hers ... most of
> them. And where would we be with-
> out mothers? ... But for the athlete ...
> the athlete has to think about ...
> conserving his strength ... You under-
> stand what I mean?
> I feel great, Coach ...
> Well, I know that, Billy. And you're
> pitchin' real good. Real good. You're
> approaching greatness ... But what I
> mean is that ... the night before a
> game you shouldn't ... I mean you
> *should* ... be in bed early ...

Ballmeyer was unable to say, "in bed *alone*." ... He was never sure just how much his students knew about such things.

Bill pitched through the pain, afraid to even think about it, testing it in secret moments, hoping it would go away. Or at least not get any worse. Clinton made it to the play-offs with ease, capturing their own league title undefeated. There was talk of Bill Mahoney being All-State, All-American, even, as some wag suggested in the Valley Greensheet, All-World. Big league scouts, stringers, anyone even casually connected with baseball called to offer him contracts, bonuses, advice and admonitions. Perfect strangers told him how to throw the curveball, screwball, change, knuckleball and slider. He re-

ceived unsolicited advice on how to invest money he didn't
have, how to pitch to batters he never heard of, how to avoid
summer colds, and a list of the best restaurants in New York
City.

Then in the first game of the play-offs, against the second-
place finisher from the Harbor League, the crummy *Harbor*
League, against a team with a nine-win, seven-loss record, an
unbelievable thing happened: Bill Mahoney had a bad game.
No zip on the fast ball. No curve on the curve. Ernie Ballmeyer
watched with grinding apprehension as the innings rolled by.
Two walks. A base hit. Two more walks. A strike-out.

That's it, Billy boy. That's the old zip, kid.

Then another walk. Two hits. Ballmeyer was not prepared for
Bill to have a bad game. Ever. But especially not in the play-
offs. Against a team from the crummy *Harbor* League. Lawndale
High School. Who ever heard of *Lawn*dale? And since Bill had
not had a bad game in nearly two years, Ballmeyer didn't have
anyone else who could pitch. Oh, he had a kid he brought up
from the junior varsity squad for the play-offs, a kid who could
throw some. But not a real pitcher. The score was 9-0 when
Ballmeyer reluctantly trudged to the mound and took Bill out
of the game. In the corner of the dugout where Bill sat alone,
the Coach approached and hissed his fervent accusation.

You were out *screwin'* last night,
weren't you? growled the Coach,
quietly enough so that everyone could
hear, the tone of his voice like that of
a bargain basement barrister accusing
the defendant of murdering a mild-
mannered priest, a crime he would
have considered no more heinous ...
Out screwin' ... *Jes*us, Mahoney ...

Bill did not look up. The kid from the J.V. squad threw two
shutout innings. Clinton rallied for six runs in the sixth inning.
But it was not enough. Mighty Clinton was felled by Crummy
Lawndale.

Chapter 1

The gaunt middle-aged man in the white Panama hat was heard to remark to the young phenom as he left the dressing room:

Hell's bells, kid ... No balls ...

though he did spare him the story of the time he played with a broken ankle in Shreveport. Dorothy Mahoney clucked her condolences (she had never been to a baseball game) and offered her son a large bowl of peach cobbler. He was not hungry, though he weakened when the ice cream was mentioned. The white Panama hat sat in the living room and read a newspaper that was two days old.

It was Prissy, that emissary from the natural order of grace, Prissy in her Daddy's four-door Nash, with her pulsating young body—it was Prissy who brought him respite from the pain. Curled up in the back seat, his cheek pressed against the naked curve of her teen-age tummy, he let the tears of frustration flow; tears that dropped unevenly on her lower abdomen and trickled down between her legs. He denounced Life and its unfairness into the moist triangle of her pubic hair. There there, she said. Later she told him it really felt freaky, but then she just stroked his hair and sobbed along with him.

One bad game does not a pitcher break; the scouts were just as eager as ever. Bill was certain that rest would heal his arm. He signed with the Chicago Cubs in the summer of '60 for a small bonus and headed for Rookie League with high hopes. He and Prissy pledged their undying love. In later years he would look back and wonder how things could have gone so wrong. But in the summer of '60 it seemed like a dream come true.

Bill gazed in at the stubby index finger that Loony displayed in the V between his thighs. He nodded his agreement, went into his windup and stepped forward, pushing hard off the pitching rubber. It was a good running fastball that moved in on the right-handed batter. The farmboy swung, but the pitch was in on the bat handle and he popped it harmlessly back to the screen. Maybe J.C.'s right, he thought. Maybe this guy can't hit the inside fastball. The next thought was less comforting: Maybe I can't throw another one inside.

Seventeen inches across home plate: a harsh and unrealistic width. Ask any pitcher. The difference between grooving it right down the middle and getting one in and tight was some eight inches. At most. More like three or four. A mistake would be a matter of a few paltry inches at a distance of sixty feet, six inches—or, as he figured it one day, 726 inches. You had to think the ball into an area that small; trying to actually *throw* it inside was useless. He always overcompensated—inside sent the batter scrambling for safety, outside was a foot outside. He knew he had to *think* Inside and Tight so that in some mysterious way his brain would communicate the tiny adjustments to his arm and fingers, perhaps even imparting to the ball itself a certain cellular intelligence, a rudimentary comprehension, directing it to the proper spot. He tried to concentrate, to block out the daily march of trivia that assaulted his mind like an eager Mongol horde, tried to focus and allow that Thing, that psychic, ball-guiding Thing to speed the ball on its way, homing it Inside and Tight.

"I gotta beer says this guy gets a base hit," boomed Harry from the first-base side of the stands.
"You're on," yelled Dean.

Inside and Tight, he thought, going into his windup. Inside

and Tight, speeding the small white sphere on its way toward the round brown mitt positioned just under the batter's hands. Unknowing, unthinking, its flight an afternoon gamble, the ball drifted Up and Out. The farmboy swung, meeting the ball squarely as it furrowed the air toward the safety of Loony's mitt. *Cra-a-a-a-ck!* ... The nostalgic sound of good dry ash hitting a baseball; a sound so clean, so joyous, so American, so urgent, that all idle activity in the stands came to a halt.

The ball was a blur as it headed toward short. Oh shit, said Bill. He knew it was too low to go out, but if it got over the shortstop it might find the gap in left-center and go all the way to the wall. Be an easy double. Maybe a triple if the farmboy had any speed. The shortstop, Charley Soprano, took a quick crossover step, leaped high in the air and snagged it for the out.

"All right, *Soapy*," yelled Frank Tenor from his third-base position.

Soprano and Tenor. Soapy and the Songbird. The singing infield. Dubbed the Dynamic Duet by a sportswriter from the *Lodi News Sentinel*, part of the tightest infield since Scrooge. (There were some irreverent references to the Virgin Mary, though not in print.)

Bill jogged off the field with the rest of the team as the *ooohhhhs* turned into appreciative applause.

"Good job, kid," said J.C., his right cheek bulging with Red Man chewing tobacco.

"Better thank Soapy," said Bill, knowing he'd been lucky.

"Ya done okay," said J.C. "Ya got 'em out. Dat's what counts ... Dance wit what brung ya."

Dance wit what brung ya: in a tight spot, use the pitch that *brung ya* to the big leagues; though California Class A baseball was not the big leagues, was in fact only slightly removed from Rookie League jungle ball as played in the provincial regions of Lethridge and Idaho Falls. To John Christianson, that pitch was always the fastball.

It was an expression he first heard when he arrived in the big leagues with the St. Louis Browns after a lengthy but undistinguished career in the minors. He was thirty-one at the time, a

Philadelphia-born, street-raised, splay-fingered catcher (each oft-broken finger like a signpost to a different city), already on the down side of a mediocre career. But he had been There, to the place they all dreamed about, that mythical kingdom, the Camelot of baseball: the Bigs. The Major Leagues. There were thirty, forty, sometimes fifty thousand people at those games. There were infields manicured to perfection by ground crews who magically transformed treacherous terrain into smooth, inviting, true-bounce carpets; nature-loving elves who kept outfield grass miraculously green and lush during the hottest months. There were dressing rooms, clubhouses like bridal suites at the best hotels; first-class travel, sums of money that would make oil sheiks green with envy; nubile young groupies, legs akimbo, living only to grasp a real major leaguer in their eager thighs; trinkets, treasures, baubles beyond their wildest dreams. The Bigs. Oh man ... the Bigs ...

Playing for the St. Louis Browns in 1941 had been none of those things. At least for John Christianson. He was a backup catcher, third string, who appeared in only ten major league games. His memory brought him a better picture, one that was kinder to an old man. Early in 1942 he traded his baseball uniform for the olive drab of the Marines and spent the next few years in the equatorial latitudes of Micronesia, occasionally assaulting a beach at Tarawa, Kwajalein, Truk or Saipan. He caught a mortar shell on Saipan and gonorrhea in Pearl City, but otherwise emerged unscathed.

After the war he went back to baseball; here, there, the minors, not much wanted. He was 36 in '46, a man of limited skills and mobility, a rough-hewn rock of rugged baseball sculpture, twenty-some years crouching behind that 17-inch slab, his hands a crooked testimony to the caustic bite of foul tips, his knees a watery reminder of what it was like to squat a hundred fifty times a day. He was wed in 1948 to Bobby Jo Worsten, a dumpy lady twice divorced from the same stubborn trucker, her face like Arizona flint, her heart like sluice-pure gold. But baseball was the only thing that John Christianson ever really loved: its sights, its smells, its special jargon. It ran through the middle of his heart. And baseball took care of him.

He managed and coached with several minor league teams, finally hooking on with the Dodger organization in the early '70s. Oh, he knew baseball, but nearly any decent high school coach knows enough to coach in the minors. The Dodgers recognized his greatest asset: he loved his kids. They put him with one of their low minor league teams where he was father, mother, Band-Aid dispenser (though they had a trainer to do that), counselor; his rag-bag face corrugated with concern as he watched his callow charges.

He still loved to take his old fungo bat and hit the pregame warm-up drills, singing his special chant through a cheekful of Red Man.

> Okay secun' base no-o-ow, hit da cutoff
> ... way to hum, kid. Get one now, one'n
> cover ... wayda *shoot*, kid. Glove down
> now, glove down, stay'n front. Two now,
> get two ... wayda *shoot*, kid. Roun'a horn
> now. Boom boom boom ... Who's
> coverin' eh? *T'row* it ... one'n follow ...
> bring it in ... Lookin' good now ... good
> t'rows now ...

The old fungo bat, cogent as a bishop's crozier, lovingly taped around the barrel to keep it from splintering, was like a magic wand in his gnarly hands. He could make a baseball dance with topspin, backspin, sidespin, make it curve like a banana, make it stop like a five-iron shot to the green. And he could hit those towering, twisting pop flies that had young catchers turning in circles till they were dizzy.

"Helluva play, Soapy," said Tenor.
"Nice grab," said Bill.
"Thanks," said Soapy, his eyes on the dugout floor, trying to avoid the praise. He knew it belonged to Jesus.

"*Ev*erybody rise for the seventh inning *stre-e-ee-e-etch*," said the announcer.
The organ warbled "Take Me Out to the Ball Game" and the fans sang along. All who could, stood to sing: old men with

tractor hats and roadmap faces, old women in sunbonnets—parents, grandparents, kids, infants cradled in the withered arms of the aged. Generations ...

> ... for it's *one, two, three* strikes you're out
> at the o-o-o-o-ld ba-a-a-ll ga-a-a-a-me ...

"Now turn to page twenty-two in your *pro*-gram (continued the public address announcer) and check your *lu*-cky *num*ber. This one's for two free passes to the *Cher*-o-kee *Roll*ercade. The lucky number *is* ... two one eight ... six ... *se*-ven ... Just bring your lucky *pro*gram to the press box and collect your two free *pass*es."

On the mound for the Giants, Ted Simpson was completing his warm-up tosses. He was a twenty-year-old right-hander who decided to forgo his final two years at U.S.C. when the San Francisco Giants made him an offer he couldn't refuse. The program had him listed at six-feet three, and two hundred twenty pounds. He had a fastball that had been clocked at one hundred miles an hour, an arm like a snake and a disposition to match.

"Your lucky baseball *bingo* numbers for the seventh *inn*ing are ... G twenty-three ... a-a-a-nd ... B fourteen. That's ..."
"*Bingo!*" yelled Harry.
"*Bingo!*" yelled Dean.
They had both been yelling "Bingo" since the first inning. Neither had a bingo card.

"Base hit now," said J.C. "We need a couple." He clapped his hands.
Gunner Gunderson, the lanky first baseman, stood in the on-deck circle swinging a weighted bat.
"One base hit comin' up," he said, striding toward the plate like a man with a mission.

The only Dodger coach, Art Sly, positioned himself in the third-base coaching box, ready to relay signs to the batter. Between pitches the batter looked Sly's way as he went through his intricate hand ballet: right hand to the bill of the cap, left hand to the ear lobe, right hand to the belt buckle, then brushed down the thigh, left hand across the chest, both hands to the bill of the cap. Was it the Hit and Run? The Take? The Sacrifice? ... Designed to confuse the opposition, to provide an element of surprise, they often merely confused the young Dodgers. Sly had a standard speech:

> ... Now I don't have to tell you guys
> it's the sign *after* I brush across my
> chest. *After*. Brushing across the chest
> is the *key* today. The *key* is to alert
> you to the *next* sign ... which is *it*. If I
> don't brush across my chest then
> *noth*in's on. You can stand at the plate
> and jerk *off* if you want. How many
> times I gotta go *through* this with you
> dummies? I'm gonna have big *signs*
> painted ... *Flash* cards. I'll just hold up
> the right one. Only maybe some of
> you guys can't *read* even. Now to*day*,
> the key is the hand across the chest.
> To*morro*w, the key will be different.
> So you only have to remember the
> key for maybe a couple of hours. Try
> to remember that the key changes
> every day. Every day you take a shit
> and every day the key changes. Now
> tomorrow, one of you dumb sonsa-
> bitches is gonna miss a sign and
> you're gonna say (he made his voice
> high and squeaky) "But I thought the
> key was the hand across the chest,
> Coach" ... I mean, am I askin' too
> much? Is this too much to remember?
> Should we go to *verbals?* ... Bunt-the-
> ball-Ramirez ... Come on now you
> guys ... Suck it up ...

Simpson's first pitch sailed over Gunner's head.
"Good eye, Gunner," said Bill.

"Nice pitch, Simpson," yelled Tenor.

"Yogi Berra used to swing at dose," said J.C.

"Yeh?" said Coleman. "How'd he manage to stay in the big leagues so long?"

"Yogi could *hit* 'em."

"... Jesus" said Coleman.

Bill sat in the dugout with his warm-up jacket on. No matter how hot it was, he always put it on between innings. He tossed a baseball from hand to hand.

"Base hit, Gunner," he called.

Then to himself:

"I'm gonna need all the runs I can get."

He stopped tossing the baseball long enough to gently massage his right elbow.

"... Bill calling Arm ... Bill calling Arm ..."

"Who you talking to?" said Coleman.

"Oh ... nobody ..."

Gunner lined the second pitch over second base for a single.

"The batter ... Char-ley So-*prano* ..."

"Sing it to me," said Harry.

"I'm just wild about Char-ley," sang Dean.

"Melodious," said Harry.

"Thank you," said Dean.

Soapy looked to the third-base coaching box where Sly was going through the signs like a speaker at a convention for the deaf. Left hand, right hand, pull, tweak, tug, hand across the chest, hand to the belt: the bunt. It would come as no surprise. Bottom of the seventh, one on, nobody out, down by a run. The book would call for a bunt. The Olde Tymers looked at one another and nodded. Bunt, said the nod. Yep. Bunt ... Move the runner to second so's he can score on a single. Stay outta the double play. Yep, said the eyes ... Good baseball.

Soapy never had a chance. He disguised his intent to bunt until the last moment, but the pitch was high and tight, right at his head. He shortened his grip on the bat, tried to turn and lean back. The ball crashed off the side of his helmet, hit his cheekbone and flattened his nose before careening to the backstop.

"Oh, Jesus," said J.C., stumbling up the dugout steps and heading toward the plate.

Doc Hardin, not really a doctor, though his three hundred pounds should have qualified him as something more than a trainer, muddled after him. Bill, Tenor, Chewy Ramirez and a few others were close behind. Some did not want to see, did not want to know what a face looked like after being hit by a baseball traveling at close to one hundred miles an hour.

"S'okay, kid," said J.C., kneeling beside him, the statement more hope than observation.

He eased off the helmet. The ear flap was shattered; an abandoned white web spun out from the point of impact on the dark blue surface. Soapy lay on his side, his right knee drawn up toward his chest.

"Don' worry," said J.C. "You ain't hurt bad."

The left eye was already swollen shut. Blood poured from his misplaced nose. His other eye, though open, did not appear to focus on anything. A small bubble of blood appeared at the corner of his mouth.

"Somebody call a amb'lance," said J.C.

Ted Simpson stood on the mound, hands on his hips, and stared at the center-field fence.

Fans oozed from their seats to stand in the front row and get a better look. Everyone talked in whispers. Olde Tymers drew on rusty memory banks labeled "Beanballs I Have Seen" and talked in low voices of batters hit and maimed, careers ended, by the haunting treachery of the inside fastball. Some claimed to have been present at the old Polo Grounds in New York the day Ray Chapman was killed, but so many could not have been there. Some even claimed to have been close enough to see his left eye pop out of the socket and dangle on his cheek, suspended by small, pink threads. Chapman got up that day— as though in some far region of his rapidly dying ballplayer's brain he knew that he should go to first base—got up, took two steps, collapsed, and never regained consciousness.

Dean walked over to the first-base side and sat next to Harry. They talked quietly. Though they were friends, they never sat together, preferring to exchange their seasoned remarks across the folding chairs and the long wooden benches.

J.C. sat on the ground and cradled Soapy's head in his hands till the ambulance arrived. Two burly paramedics carefully slid Soapy's crumpled form onto a stretcher and eased him into the back of the ambulance.

"See you later, Soap," said Tenor, not sure whether the shortstop could even hear him. "We'll get this prick for you. ... Promise ..."

Then the ambulance was off with flashing red lights and a wail of its twin sirens, disappearing out the big gate down the left-field line, the fading lament like a dying quail.

"He'll be okay," said Bill to no one in particular. ... He'll be okay."

"I'm gonna get you, Two Six," yelled Loony, pointing a blunt finger at the numbered back of Ted Simpson.

Two on, nobody out. The umpire warned both managers about retaliating. Snake Simpson turned back toward home plate as if nothing had happened.

J.C. stepped outside the chainlink fence and washed the blood off his hands at a small drinking fountain. Several young boys stood watching, their eyes as round as startled owls, their mouths like soft spaghettios.

"Now running for So-prano (said the P.A. announcer) ... Larry Du-ffy."

Duffy sprinted out of the Dodger dugout, his bushy black Afro sprouting around the bottom of a baseball helmet that didn't quite fit. He did a few frog jumps at first base and signaled his readiness.

Manny Sosa strode to the plate.

"The bunt is called for," called Harry.

"Correct," said Dean.

Manny got the bunt down and the runners moved to second and third.

"Nice move, Harry," yelled Dean.

"... Elementary," said Harry.

"I know," said Dean.

Chewy Ramirez, the Dodger second baseman, got a base hit to right, scoring Gunner and Duffy. Tenor drilled one up the middle, then stood at first base and said something uncomplimentary about Simpson's mother. Before the inning was over, the Dodgers scored three more and led 7-3. Bill prepared to take the mound for the top of the eighth.

"Shazam," he whispered. "Come on, Arm, do your stuff."

"You know what to do, kid," said J.C., as Bill stripped off his jacket and headed toward the mound.

Sure, he knew what to do. Hit one of their batters. The obligatory plunk, as old as baseball itself. The warnings and fines were useless. It was a primal law. Protect your own. An eye for an eye. A plunk for a plunk. He'd never had much heart for it, even when he was young. The man in the white Panama hat was fond of telling him that he wasn't *mean* enough to be a pitcher. Pitchers, the good ones (he always mentioned Sal Maglie—dubbed the Barber for his tendency to throw at a batter's chin—as one of his favorites), all have a mean streak. Hitters re*spect* a mean pitcher, he'd said. Maglie ... Gibson ... Drysdale. Mean ...

Bill took his eight warm-up pitches. He knew it had to be done. One of the unfortunate aspects of the Designated Hitter Rule was that it was no longer possible to plunk the Plunker. The Plunker no longer batted, was no longer exposed to the mean street hum of the inside fastball. He sat in the dugout shouting encouragement while his teammates bore the brunt of the brushback bruises.

He managed to hit the Giant leadoff batter on the arm with his second pitch. The umpire quickly informed John Christianson that his pitcher would be fined for retaliating. J.C. nodded without looking at the umpire, showing his disdain by spewing some wet Red Man from the side of his mouth.

But it was done; the debt had been repaid—though there was certainly some difference between a man with a bruised triceps muscle and one being rushed to the hospital, possibly in danger of death. But for the present, honor and manhood had been preserved. The challenge had been met. Fire for fire. Fastball for fastball. Though he did not look, Bill knew that the man in the white Panama hat, chin resting on the curved hook of a hickory cane, would be nodding his approval.

Bill pulled at his cap. Balls, he thought. Big balls ... I got balls weigh a ton ... He took a deep breath and tried to concentrate.

But even with a 7-3 lead, it was not to be an easy day for Bill Mahoney. He reached back for something extra but there was nothing there. Baseballs jumped off the bats of the Fresno Giants like popcorn in a party skillet, landing with some shrewd interior logic in unoccupied portions of the field. Several caromed off the willing but inarticulate hands of Country Klinger who had gone in to play shortstop for Soapy. The Giants scored three in their half of the eighth. Pedro Guttierez got the Dodgers two more in the bottom half with a towering home run over the center-field fence, the final indignity that sent Snake Simpson to the showers. Loony gave him the raspberry. Tenor gave him the finger. It was 9-6 Dodgers when they took the field in the top of the ninth. Bill went out determined to hold the lead.

"Smoke 'em, kid," said J.C.

"Suck it up," said Sly.

Though he'd only been pitching since the fifth inning, he was tired. Three innings plus, and he was beat. His head knew what to do, but his arm felt like lead. He remembered an old pitching coach talking about his final year in the majors:

> I was throwin' just as hard as ever. It
> just wasn't getting there as fast ...

Some of it was the heat. He was grateful that they only played one day-game a week; the others started at a more merciful seven-thirty. But the heat was only part of it. There was the physical pain—and the memories of thirty-nine years that played like a bad dream.

And in spite of the heat, the pain, the weariness, there was something about the game itself that kept him going. Maybe it was because it was the only thing he'd ever been happy doing. Sometimes, when he was in a groove, when the pain wasn't too bad, he wanted the game to go on forever. Hundreds of innings. Thousands maybe. He wanted to go on feeling what it was like to catch the corner with that good fastball, go on feeling the rush when the curveball broke down in the dirt and the batter went after it anyway. That was something. One on one. Here it comes. Hit it if you can. When it was good, when the heat was there, nobody could touch him. Nobody. He was the King ... He felt safe out there on the mound, his fingers touching the cowhide cover, the red cotton stitches. Safe. Smoke 'em, kid. Hum it.... There was nothing like it. Nothing.

He rubbed up a new baseball. And then there was the man in the white Panama hat. The Judge. The Jury.... He tried to tell himself it didn't matter.

He took off his cap and wiped his forehead on his right sleeve. It was part of the Road Back. He knew that. Maybe the end of it. All the way from Sleeveless John's. From Rudy's. Great places ... to be from. Where have *you been, Billy Boy?* Somewhere over the ruinbow. Somewhere. Thirty-nine years old. Thirty-*nine* ... And some of those years he didn't remember. Too many intermissions. Lights on. Lights off. Couple of bricks short of a full load. That's what Lushwell said ...

Loony displayed the practiced one finger between his thighs. Bill got a quick strike on the batter; fastball on the outside corner. Nice pitch, Mahoney, he said to himself. Good rotation. Remember how you did that. The second pitch caught the inside corner, but the ump called it a ball. Bill gave him his What-Do-I-Have-To-Do-To-Get-A-Decent-Call look. The batter hit the next pitch down the left-field line, kicking up some chalk just behind the bag. Tenor dove for it but couldn't make the play. Bill stepped off the mound and wiped his forehead with the long thumb on his leather glove. He surveyed the grandstand. Everything was blue; bright Dodger blue. He could see Harry trying to balance an empty popcorn bucket on his head.

"You oughta be in the *circ*us," yelled Dean.

"I thought this *was* the circus," said Harry.

Bill stepped back up on the hill.

"Go at 'em, kid," said J.C. "Dance wit what brung ya."

The next batter hit a sharp grounder to short. Easy double play. Easy. Bill breathed a sigh of relief; maybe it wouldn't be so tough after all. Country scooped it up. Dropped it. Picked it up. And dropped it again. He stood looking at it as if it were some foreign object that had unexpectedly materialized at his feet. His long country face was as sad as a Kansas sky.

"Surround it and *fall* on it," said Harry.

"How do you *eat* with hands like that?" yelled someone in the Giant dugout.

He picked it up and tossed it to Bill. Two pitches later, a skinny kid who looked like he should be up in the stands chasing foul balls rapped a sharp single to right.

J.C. called time and strolled out to the mound.

"How ya feelin', kid?" he asked, both hands stuffed in his back pockets.

"Okay, Skip ..."

"... Tired?"

Bill could see Vince warming up in the bull pen. The Animal. Opened pop bottles with his teeth. Chewed light bulbs. Philly Vince Keane.

"Naw ... Just havin' a little trouble hittin' the spots."

"... Uhuh," said J.C., "... you get tired ya lemme know, eh?"

"Yeh ... Sure ..."

"Go at 'em, kid. Show 'em the dark one."

J.C. turned and walked slowly back to the dugout, stumpy arms swinging lightly at his side. Bill noticed the thin paperback book peeking out of his back pocket. *This Time It's Love* ... Barbara Cartland. He remembered someone who read Barbara Cartland novels. She had marcelled hair. Hazel? Ethyl? ... Just someone ... He couldn't remember the name.

Bill placed the baseball in his glove. The Dark One: a baseball expression for a ball thrown so swiftly that no one could see it. The Hummer. The Heater. The Dark One.

Two well-placed fastballs and a good slider and the next batter was down on strikes.

"Billy the Kid," said Tenor. "Fastest gun in the West."

Two on, one out. Come on, Arm, he said ... A pop fly to Gunner near first base ended the farmboy's hopes of giving the Giants the lead. Two out ... Chewy got the final out, neatly short-hopping a line drive that exploded at his feet and tossing to Gunner at first base.

Bill headed for the dugout, exhausted.

"Good job, Pops," said Gunner.

"Nice game, kid," said J.C.

It was over. It wasn't pretty, but it was a win. He'd take them any way they came.

After they showered and dressed, several of them went to the small Lodi Emergency Hospital to see Soapy. He was propped up in bed, the left side of his face badly swollen, an angry red welt on his cheekbone, cotton packing in each nostril. But his right eye was open and that side of his face tried to smile.

"Well?" said Bill.

"Ahm godda lib," he said.

"I *hope*," said Tenor. "You shoulda seen Country at shortstop. Guy's got hands like *con*crete."

"Didja wid?" said Soapy.

"Goin' away," said Bill.

"Wha'd they say was wrong?" said Chewy.

"Head's okay," said Soapy. "Cheekbode's broke ... Node's broke." Pointing to each spot.

"Glad it's nothin' serious," said Bill.

"When you comin' back?" said Tenor.

Soapy shrugged.

"You know, I broke my nose in college once," said Gunner.

"Yeh?" said Loony.

"Yeh. Some chick rolled over on it. I never had a chance."

"Figures," said Chewy. "You college guys ..."

"High inside thigh," said Gunner. "Never saw it comin' ..."

"... Big deal ..." said Chewy.

"Actually ... It was this *Mex*ican chick who ..."

"Get fucked, willya Gunner?" said Chewy.

"How'ja break it?" said Loony.

A bulky nurse, looking not unlike a bale of cotton in her ill-fitting uniform, sent them away after a few minutes, scolding about the patient's need for rest.

"Wid wud for de Soap," said Soapy as they trooped out.

Bill Mahoney spent the first two years of his life in a small brick bungalow on Saratoga Street. In 1943, just before the Zoot Suit Riots in Los Angeles, Thomas Mahoney moved his family from the steamy cauldron of Boyle Heights to the rural township of Chatsworth. Nestled at the foot of Oat Mountain, Chatsworth was a small collection of wood-frame buildings surrounded by acres of orange and lemon groves. North was the Santa Susanna Pass to the Simi Valley, south two twisting lanes to the more affluent communities of Encino and Woodland Hills. It was forty-one miles northwest of downtown Los Angeles, closer when the freeways came.

Thomas bought a two-acre plot of land at the corner of Tulsa and Desoto with the few thousand dollars inheritance he received from his father who died that same spring. The resident fig trees he uprooted with a Vandyke shovel and a double-bladed ax, nine-year-old Christopher at his side, ready to lend a grunt or a groan to a particularly tenacious tree. When the land was cleared, Thomas began construction on the chicken houses. Soon, sparse wood-frames began to rise from sterile cement slabs. Thomas did most of the work himself, though on occasion itinerant carpenters toiled nearby. One of Bill's earliest memories was the sound of the dual hammers; odd staccato *pahs* that echoed against the barren hills, one always faster, or slower, than the other. Just as one would catch up, the other would stop. He was fascinated by the formidable figure of his father burying nails in the siding with two or three deft strokes. He often went to watch, unnoticed.

Toward the end of the second September, two hundred, day-old chicks arrived in peek-a-boo cardboard cartons. It had been a week of preparation and excitement. The gas-heated hoods were tested. Small mesh wire was stretched and tacked to the simple two-by-four frames, bales of straw scattered on the concrete floor.

The mongrel dogs from the Mexican shanty town west of the Mahoney place ran to greet the old battered Dodge that early Friday morning when the baby chicks arrived. Bill watched from the back porch as Thomas gently lifted each carton and carried it inside. He had been forbidden to get any closer. It really wasn't fair; he could hardly see from where he was. The worst thing was that Christopher got to help and he didn't. And lately Christopher had been calling him Piggy because he wouldn't take a bath. What did taking a bath have to do with anything?

Later in the day he was allowed in to see and touch the baby chicks. He even got to hold one and feel its heart flutter in the moist cup of his hands. He held it tight to keep it warm, held it until he couldn't feel the heart beat any more. Then he gave it back to Thomas.

"Hell's bells," said Thomas, tossing the dead chick in the corner. He grabbed Billy by the ear, marched him to the door and shoved him outside.

"You killed it," he snapped. "Now stay outside."

Bill tried to get back in, but was quickly shoved outside again.

"Dummy," said Christopher.

Billy kicked the door and ran away to the orange grove where he attacked the trees with his bamboo stick and yelled all the bad words he knew.

"What's a killdit?" he asked his mother later.

"... A killdit?"

He nodded and waited for an answer.

"Hmmmm ... A killdit." She worried her hands on her apron. "It might be a bird ..."

Bill thought about that.

"... Maybe." But he wasn't sure.

The fragile young chicks were not yet into their fifth day when Thomas went out to check them one chilly morning and found them all dead. Too much heat from the gas hood. One hundred ninety-nine small yellow balls of fluff betrayed by a sheet-metal surrogate mother.

"Hell's bells," said Thomas.

They were buried without ceremony in a shallow mass grave behind the Incubation House, violated a few nights later by hungry coyotes who emerged from the moonlit hills. Thomas reread Incubation Techniques, made adjustments and installed a thermometer in the hood. Subsequent generations fared much better.

By springtime the flock had grown to nearly a thousand, a cacophonic chorus of baby chirps and more adult clucks. Thomas read an article in the *Poultry Digest* suggesting that if lights were installed in chicken houses and turned on several hours before sunrise, chickens would rise to a false dawn and spend more time laying eggs. The article implied that not even the smartest chicken could tell the difference between a 200-watt G.E. bulb and a ball of hydrogen ninety million miles away. What does a chicken know? Very little, the article concluded.

Thomas installed the lights and was delighted with increased productivity. The chickens, biological clocks gone awry, dutifully rose to the glowing bulb and settled down to a long day. Eggs were nearly a dollar a dozen; even fifteen minutes could be important. Thomas turned the lights on earlier and earlier until even the most stable of the flock began to show signs of severe disorientation; pecking at one another, only toying with well-balanced meals of mash and barley. When production began to decrease, he relented and allowed them a little more sleep. Many became burnt out cases, providing a Sunday meal long before their time.

The Mahoneys set up an assembly line to ship the Grade AA, farm-fresh eggs. Thomas did all the feeding and collecting. Dorothy cleaned and candled and generally supervised activities in the Egg House. Christopher was old enough to help clean and pack the eggs.

Though he wanted to help, Bill was deemed useless by Thomas and left to wander the two-acre plot, exploring underneath rocks (intrigued by the flurry of moist, multi-legged creatures who scurried for cover—sow bugs, silverfish, potato bugs), poking at gopher holes, a ready rock in his small right hand. Later he learned to set traps for the gophers, disguising the sharp metal prongs with succulent greens, anchoring the traps with small wooden stakes after several were dragged down into labyrinthine gopher tunnels by their mortally wounded victims. He received twenty-five cents per dead gopher at Dorothy Mahoney's Trading Post. Trapper Bill. (Carefully saving his gopher and Tooth Fairy money, he had amassed an estate of more than fourteen dollars by the time he was ten years old.)

Santa Claus brought Billy a book that Christmas, though he couldn't read yet. He put it on the desk in his room alongside the praying mantis that was struggling for life in a large Mason jar. They had turkey and parsnips and yams for Christmas dinner. Bill only picked at the parsnips and yams and refused to eat any of the pumpkin pie. His mother told him it was tra*dit*ional to have pumpkin pie for Christmas, and Thomas told him that *every*body liked pumpkin pie. But even after tra*dit*ional was explained, he still wouldn't eat any.

"Tastes like mush," he said.

"And what does mush taste like?"

"... That," he said, pointing to the pie.

"Oh, Billy," she said.

They listened to Lionel Barrymore doing Scrooge on the "Radio Theater," his voice a raspy cavern of annoyance ...

> ... Cratchit? .. *Cratchit?* .. Where i-i-i-is
> that boy? ...

Christopher punched him in the face that Christmas day, then lied and said he never did it. The mantis died two days later.

That was the year he first saw his reflection change when he looked in the mirror.

"Who are you?" he whispered, but the face didn't answer.

If he looked for a long time, his eyes would begin to glow like red-hot coals. That frightened him, though it didn't stop him from staring at the mirror. He wondered what goblins looked like.

The house at the corner of Tulsa and Desoto was an old, two-story, wood-frame house. There was a porch in front, fully screened, though the screen was full of holes and not much good for anything. A rickety, three-step porch tumbled from the kitchen door to the backyard. A fieldstone fireplace spanned both levels on the north side, a horde of musty-smelling geraniums clustered at its base.

Bill's room faced north with a view of Oat Mountain, gently rolling humps and bumps that eventually rose to a little over three thousand feet. In the summer it was varying shades of gold; clump grass, dry cactus, midget sage, anonymous ground cover that crackled in the California sun. In the winter it attempted to be green, though all it ever managed was a pale imitation of a real green mountain. Some years there was snow at the top. When he was older he climbed it. Christopher said it was exactly seven miles to the top, but never said how he knew that.

In the '40s (before they put in the Nike Base and fenced the road), they hunted in those hills: rabbits, squirrels, a few quail. But Dorothy never cooked anything they killed anyway, wouldn't even look at a dead rabbit. After viewing a steady procession of dead gophers brought in by Trapper Bill, she finally told him that he just had to *tell* her when he killed one. That would be enough.

"What if I lie?" he said.

"You won't," she said.

"How will you know?"

"Mothers know," she said.

Some nights she read to him: *The Brothers Grimm, Alice's Adventures in Wonderland, Winnie the Pooh ...*

> *I can swim,* said Roo. *I fell into the river
> and I swimmed. Can Tiggers swim?*
> *Of course they can,* said Tigger. *Tiggers
> can do anything.*

He wanted to be like Tigger. She recited poetry from the cluttered collection she kept in her head:

> We are all in the dumps
> For diamonds are trumps;

The kittens are gone to St. Paul's.
The babies are bit,
The moon's in a fit,
And the houses are built without walls.

He often sat by the window and looked at the mountain, clutching his sightless teddy bear, making up impossible stories about peg-legged pirates and fire-breathing dragons that roamed the woolly hills. Tiggers can do *any*thing, he said. There was a witch there. On the mountain. He knew that sure as anything. Sometimes he could even see her. But he didn't know her name ... Not until later.

He begged to be allowed to help with the chores until Thomas finally relented and assigned him the entry-level task of removing the eggs from the big wicker baskets and placing them on the cleaning table. He was cautioned to be *care*ful and not break any of the *eggs* ... He was caution itself, taking each egg and transporting it with single-minded, double-handed intensity, his chubby fingers gentle as a surgeon's. Still, he managed to break a few. Some were already cracked, some deceptively thin-shelled, produced by chickens markedly deficient in calcium. Chris always sneered when Bill broke an egg. Dorothy was apt to recite a nursery rhyme:

> ... and all the king's horses
> and all the king's men,
> couldn't put Humpty Dumpty
> back together again ...

On the rare occasions when Thomas was present, he would tweak Bill's ear and mutter, "Hell's bells. Be careful with those things" ... Eggs were nearly a dollar a dozen; each one was important.

As Thomas saw his empire expand, he felt the need to protect it. The perimeter was fenced with Sears Finest Chain Link, the first in a community that did not feel the need to protect itself. There came a succession of dogs to the Mahoney ranch. The first was a Doberman named Prince, a war-dog fresh from K-9

School. Billy never liked him. Prince died near the end of his first year in residence, his Armageddon an attack on a gravel truck that passed his domain each day on its way up to the reservoir to repair the road. Usually Prince had to be satisfied with snarling his defiance from inside the chain link fence, but one day the gate was left open and Prince seized the opportunity to attack and destroy the troublesome truck. He barely got his teeth into the twelve-ply tire before his head was flattened under it, leaving only his brindled legs to continue the attack for several moments. Billy breathed a sigh of relief.

A big black Labrador replaced the Doberman. Though given to occasional snarling and almost constant flatulence, he was at least approachable. He lasted only four months. Thomas himself ran over him with his war-surplus Jeep as the dog lay sleeping on the decomposed granite driveway: his final flatulence.

"Hell's bells," said Thomas. "Dumbest dog I ever saw."

Then there was the golden cocker spaniel that Chris named Salty, a beautiful, sad-eyed dog with floppy ears and an unfortunate susceptibility to canine disorders. Bill suggested sleeping arrangements for the dog.

"No, he may *not* sleep in your room," said Thomas.

"He's not *your* dog," said Chris.

"He's not yours neither," said Bill.

"He's *every*body's," said Chris, "so he can't sleep in just *your* room."

"Hell's bells," said Thomas. "He's an out*side* dog."

One day Thomas carried the sickly dog to the back of the property, placed the muzzle of the twenty-two caliber, pump-action rifle a few inches from one floppy ear and pulled the trigger. Distemper, said Thomas, as if he knew. He's better off dead ... Chris dug a hole near the lime pit and buried him.

There were creepy crawly things that lived on the land: garter, king, and gopher snakes; tickle bugs; lizards with pink and blue bellies; the rare but terrifying, fuzzy brown California tarantula. There were even bats, winged predators suspended upside down from the rafters in the barn, nocturnal creatures who sucked the blood of children foolish enough to wander out after dark. Bill always carried his stout bamboo stick.

In the latter part of the war decade, other animals came to grace the two-acre plot; a Guernsey cow called Bossy, horses named King and Scout, three pigs that were nameless and smelly, six rabbits that multiplied and died in the hot summer months.

He walked the mile-and-a-half to Chatsworth Park Grammar School each day, past the McFadden's place and along the railroad tracks. The very first day he talked in class and someone wrote his name on the board. The third day he got into a fight with Manuel Lima and lost. His first-grade teacher was Mrs. Gore, a tarnished jewel whose only interesting facet was the fact that her thumbs were double-jointed. She sent him home several times for wetting his pants in class.

At his mother's insistence, he took piano lessons from a Robert France, a local resident whose long hair and distant manner were considered marks of artistic temperament. Mr. France had played for the Encino Chamber of Commerce New Year's Eve Gala the year previous and came highly recommended by Mrs. Stuart, who said that her son could play just like a little Chopin after only six months of lessons. Bill practiced his scales, his snow-capped-knuckle exercises and, in a few short months, mastered both "Snake Charmer" and "Tarantella."

In the Mahoney front room (Mr. France insisted that pupil and teacher should be left alone for the lessons), Mr. France spent more time with his hands in Bill's pants than on the keyboard. Bill squirmed but said nothing.

Duuuum da da *duuuuuuum* da da da
duuuuuum
That's it, Billy. Tha-a-a-t's it ...

Then one day Mr. France disappeared, never to be heard from again. Bill continued to play, learning pieces like "Deep Purple" to please Thomas, and his mother's favorite, "Missouri Waltz," making a comeback during the presidency of Harry S. Truman.

But mostly he roamed the dusty streets, walked in the freshly furrowed grooves between trees in the orange groves, threw dirt clods at imagined pursuers, and sometimes hid in the tree house across the street. He secretly followed Thomas, trying to leap from footprint to footprint with the same giant stride. He watched him load hundred-pound sacks of grain on his shoulder, prop one hand on his hip, and march off as if the sack were no more than a feather. Bill took a small sack of flour from the pantry and practiced out behind the barn. Up she goes, he said, hoisting the ten-pound sack to his shoulder, trudging off to feed the chickens, dreaming of the time when he would be big and strong enough to lift hundred-pound sacks himself.

He dueled with the big oleander bush near the gate, thrashing it with his bamboo stick till the slender stalks were pulpy and limp.

"Enough tree? ... You had enough? Or does Sir Billy have to kill you?"

And the tree, oozing mortal green marrow, would silently surrender.

"Smart tree," said Sir Billy, sheathing his staff in an empty belt loop.

They ate in the alcove off the kitchen. Bill sat near the window because he was the only one small enough to fit in the corner. Dinner conversation ran mainly to sports. Thomas discussed only major league teams, refusing to acknowledge the Hollywood Stars or Los Angeles Angels as worthy of comment. Chris was then in his junior year at Clinton High. Bill traced his name on the windowpane.

"Don't *do* that," said Thomas.

Bill wiped his finger on his shirt.

"Finish your dinner."

Bill looked at the mound of chicken à la king on his plate and halfheartedly sank a fork into it.

"You don't eat, you don't grow," said Thomas. "That's nature. You wanna be little all your life?"

Bill shook his head.

"Then eat."

Bill began to eat.

"Well, Bucko," said Thomas, turning his attention to Chris, "you got the center-field job nailed down?"

"I think."

Bill wished he had a nickname like Bucko. Or Duke maybe.

"Who else?" said Thomas.

"Jackson maybe."

"Baloney," said Thomas. "Kid's not half the ballplayer you are."

"He's not bad. Good stick."

"Huh ..."

"I scored a goal today," said Bill.

"Did you?" said Dorothy.

"Yep."

"A goal?" said Thomas. "You playin' soccer?"

"... Kickball."

"Kickball? ... What's kickball?"

"They have this ball ... like a basketball. Only you kick it."

"That's soccer," said Thomas.

"Kickball," said Bill. "It's kickball."

"You might call it kickball, but it's soccer."

"... Kickball," said Bill under his breath.

"Jesus ..." said Thomas.

Dorothy closed her eyes for a moment.

Bill scrutinized his plate.

"You like to play, Billy?" said Dorothy.

He nodded, pushing the chicken around his plate.

"My boy, the kickball champ," said Thomas. "Jesus ..."

"... Chicken's really good, Mom," said Chris.

"I'm glad you like it," she said. "Have some more." She pushed the bowl toward him.

He hesitated, then took the ladle and spooned another helping on his plate.

"See?" said Thomas. "That's how you get big. You eat."

"More, Billy?" said Dorothy.

Bill shook his head without looking up. He felt sick.

"Don't mumble, honey," she said, brushing the hair out of his eyes with her hand.

"Jesus ..." said Thomas. "You gonna end up being a midget. Wait and see."

Bill took another bite and went back to staring at the window. He saw his father catch fire and burn in the wavy reflection. He sucked his thumb and watched.

"Hell's bells," said Thomas. "Don't suck your thumb."

Dorothy Krueger Mahoney was a wisp of a woman, barely five-feet tall with dark, saintly eyes. She liked to sit outside on summer evenings and say the rosary, lips moving slightly as the hardwood beads slipped easily through her fingers. She worried about the children, perhaps (she thought) fussing too much over the youngest. She prayed that God would forgive her lapses of faith, her many transgressions. Such a long time since she had been to Mass. Our Lady of Sorrows, only five miles away in Encino, might just as well have been in Oregon. She didn't drive. There were no buses. Thomas would not take her; he thought the whole business was foolishness. He had discarded his Roman legacy along with his short pants.

In her youth, she had entertained the idea of entering the ranks of the religious, seeing in the framed, pinched faces of the nuns expressions she misinterpreted as joy. But she understood that all nuns were virgins, eternally married to Christ in blissful, inorgasmic ceremonies, and she felt disqualified when she fell from the ranks of the chaste while still in her teens.

Thomas was six years her senior, a maverick who had toiled briefly in the minor league vineyards as a property of the New York Giants. He was the handsomest man she had ever seen. They met at a downtown cafeteria where she was employed as a Salad Lady, a vision of loveliness standing primly behind the bowls of individual greens. They married in the midst of the depression, oblivious to the times, unerringly in love. They welcomed Christopher in 1934 in the waning throes of that love. He was a bright and curious child, compliant and eager to please, a patchwork gift to a tattered marriage, filling in the gaps that love no longer covered.

They lived in a bruised little house in Boyle Heights. Thomas read the *L.A. Times* by the light of the walnut floor lamp, its silken shade a gossamer shroud of silver threads. Dorothy embroidered "Home, Sweet Home" potholders by the dozen and thought about going to work at the May Company where clerks were making more than thirty cents an hour. Christopher grew tall and handsome.

Bill's arrival in 1941 was not a particularly joyful event. Thomas was then thirty-five, on the eve of discovering what he had suspected for some time: that there was no pot of gold at the end of the rainbow—that perhaps the rainbow itself had been an illusion. Dorothy was troubled because she knew that Thomas didn't want another child. Only Christopher seemed happy, patting his mother's tummy, putting his ear to the bulge in her dress.

The death of his father allowed Thomas to move from an area that was already beginning to show signs of ethnic overload and buy the two choice acres in Chatsworth. There were elements of beginning anew that temporarily revitalized him.

Chickens, he thought, viewing the rows of fig trees. No money in figs. Chickens it would be, eventually thousands of them. A cow. A few horses. Assorted barnyard animals. He and Christopher rode the hills on King and Scout, long guns tucked in saddle scabbards, a scourge to squirrels and rabbits. They sat astride their mounts on the sunset knoll overlooking the valley. Thomas watched with the narrow gaze of a plantation owner, already affecting the snap-brim, white Panama hat that would be with him the rest of his days. His Morgan stallion pawed the ground after a hard ride, both horse and rider summarized in the fading day.

They watched the sun set. Together they galloped down the hill, King always in the lead, Scout a close second. Thundering hoofbeats. A cloud of dust. Hi ... ho ... Mahoney.

The ride to Rohnert Park only took about two hours the way Chumley drove the old silver-and-blue huffnpuff Dodger team bus. Took two-and-a-half maybe three hours by car, normal driving. But there was nothing normal about the way Chumley drove. A wizened old man with trifocal vision, he raced away from Lodi as if from a launching pad, dumped the first stage rocket as he sped down Highway 120 to Antioch, left the second stage as he found the four-lane comfort of Highway 4 through Concord, whizzed across the Bay on the San Rafael Bridge (past the deceptively domestic-looking San Quentin with its pinkish trim) up 101 through Novato, Petaluma, to the windswept splendor of Rohnert Park, the latest addition to the California league, its newest stadium.

Bill smiled. On the road. Two games here. Three there. Four maybe. Long bus rides. California midsummer heat. Sweaty uniforms. Laundromats. Fast food restaurants. Endless bull sessions. Dreams ... On the road again. The routine of minor league baseball. He didn't mind.

It was June 13, 1981, the day after the Major League baseball strike began. Larry Duffy cradled his larger-than-life radio/tape deck in his arms, bent his ear to the round, mesh speaker and listened to the artful blues of B.B. King.

"Doo-be-doo-be-doo-be-daaaaaa," he crooned.

Gunner Gunderson scanned the *Lodi News Sentinel.*

"Says here they got an electric car that runs on an electric highway and charges itself."

"... Like jackin' off," said Tenor. "I always get a charge outta that."

"I'm *ser*ious," said Gunner. "It's right here ... Says the car gets its power from a magnetic core that's embedded down the center of the road."

"That mean everybody has to drive down the middle of the road?" said Bill.

"Think of the fuckin' *wrecks* it'd cause," said Tenor.

"Jesus, you guys never take anything *serious*," said Gunner. "This is big news ... Energy conserva ..."

"Sure make it tough on the hitch-hikers," said Chewy Ramirez. "Everybody drivin' down the middle of the road like that ... Chingaso ..."

"Leave it to a ... a mi*nor*ity person to think of that," said Gunner. "If your people would go to *work*, Chewy, instead of sittin' around takin' si*est*as all the time, they wouldn't have to worry about hitchhikin'."

"Big deal," said Chewy.

"It only goes thirty-five miles an hour," said Tenor, reading over Gunner's shoulder.

"That kills it for us," said Bill. "Chumley wouldn't stand for it. Can you imagine him goin' thirty-five miles an hour?"

"In the parkin' lot, maybe," said Tenor.

Charley Soprano sat quietly in the back of the bus reading his Bible. Though he made the trip, his first since the beaning, he would not play; he was still plagued by recurring headaches and double vision.

"Here's a hot item for Duffy," said Gunner. "The Mormons have revoked their one hundred forty-eight year old policy excluding black men from the priesthood."

Duffy eased the radio away from his ear.

"I don't wanna be no muthafuckin' priest," he said.

"Right on," said Tenor.

"... Thought I'd let you know," said Gunner. "In case baseball doesn't work out. You could always ..."

"I *be* there, chump. In the big time, if you get there, look me up. *If* you get there. I be the one just broke the base stealin' record. The one makin' all the bread. I be wearin' diamonds and fine threads. Just ask for Duffy, chump. Eve'body know me ..."

"What about the strike?" said Loony.

"Three strikes and you're out, Loon," said Gunner. "You oughta know that. Marquis of Queensberry rules."

"Fuck the Marquis of Queensburg," said Loony. "The *base*ball strike, man."

"What section?" said Gunner, thumbing through the paper.

"The comics," said Bobo Crutchfield, one of the young pitchers.

"Da comics," said Keane, laughing mirthlessly and rubbing his crotch. "Da fuckin' comics. Ha ha ha. You're too much, Crutch ... Ha ha *ha*. Too *much*, Crutch. Get it? Now *dat's* funny."

"Whada they feed you guys from Philly?" said Tenor the Songbird. "Soot? ... A bowl of dirt for breakfast?"

Vince stopped laughing but continued to massage his crotch.

"Birds," he said flatly.

"Can you rub your balls and pat your head at the same time, Vin?" said Tenor.

Keane stood in the aisle, thrust his hips forward and pointedly squeezed his fly.

"How can you talk when I'm chokin' ya?" he said. "Ha ... ha ... ha ..."

"*Here* it is," said Gunner, folding back the Sports section. "What is it you'd like to know?"

"The *strike*, man," said Loony.

"The strike," said Gunner, scanning down the page.

"Gimme the goddam paper," said Chewy, reaching across the aisle.

Gunner pulled the paper away.

"What are you gonna do, wipe your ass with it?" he said.

"It's got print on it, Chewy. Printed *words*. In English. Wouldn't do you much good."

"I can read," he said indignantly. "You college pricks think that just cuz ..."

"How come you got your hand on your nuts alla time, Vin?" said Tenor.

"Cuz de're heavy," he said darkly.

"Don't squeeze too hard," said Tenor. "You'll give yourself a headache."

"Never mind," said Gunner. "I found it ... Says the strike is definitely *on* ... Last minute legal moves have failed and baseball's first midseason strike is underway."

"How long's it gonna last?" said Loony.

Gunner gave him a fishy look.

"I'll check the horoscope section and find out."

"No, really," said Loony.

"As a matter of fact, nobody knows," said Gunner. "It's a classic confrontation between labor and management."

"What's that mean?" said Loony.

"It means ... that nobody knows how long it will last."

"Hope it's over by the time I get called up."

"Won't last that long," said Tenor.

"Whadaya think, Pops?" said Loony, turning to Bill. "How long's it gonna last?"

"A while, I think," said Bill.

"Really?" said Loony, his bulldog face sagging in despair.

"Well, not for*ever*," said Bill. "I'm talkin' a few *weeks* ... a month maybe."

"Oh ..."

"What would summer be without baseball?" said Bill.

"The fans would re*volt*, said Tenor.

"Right on."

"They'd tell President ... eh ... President ..."

"Portillo, Chewy," Gunner said dryly. "José López Portillo ..."

"Get fucked, willya Gunner," said Chewy.

"Reagan," said Bill.

"Yeh. Reagan ... They'd tell Reagan, Hey man, We-want-baseball, We-want-baseball ..."

Duffy raised a clenched right fist.

J.C. smiled and shook his head. Kids ... He went back to reading his Barbara Cartland novel.

> The words burst from Rex, deep and
> low as if they were spoken in the
> extremity of pain.
> "Do understand," Fenella pleaded.
> "You've got to understand."
> "And if I don't?"
> He spoke the words harshly, then
> suddenly his hands went out towards

her, taking her by the shoulders,
drawing her nearer to him. "I loved
you," he said. "I loved you more than
I believed it possible to love any
woman—and now this has happened.
It isn't your fault and it isn't mine; Fate
has been too strong for us ..."

Gunner folded the newspaper and dropped it in his lap. He
turned to Bill.

"You know, Mahoney, I'm hittin' a ton," he said.

"I know."

"One fuckin' ton."

"... Heavy hitter," said Bill.

"Poundin' the old apple."

"Show no mercy ... Take no prisoners."

"I'm on my way to the big leagues," said Gunner.

"Look out here you come."

"Yeh ... Look out. Here I come."

"Your name up in lights," said Bill, framing a large sign with
his hands.

"... Yeh ..."

"Gunner Gunderson Hitting One Fucking Ton ..."

"In lights," said Gunner.

"I said that ... Bright lights ..."

"Yeh ... And here comes his roomy, Bill Mahoney." He thrust
an imaginary mike under Bill's chin. "And where are you
headed, Mr. Mahoney?"

"I'm waitin' for the bus," said Bill.

"To where?"

"The amusement park. I wanna have some fun ... I'm over-
due."

Gunner shook his head.

"You're too much, Mahoney. Too much."

"I know," said Bill. "And don't think that doesn't worry me
sometimes."

Chumley pulled off on Labath Avenue and slid the bus to a
stop in the gravel parking lot.

ROHNERT PARK STADIUM

Home of *THE REDWOOD PIONEERS*

Gen. Admission	$2.25
Student & Senior Citizen	$1.75

"Look, Bill," said Gunner. "You can get in for a dollar seventy-five."

"Here," said Bill. "Stick this in your nose. It'll clear your sinuses."

J.C. closed his book and shoved it in his back pocket, a hint of moisture in his eyes.

"... We-want-baseball ... We-want ..."

"Okay," said Coach Sly. "You guys want baseball so bad, get your asses out and *play* some baseball."

Bill Mahoney was barely ten years old when he ran away from home for the first time. He didn't know why, or at least he could never tell anyone why; in his memory it was a vague and desperate event. He knew it had something to do with his father, though he didn't know exactly what. He left a note in the Mahoney mailbox at the corner of Tulsa and Desoto.

I am going away. Do not wory. I hav
14 dolars.

Bill

And off he went, when he was sure Thomas would be down feeding the chickens, his mother and Christopher busy in the Egg House scraping dried excrement off the wholesome Grade AA, farm-fresh eggs. Armed with his sleeping bag, his favorite Captain Marvel comic book, two peanut butter sandwiches, canteen, flashlight and five-bladed Swiss Army knife, he scampered across Desoto and into the Abernathy's orange grove. He took no clean underwear. Walking swiftly in the center of the furrows, heart pounding furiously in his chest, he doubled back through the Shulter's grove, across Owensmouth, across Mason and into the dark interior of the Larsen's ten-acre orchard. He slithered under the drooping branches and into the welcome womb of the Designated Tree. He sat quietly and listened for pursuers. There was only the distant whisper of eucalyptus trees rubbing slick green leaves together in the afternoon breeze. He breathed a sigh of relief. Safe ... So far. The triphammer beat of his heart lingered like the taste of sour apples.

Sluggo Larsen, sole heir to the miniature Larsen fortune, his whalewhite belly exposed in the airy gap between tee shirt and blue jeans, arrived at the appointed hour. He whistled the code from a distance of two trees.

tweet tweet ^tweet^ ... like a beginning bobolink, two lows and a high, fleshy lips pursed for a kiss.

Bill, aware of the clumsy windward approach some minutes before the signal, whistled the coded reply.

^tweet tweet^ *tweet* ... two highs and a low. A mirror-image code. They had worked it out at recess.

Sluggo advanced with the stealth of a water buffalo, crashed through the leafy barrier and plopped down next to Bill.

"Cheeso ... You *did* it," he said.

"Sure," said Bill.

"Your old man's gonna *kill* you when he finds you."

"Huh," said Bill. "*If* he finds me."

"Yeh ... if," Sluggo said thoughtfully. "Cheeso ..."

He sat Indian-style, or as close to Indian-style as his fat thighs would allow, his cheeks twin freckled bubbles, the roll of his tubular tummy punctuated by the wink of a hidden navel.

"Whadaya gonna do *now?*" he asked.

"Oh ... Maybe hop a freight," said Bill.

"Yeh?"

"Yeh," said Bill, straightening his legs and leaning back against the tree.

"Where to?"

"Oh, I dunno," he said casually, pulling his battered Yankee baseball cap low over his eyes. "St. Louis maybe ... New York ... Chicago ... Somewhere ..." A random wave of his right arm indicated the length and breadth of the world.

"Cheeso," said Sluggo. "Hop a freight ... Wish I could go with you."

"Come on," said Bill, tilting his head back and staring up into the tree.

"You *kiddin?* ... My old man'd *kill* me."

"He'd never find us."

"He'd find *me*," said Sluggo.

"Maybe .... maybe not."

"Oh yeh ... He'd find *me*."

Bill flipped open his five-bladed Swiss knife and began to

clean a hopelessly chewed fingernail.

"Where'd you get that?" said Sluggo.

"Oh ... I had it," said Bill.

"Can I see it?"

"Nope," said Bill.

Sluggo pondered that for a few moments before he spoke again.

"Cheeso ... St. Louie, eh?"

"Maybe."

"Chicago ..."

"Maybe."

"Cheeso ..."

They sat in silence, quiet moments when the very shape of destiny is changed.

"Wait'll old Dingleberry finds out," said Sluggo, grinning, his eyes mere slits above the porcine sheen of his bubblegum cheeks. He referred to Mrs. Mayberry, a storybook spinster who doubled as fifth-grade teacher at Chatsworth Park Grammar School.

Bill allowed himself a smile.

"Can't you just hear her?" said Sluggo, going into his warbling imitation of Mrs. Mayberry, his rubber-band mouth moving like a food-crazed guppy. "... Billy? ... Billy Ma-*ho*-ney? ... Yoooo ... hoooo. Bil-ly ... You say he's gone? Ran away from ho-um? Where? ... St. Lu-lu? ... Lu-lu? ..."

Bill joined the jelly roll laughter; Sluggo held his stomach and rocked back and forth.

"St. Lu-lu ... I can hardly *wait*," he shrieked.

"Not so loud," said Bill.

"Oh," said Sluggo, instantly sobered by the thought of detection, swiveling his head for a glimpse of pursuers. "Yeh ... Almost forgot."

The early October sun slumped quickly behind the mountains to the west. The light fled, sucked away by the fading day. The Mahoneys would be sitting down to the evening meal. Chicken salad perhaps. Or chicken casserole. Chicken cacciatore. Fried chicken. Baked chicken. Roast chicken. Disguised chicken. Maybe a vegetable. Corn. Lima beans (Bill hated them; called them slime-a beans). Mashed potatoes. And gravy; thick, delicious, dark brown gravy from a recipe known only to his mother.

"Gettin' cold," said Sluggo, hugging himself.
Bill pulled up the collar on his wool shirt but said nothing.

It would be warm in the kitchen. It was always warm in the kitchen. The window would be glazed with moisture, darkly reflecting the diners. The chair nearest the window would be empty ... The Fall Classic was in progress. Two New York teams; the Giants and the Yankees ... Although he loved his Yankees, Thomas bemoaned the fact that the Barber got clipped in the fourth game. He retraced portions of his own two years in organized baseball, lamenting the broken ankle in Shreveport (played on it for a week) that cost him a step or two down the line. And maybe a major league career. He avoided any mention of the empty chair. Dorothy studied the salt shaker. Christopher ate enough for two.

"Where's St. Louie?" said Sluggo.
"Oh ... North ... and east a ways."
"Further than ... Arizona?"
"Yep ... Long ways."
Sluggo began to shiver.
"We oughta get Patsy Renfro down here to keep us warm," said Sluggo, gleefully rubbing his palms together.
"Yeh," said Bill.
"We could ... do it to her," said Sluggo, nearly a year older, slower at some things, swifter at others.
"Yeh?"
"Sure," said Sluggo. She took off her pants for me one day."
"... Yeh?"
"Sure ... She told me she did it with her brother."
"... With her *brother*?"
"Cross my heart," said Sluggo, doing just that. "I seen people doin' it."
"Really?"
"Sure," he said smugly. "I seen my *folks* doin' it."
"... Awwww ..."

"Honest a God," said Sluggo, raising his right hand for verification.

"Awww-w-w-w-w ..." said Bill.

"You think your folks don't do it? You think some *stork* brought ya?"

"... Course not."

"That's how they *make* babies."

"*I* know that."

That unsavory bit of information was left to dangle in the air. Bill squirmed uncomfortably. Sluggo drew lines on the dirt with a small twig.

"I'm goin' to the circus next week," he offered.

"Oh?" Bill tried not to sound interested. He had gone with the Larsens the year before and loved it. Especially the trapeze people. Jeez ...

" 'Member the little car with about fifty clowns in it?" said Sluggo.

"Fifty? ... No way," Bill scoffed.

"Twenty anyway," said Sluggo.

Bill found his own stick and dug at the dirt.

"... There were lots," said Sluggo.

Bill agreed with a nod. There were lots.

"I could join the circus," he said.

Sluggo poked at a rotten orange.

"Maybe," he said.

"Sure bet," said Bill.

"Rotten oranges stink," said Sluggo, wrinkling his nose.

"Yeh."

"I gotta be goin'," Sluggo said abruptly.

"Right now?"

"Yep."

"You comin' back?"

"Tomorrow," he said as he crawled under the branches. "After school."

He lumbered away, the sound of his exit fading in the soft evening soil. Bill listened until he was out of sound, until there were only night noises magnified by the absence of sight. A dog barked. Others answered; a mournful, nocturnal chorus.

Crickets chirped noisily. He wondered if it was true that they made that sound by rubbing their hind legs together. It didn't seem possible. A train whistled through the crossing near the depot on Devonshire, then chugged slowly up the grade toward the tunnel. He heard something crawling on the leafy mulch nearby. What if there were tarantulas under the tree waiting to attack; row upon row in assault formation? He was afraid. He fished in his sleeping bag, retrieved the flashlight and flicked it on. The pale finger of light flickered for a brief moment and then went out. Darkness ...

What if a tarantula crawled in his mouth when he was asleep? The thought of it made him shiver. Joe Eckels said he had a friend who went camping and a lizard crawled in his mouth and killed him. Choked him to death. But Joe was in the seventh grade and Bill could never be sure if he was telling the truth.

He shook the flashlight and flicked it on again. Nothing. In his mind a phalanx of fuzzy brown tarantulas advanced from all sides. Surrounded! he thought, squeezing his eyes shut. Shazam, he whispered. .... Something landed on his leg. He brushed at it wildly, got up and dove through the overhanging branches. He rolled over and over in the shallow furrows between the trees, sure that the motion would dislodge the unwelcome invader. He spit the dirt out of his mouth and lay still; all he could hear was the frantic thumping of his heart. Tears welled up in his eyes and he began to sob ... A dog howled. Or was it a coyote, a nocturnal scavenger from the barren hills? The leader of a pack, his followers rib-hollow hungry ... Fang, Dog of the Hills ...

Bill wanted to go home, but he knew that he couldn't. Not then. Not ever ... Better to be eaten by a hundred hungry tarantulas, shredded by the ice-pick teeth of ravenous coyotes than face the red-rock wrath of Thomas Mahoney. Better anything than that. He stopped sobbing and held his breath ... Only the leaves. But how much noise would a tarantula make on the freshly plowed soil? Or even a hundred tarantulas? Perhaps they were even now gathering at the top of a furrow, teeny red eyes ablaze in the night, a veritable army of fuzzy brown killers. Too frightened to go back under the tree and get his sleeping bag, he got to his feet and began to walk in the furrows between the trees, up one row and down the other, safe as long as he kept moving.

How would he sleep? To lie down would be to invite the bite of numberless nocturnal jaws, eager mandibles famished for the taste of soft young flesh. They waited in the darker shadows beneath umbrella leaves, their eyes a cold testimony to innate cruelty, patient as only killers can be. When he fell from exhaustion they would be on him in an instant, tiny jaws tearing at his skin, his body carried away in a million small stomachs, his bones left to greet the dawn, to bleach in the cool October sun. He had seen it in a movie: a listless cow wandering into a South American river full of small fish with large teeth. A sudden flutter at the surface, a dark pool of blood, the cow stripped of its hard-earned hide in a matter of seconds. He pictured a similar fate. He wondered how long he would remain alive under the onslaught? Would he notice the spiders tearing at his eyes, dividing the delicate spoils before he could raise a skeletal hand to brush them away?

Hands shoved deep in pockets, he wandered through the grove. Still early, he thought; only eight or nine o'clock. He glanced up at the sky; a vast blackboard dotted with chalky points of light so distant, so numerous that they looked like white dust. He spotted the Little Dipper and followed the handle to the North Star. His stomach growled for food but he dared not return to the Designated Tree, sure that by now the tarantulas had overrun the area. He crossed Mason street, then Owensmouth. He looked down a narrowing row between trees and was surprised to see his own house. He jumped behind a tree as if the very sight might betray him. He peeked through the leaves: the upstairs dark, the downstairs light diffused through drawn shades. They would be sitting in the living room, he decided. Probably watching the new TV. Boy that was something. Television. Maybe the wrestling matches. He wondered if Wild Red Berry would be on. Or Man Mountain Dean. Six hundred and forty pounds. Jeez ... Bill didn't see how anyone could beat him. Six hundred and forty pounds. What if a guy like that just *fell* on you? .... Be nice to be inside watching.

Be warm in there. On the couch. Maybe have a bowl of ice cream. He sighed ... A pale and icy moon rose like a shooter marble over the eucalyptus trees, its light vague and unfriendly ... The tree house, he thought, staring at the windbreak row of towering trees. Of course! A perfect place. He'd be safe there (he decided that tarantulas couldn't climb trees). He hurried to the tree, climbed to the makeshift tree house and settled down behind the narrow siding. It was actually an old shipping crate that he and Sluggo had discovered down by the dump. They had dragged it back, pulled it up into the tree with a rope, placed it atop two parallel branches, hammered it in place, and secured it as best they could with the rope.

It wasn't much. It barely held two people. It was only the height of the top of the orange trees. But it was hidden. They'd cut some small branches and draped them over the sides so that even if you were looking right at it, it was hard to spot. They took a solemn oath never to tell anyone where it was. Ever.

He leaned against the back of the crate, folding his arms across his chest and pulled his knees up. Better. Warmer. The camphorous smell of eucalyptus leaves was familiar. The slick leaves rustled rhythmically. He drifted into a fitful sleep. He woke several times, once plummeting from a high cliff, once from a dream of Thomas stuffing oily rags in his mouth and setting them on fire ... With the first silver streaks of dawn, he crawled out of the tree house and dropped to the ground. He was cold and hungry, but the sun was coming up. He had made it through the night.

He found his cache near the Designated Tree, no evidence that an army of killer tarantulas had bivouacked in the area. Even his peanut butter sandwiches were undisturbed, undiscovered by the few harmless black ants wandering aimlessly near the base of the tree. He wolfed down one of the stale sandwiches, shook out his sleeping bag, crawled into it and quickly fell asleep. Dappled patterns of morning light peeked mischievously through the leaves.

Thomas Mahoney, his eyes the color of sewer pipes, sped up and down the rutted dirt roads in his dusty Jeep, the grating sound of shifting gears an indication of his mood. He scanned the groves with pinched and wrinkled eyes, searched near the dump and behind the drugstore, hoping for a glimpse of his wayward son. He did not share his wife's concern for the youngest Mahoney. He was simply furious that the boy had run away. "Hell's bells," he said, taking a corner too fast, sending the squat little Jeep skidding across the road. "Goddam him." Chris, he knew, would never have done such a thing. Even when he was younger, Chris had a certain ... moxie that set him apart from kids his own age. He was more a man. But Bill ... well, Bill was mostly just aggravating. Never seemed to really listen when you told him things. Hell's bells ... Well, he can't be too far away, Thomas decided, slamming the Jeep into second gear at the corner of Devonshire and Desoto.

Billy slept till nearly noon. When he got up, he devoured the last of his peanut butter sandwiches, got a drink of water from the faucet near the edge of the grove and set out for the railroad tracks near the grade. He went from tree to tree, aware that the rows between trees could be seen from the road. He crossed the streets with great care, waiting till no cars could be seen in either direction, then dashing across to the next welcome cover. He spent the afternoon watching the trains, mostly freight, an occasional passenger. There were boxcars, flatcars, open cars bulging with sugar beets; Burlington Northern, Lake Erie, Central, Great Northern, Rio Grande, trains on the move, going places. He wondered if any of them were going to St. Louie. Or New York. ... They were slow going up the grade. He ran in the gully alongside the tracks to see if he could keep up ... Almost. Maybe if he got close enough he could grab a ladder on a boxcar and pull himself aboard. But the tracks themselves were raised, with gravel on both sides. He didn't think he could get close enough without slipping on the gravel. He tried it when no trains were passing. Awful slippery. Maybe there was another place farther up the line. He'd look later. There was no hurry.

He sat under a tree and watched. The day was warm. He thought about being a hobo (though he didn't rule out the possibility of joining the circus). Have a stick slung over his

shoulder with a little cloth sack on the end. Just goin' from
town to town. Work when he needed to. That's the way hobos
did ...

> Pardon me, ma'am. I was wonderin' if I
> might feed the chickens for you. Maybe
> hoe the weeds ...
>
> Why surely, mister. You've come just in
> time. My husband has just been run
> over by the train. Cut clean in two ...
>
> Sorry to hear that, ma'am. I'll do the
> chores. I'd be much obliged if I could
> stay for dinner ...
>
> Oh surely ... Stay as long as you like ...

He'd stay and help. But not for long. He wouldn't be one to
wear out his welcome. A hobo never did that.

His father wouldn't be able to find him. He'd look and look
and never find him. Bill'd be gone for good. On the road. Free.
He pulled his Captain Marvel comic book out of his back
pocket and opened it to his favorite story:

> Whenever Billy Batson, famous boy
> newscaster, says the word "Shazam"
> he is miraculously changed into
> powerful CAPTAIN MARVEL, the
> WORLD'S MIGHTIEST MORTAL ...
>
> Once again, the evil Dr. Sivana has
> escaped from jail. He has joined the
> Trio of Terror and the Black Magician
> in a plot to steal all the gold from Fort
> Knox.
>
> When the grim news hits the Teletype,
> Billy and his two companions, Mary
> Batson and Freddy Freeman recognize
> disaster ...
>
> SHAZAM!
> SHAZAM!

CAPTAIN MARVEL!
As the youngsters utter these key
words, thunderclaps shatter the air and
blazing bolts of lightning crash down
to change them into their other forms
of CAPTAIN MARVEL, MARY MARVEL
and CAPTAIN MARVEL JR.—better
known as the Mighty Marvel Family,
champions of those in distress.

Ooooooooooowweeeeeeeee. ...
A train muscled up the grade and fled into tomorrow. Bill
watched dreamily.

Sluggo was so excited that he approached the Designated
Tree without whistling the code.
"*Cheeso*," he exploded. "*Every*body's lookin' for you."
"The code," Bill said calmly.
"The what?"
"The code, Slug. You forgot the code."
"Oh ... the code. I forgot."
"It's okay," said Bill. "This time."
"Yeh. Sorry ... The whole *town's* lookin' for you."
Bill grinned.
"Everybody thinks *I* know," said Sluggo.
"You didn't tell ..."
"You kiddin'? Cheeso. Scout's honor, Bill ... When you leavin'?"
"Leavin'?"
"Hoppin' a freight ... for St. Louie."
"Oh ... soon," he said casually. "I checked it out today. Gotta
find a better place to hop it. Too much gravel where I was."
"Yeh?"
"Yeh. .... You know, Slug, I got fourteen dollars."
"Cheeso ... Fourteen *dol*lars."
"Yeh ... We could get some comic books. Some candy."
"How?"
"You can buy them ... At the *drug*store."
Sluggo looked doubtful.
"What's wrong?" said Bill.

"I dunno," he said. "They're watchin' me pretty close."

"Yeh?"

"Yeh ... My old man said if I knew where you were and wouldn't tell him he was gonna *kill* me."

"Yeh?"

"Cross my heart. I had to tell him I was goin' to Schwartzy's to do homework so I could get out."

"Oh ..."

"Maybe we could get Schwartzy to go."

Bill shook his head.

"He wouldn't tell," said Sluggo.

"You sure?" said Bill.

"Scout's honor."

"Well, okay," said Bill, still doubtful.

"Gimme the money. I'll get him to go right now."

Bill dug into his pocket and withdrew the fourteen carefully folded one-dollar bills.

"How much you need?" said Bill.

"Just gimme all of it," said Sluggo.

"Not *all* of it."

"Sure."

"Comic books are only a dime, Slug."

"I know, I know," he said. "We'll get lots."

Bill peeled off five ones.

"Get some Captain Marvel ... and Plastic Man. And some Milky Ways."

"And Snickers. I love Snickers."

"Okay."

"And some hamburgers ... How about some *ham*burgers," said Sluggo.

"Yeh. Hamburgers," said Bill, catching some of the enthusiasm. "From Bud's, eh? Have him go to Bud's and get some hamburgers ... How much are they?"

"Oh ... two bits," said Sluggo. "Thirty-five maybe."

"I could eat two," said Bill.

"At *least*."

"No pickles."

"Everything but pickles," said Sluggo.

"I hate pickles. And onions ... No onions either."

"Everything but onions and pickles ... I *love* pickles. I'll get pickles on mine."

Bill peeled off three more ones and Sluggo was on his way. He leaned back against the tree and smiled. This was more like it. Comic books, candy, hamburgers from Bud's Little Log Cabin Diner. ... There were four for dinner that night—Bill, Sluggo, Schwartzy and Johnny Bricenio, the latter encountered on the way back from the diner and promptly invited. They devoured the hamburgers and candy as if they had not eaten in days; they laughed and giggled for a time. But they scampered away before sundown, each to his own warm house, leaving Bill to while away the long fall night amid the scattered wrappings and the stack of comic books. It was then that he realized that he had forgotten to get batteries for the flashlight. Hell's bells, he mumbled, picking up the flashlight and testing it once again. Did he dare risk going to the drugstore himself? Would it even be open this late? ... He decided to chance it.

Mission accomplished, he sped back to his encampment, fumbled the batteries into the flashlight, thumbed the light on and surveyed the ground under the tree. Just the hamburger and candy bar wrappings, the comic books, the leaves mashed flat. He thought about moving his camp, but decided he would be safe there for the night. But tomorrow for sure, he said, gathering the greasy papers and stuffing them into a large brown bag. He slid into his sleeping bag and settled down to read a Captain Marvel comic by the light of his rejuvenated flashlight. He loved Captain Marvel comics best of all. Sometimes he would stand in front of the bathroom mirror and say *Shazaaaaam ... Shazaaaaamm ...* hoping he would actually become Captain Marvel, cape flowing in the wind, zooming off into the sky. Jeez ... He even had a Captain Marvel Decoder to read the secret messages. Only he left it at home. Maybe he could send away and get another one.

Only a few minutes had passed until he thought he heard voices. He turned the flashlight off, scrambled out of his sleeping bag and listened intently. There *were* voices. A probing cone of light searched the trees several rows away. He slipped out from under the tree and moved to the next row. The light came closer, the voices clearer.

"Over here, Mr. Mahoney."

Sluggo!

He moved back a row and over a row, a spooky rook on leafy board.

"That tree right over there," said Sluggo.

The rustle of tree leaves.

"Huh ..." A disgruntled voice.

"He *was* here," said Sluggo. "Scout's honor. Look at all the stuff."

"Huh ..."

"He might be in the tree house, Mr. Mahoney. Over by your place. I'll show ya." Eager as a rutting sow.

The intruders withdrew, their footsteps tempered by the loamy soil. Bill returned, now diagonal as a bishop. Under the tree, his attention fixed on peripheral sounds, he patted the ground in search of his flashlight. It was time to go. He knew it. No turning back ... Pardon me, ma'am. Do you need some help? ... Sluggo had ratted on him. Like ice cream in the sun when the goin' got tough ... Where was the *flash*light? ... His hands conveyed information about comic books, paper bags, crushed leaves. But no flashlight. It was there just a minute ago. He fumbled inside the sleeping bag. Nothing to light the long bleak night. He slumped against the trunk of the tree ... Of course, he thought numbly. Thomas took it. He pictured twin fingers of light illuminating the tree house. Two-Gun Thomas, Fat Sluggo the Rat at his side ...

The grove was dark, the marbled moon too low to give much light. Bill stood beside the Designated Tree, engulfed by the night and his fear. Did he dare just walk away? Forever? ... Without his flashlight? He counted his money. Six dollars and change. How long would that last? ... He began walking between the trees.

Maybe he could still hop a freight. Maybe. St. Louie ... How would he know when he got there? Would there be signs? ... This Is St. Louie ... He'd never see his mother again. Ever. She'd be crumpled up on the corner of the couch sobbing into her flowery apron. Jeez ... He walked for the better part of an hour and turned home, lengthening his stride. He tried not to think about what would happen when he got there. He stopped only briefly at the holey screen door.

"It's me," he announced from just inside the front door. "I'm here ..."

"Oh, Billy," said his mother, tearful as a scolded bride rushing to embrace him, a half-embroidered "Home, Sweet Home" potholder trailing from her right hand. "I was *so worried.*"

He accepted her embrace stiffly, trying to keep an eye on the couch where Thomas appeared to be engrossed in watching television. He saw Christopher turn and smile.

"Go-to-your-room," said Thomas, his voice hard and flat.

He pulled away from his mother and hurried up the stairs. She seemed to be trying to tell him something, but he couldn't make out what it was. He vaulted the stairs two at a time, his heart pounding in his ears.

His room was neat as a pin; even his log set, which was always scattered on the floor, had been picked up and placed in some sequestered drawer. His bed was made, his pillow puffed, the blankets folded down at the corner.

He sat on the edge of the bed and looked out the window at Oat Mountain; pudgy knolls artlessly sprawled one upon another, the cleavage between darkened by the shadows of the rising moon. He took a deep breath ... The Witch of the Mountain; her name was Gilben. He rubbed his hand on the soft blue blanket and yawned. He was glad to be home.

It was not long before his mother arrived with a bowl of peach cobbler for the prisoner. She tousled his hair and fondled him like a blind lady, her hands curious and loving. She stayed only a few minutes, slipping quietly out the door, leaving behind a familiar aura of safety and warmth.

Christopher arrived minutes later. He sat on the bed as Bill stood gazing out the window.

"Well, how'd it go?" said Chris.

"Oh ... Okay."

"... Have any fun?"

Bill turned from the window. A thin sliver of light from the doorway sliced across the bed.

"Some."

"What'd you do?"

Chris patted the bed next to him. Bill walked over and sat down. He was dwarfed by his older brother, already well over six-feet tall, some two hundred pounds. He was even bigger than Thomas.

"Well ... I watched the trains one day."

"Great. Sounds like a barrel of laughs."

But there was a friendliness in Chris' voice that was new. Bill looked up at his brother. Chris smiled.

"What else?" he said.

"I did *lots* of things," said Bill, warming to his tale.

"Like? ..."

"Like sleepin' all night in the tree house."

"Bet it was cold, eh?"

"Cold. Jeez, was it cold. I almost froze my ... you-know-what off."

"Your ass, Billy," said Chris. "That was your ass that you almost froze off."

"Yeh. My ass ..."

"And then? ..."

"Then the next night ... to*night*, we got hamburgers and comic books and candy. Jeez, Chris, you shoulda seen all the *can*dy we got. Tons ..."

"Good, eh?"

"Great. Me and Sluggo and Schwartzy and ... eh, Johnny. We had hamburgers and candy. Milky Ways. Snickers. You shoulda seen us."

"You know Sluggo was the one who ..."

"I know," said Bill. "I saw 'em out by the tree ... (He mimicked Sluggo's squeaky voice) ... Right over here, Mr. Mahoney. This tree right here ... Jeez ... What a rat."

"Yeh."

"That's the only reason I came home, Chris. I figured the jig was up when Sluggo ratted on me."

"Yeh ... It's just as well ..."

"You think so?"

Chris nodded.

"Mom was really worried," he said.

"Yeh," said Bill, saddened by the thought.

"The old man was just mostly pissed."

"I bet ..."

"I figured you'd do okay."

"Did you?"

"Yeh."

"I was gonna hop a freight, Chris," said Bill.

"Yeh?"

"For St. Louie ... or New York maybe."

"Been a hell of a trip."

"Sure woulda ... one hell of a trip. Jeez ..."

The distant hum of the television drifted into the quiet space.

"Can you keep a secret?" said Chris.

"Me? ... Sure, Chris. You know I'd never tell."

"I know ... I'm gonna join the Marines after I graduate in June."

"Really?"

"Yeh."

"Jeez. The Marines ... How come?"

"... They got a little war goin' on and I'm gonna join up and fight."

"You're gonna fight in a *war*?" said Bill.

"Yeh. In Korea ..."

"A war," Bill said. "Is it like the last war?"

"Yeh ... A little smaller maybe."

"A war ... That's really somethin' ... With guns and tanks and everything?"

"Yep. Guns ... tanks. Everything."

"Real bullets?"

"Real bullets."

"Huh ... You won't get ... hurt or anything."

Chris laughed quietly.

"Not me, Billy ... Not me."

"Jeez ... Maybe I can go too, Chris."

"Too young, buddy."

"I'll be eleven soon."

"You gotta be eighteen."

"Oh ..."

"You wanna go throw the ball around tomorrow? I need to get in shape for baseball next year. I got a good shot at center-field ... Maybe even pitch some."

"Sure ... *Sure.* That'd be *great.*"

"Good ... Well, I'm gonna watch TV for a while. You know Man Mountain Dean got his ass whipped last night."

"Man Mountain *Dean?*"

"Yeh."

"He weighs six hundred and forty *pounds,* Chris."

"I know. Some little guy by the name of Baron Leone knocked him down and he couldn't get up. He looked like a turtle tryin' to roll over. It was really funny."

"Jeez ... Man Mountain Dean."

Chris got up from the bed.

"Bill?"

"Yeh?"

"Don't let the old man get to you. He doesn' mean anything by all that stuff he does. He's just horseshit sometimes ... Okay?"

"Okay ... I'll see you tomorrow. We'll throw the ball around, eh?"

"We'll do it, kid ..."

His wide frame filled the doorway for a moment and then he was gone, clumping down the stairs in his Chippewa boots. Bill remained seated on the bed for a long time, thoughts of Chris and baseball and war and Man Mountain Dean tumbling through his head. He got under the covers without taking his clothes off.

It was nearly a year before Chris left for the Marine Corps. Bill never remembered a happier time, trailing after his brother, an old tape-wrapped baseball ready to be produced at a moment's notice (Hey Chris, wanna throw some?). Chris even gave him his Ducky Medwick glove before he left.

"Jeez," said Bill. "What're you gonna use?"

Chris laughed.

"I won't be needin' one for a while. I'll get a new one when I get home. That one's pretty beat anyway."

Bill held it reverently. It was floppy and thin and badly scuffed; what little padding there was had shifted to the wrong places. He had never seen anything so beautiful.

It was Chris who first told him he had a hell of an arm, that he was gonna be a hell of a pitcher someday. He taught him the grip, the motion, the follow-through, how to push off the pitching rubber. He showed him how to throw the curve, but told him not to use it till he was older ... Hard as you throw, he said, you may never need it.

When Chris left, Thomas offered to catch for him, but most often Bill preferred to go up to the reservoir by himself and throw against the cracked concrete facing. He had to retape the baseball about once a week. The sound echoed through the hills ... *Pah! ... Pah! ... Pah! ....*

The Redwood Pioneers, a California Angel affiliate, were a hapless team, noted for having the rowdiest fans in the league. Only Fresno came close. There would be a game that night, a twilight doubleheader the following night, then the Dodgers would be back on the road again. Gene Autry, the Angel owner, had stocked his farm club with strong young arms, hoping to relieve the chronic third- and fourth-place finishes of the Big Club. His saddle bags stuffed with corporate gold dust, the Cowboy had been out riding the Free Agent Range for years, picking up a straggler here and there, an occasional thoroughbred, but always betrayed by mustang pitchers who turned up hobbled when they should have been in midseason form. So he stocked his farm clubs like stables, dreaming of the day when one of those rocket-fast colts would grow up to be a Nolan Ryan or a Tom Seaver.

The first half of the season would be over on the seventeenth of June; the Dodgers were still two games back of the first place Giants. A sweep here was a must; the following week they'd be in Visalia for four games with the tough Visalia Oaks who were only a game back of the Dodgers.

Eddy Kasmerzak was slated to start the first game. Gunner wandered down to the bull pen to watch him warm up.

"How you feelin', Kaz?"

" … Great," said Kaz, delivering a fastball that sailed over Loony's head.

"Looks like you're in top form," said Gunner. "Want me to get Mahoney to warm up? You might not make it through the National Anthem."

"Fuck off, willya, Gunderson? I'm tryin' to get loose," said Kaz, windmilling his right arm as he received the ball back from Loony.

"You get any looser, Kaz, we'll have to put you in restraints."

"Take a hike ... "

"Just kiddin, Kaz ... You hear my new joke?"

"No more jokes," said Kaz, going into his windup.

"This is not a Polack joke," said Gunner. "Honest ... "

"And for the tenth time, I am *not* a polack."

"I know. You're ... Don't tell me ... You're a ... what was it you said you were?"

"Why do I tell you these things? ... My grandfather came from Lithuania."

"Right. Lithuania .... You're a Lit. I remember. Anyway, there was this ... *Italian* girl walkin' down the street with a pig under her arm. And she meets a girlfriend who says, 'Where'd you get the pig?' And the *pig* says, 'I won her in a raffle.' ... Get it? The *pig* says ... "

Kaz turned his back and tried not to laugh, but his quaking shoulders gave him away.

"Funny, eh?" said Gunner.

"Terrible," said Kaz. "Go away."

"Okay ... When you get good and loose, I'll tell you some Lithuanian jokes."

The core of the rowdy fans, some ten or twelve men in their mid twenties, occupied the top few rows behind the visitor's dugout. Their calls for Jungle Jim the beer man started early in the game.

Jungle Ji-i-i-im, gimme a Bu-u-u-u-d....

They bought two apiece each time Jungle Jim struggled up to the top of the stands. Big Nick Malducci, the Dodgers hulking backup catcher, was a favorite target.

Hey, number five. What does
Nick rhyme with? ...

Kaz breezed through the first three innings, striking out four and inducing the others to pop up or ground out. The Dodgers got a run in the second and two more in the third when Gunner tripled down the right field line with two aboard.

Bill sat on the bull pen bench far down the right field line. The old Ducky Medwick glove lay folded in his lap. Gunner told him it looked like it'd been run over by a truck ... And who in the hell was Ducky Medwick? he wanted to know ... Joseph Michael Medwick, said Bill. Played with the Cards, the Dodgers and finished up with the Giants. Lifetime batting average of .324 ... How come I never heard of him? said Gunner ... Bill sighed. Education's not what it used to be.

"Looks like we can sleep tonight, Mahoney," said Danny Nesbitt. "Kaz's lookin' good."
"Good," said Bill. "My arm could use a little rest."
"Yeh ... You been pitchin' alot, eh?"
"I think so. Wait'll I ask my arm. Hey, Arm, you been pitchin' alot? .... Ye-e-e-eh ... Gimme a re-e-e-st."
"Ha ... ha ... ha," said Vince, seated on Bill's right. "Dat's funny."
"Thanks," said Bill.
" ... A talkin' arm ... ha ha ha. Now *dat's* funny."
"Wish the Skipper'd use me a little more," said Danny.
"Not gettin' much work, eh?" said Bill, knowing that he hadn't, that he'd been shelled the last two times he'd started.
"No ... Can't seem to get anything ... together. You know? When the fastball's there, I got no control. When the control's good, the fastball's out to lunch. And the curveball. Forget it ... What curveball?"
"Not breakin' much, eh?"
"No ... Not breakin at *all*. You know I threw three no-hitters my last year in high school. *Three* ... I had a curveball that went *clunk*, like it dropped off the end of a table. Clunk ... I mean I don't know what happened. I'm supposed to be gettin' *better* ..."
"Maybe you're tryin' too hard," said Bill.
Danny looked at his hands.
"Pressin' too much," said Bill.
Bill found a ball under the bench and handed it to Danny.
"Show me how you grip your curveball."
"Like this ..."
Danny showed him the grip, the ball slightly off center, the middle finger next to the short seam.

"Why don't you try it like this?" said Bill, showing him a grip with the two fingers closer together, next to the long seam. "And keep your first finger real loose, so you can hardly feel it on the ball. Then when you pull down," he bent his wrist and pulled the ball down in front of him in a release motion, "just let it spin out. Just let it go. With your finger next to the long seam you'll get four seams to rotate instead of two. Gives it more bite. And just let it go. Don't *try* to make it curve. Just pull down and let it go. Relax ... The ball knows what to do."

Danny looked puzzled.

"Try it," said Bill.

"Yeh?"

"Yeh. Try it next time out."

"... That what you do?"

"Yeh ..."

"You got a good curve ball."

"... Practice practice practice."

"An' a talkin' *arm*," said Vince.

"I think I'll try it," said Danny.

In the bottom of the fourth, the Dodger lead began to evaporate like jellybeans in a third-grade classroom. The first two Pioneers got base hits. Kaz struck out the next batter but walked the fourth to load the bases. Duffy sprinted down to the bull pen to tell Bill to warm up. If they were in trouble before the fifth inning, Bill usually got the call. He was long relief. As Duffy was delivering the message, the fifth Pioneer batter delivered a solid single to right-center.

Bill got off the bench and started to warm up. The first few throws were always agonizing; in the desolate wasteland of his frozen elbow, the grinding friction gradually eased the pain. It was better after a few minutes; at least he could throw without cringing in anticipation of the pain. And he *had* been throwing a lot lately. Doing well. Spotting the fastball (or what was left of it). Getting the curve and the changeup over for strikes. Even been working on a knuckleball. He'd had four or five good outings. Been effective.

Kaz walked the next batter on four straight pitches.

"Better hurry," said Danny. Kaz'll be in the showers any

minute."

Curious insects clustered around the glaring lights high above the field, buzzing excitedly in the tungsten glow. Bill tried to hurry his warm-up.

Maybe if he got the knuckleball perfected he could pitch a few more years. Hoyt Wilhelm was forty-seven or -eight when he finally quit. There were others. Jim Bouton came back and made it. Sort of. It was possible.

"Get ready," said Danny. "The skipper's goin' out to the mound."

Bill turned and watched J.C. plod slowly, methodically toward the mound. Though he could not see it, he knew that the Barbara Cartland novel would be peeking over the rim of the right rear pocket.

J.C. made a slight motion toward the bull pen with his right arm.

Bill draped his warm-up jacket over his right shoulder and headed toward the mound.

"Knock 'em dead," said Nick.

Bill nodded and kept walking. Kaz was tossing the ball in the air and looking up at the lights when Bill arrived. He placed the ball in Bill's glove and walked away.

"Ya done okay," said J.C.

"Next time, Kaz," said Bill.

Kaz merely shook his head.

"Holy fuck," he said.

> *Open up another can of pitchers,*
> yelled one of the Rowdies.
> *Sho-o-o-o-wer t-i-i-i-i-mme,* yelled
> another.

"Okay, kid," said J.C. "Ya got men on firs'n secun'. One out ... T'row some heat. Don' fool around wid'em."

J.C. turned his head, spit some Red Man on the mound and brushed over it with the toe of his shoe.

"Okay, kid?"

"I got it, Skipper. Sit back and relax."

J.C. smiled and departed. Bill took his eight warm-ups and got ready to face the first batter. The Rowdies were whooping it up. All two hundred twenty-eight Pioneer fans began to stomp their feet in unison. Rally time! They could feel it. A light breeze drifted across the open field. Loony settled into a crouch behind the plate and went through a series of signs. Bill nodded. Fastball ... He gripped the cowhide across the long seams, went into his windup and pushed off the rubber. The ball sailed in on the hitter who fisted it down the third-base line on two hops. Tenor gloved it, stepped on the bag and rifled it across to Gunner for the double play. One pitch. Two outs. Side retired.

"All *right*, Pops," said Tenor.

"... Nothin' to it," said Bill. "It's all in the wrist."

He gave up a harmless single in the fifth, nothing in the sixth and seventh. He worked out of a bases-loaded jam in the eighth. Between innings he told J.C. he was getting tired and suggested he let Danny pitch the ninth.

"Nesbitt?" said J.C.

"Yeh."

"He ain't been t'rowing too good."

"Give him a shot, Skip."

"... Big game."

"I been workin' with him," said Bill. "He looks real sharp."

J.C. looked out toward the horizon above the left-field fence. Hands on his knees, he rocked back and forth a few times.

"Okay," he said. "Duffy ... Tell Nesbitt to get ready. He's pitchin' the nynt'."

Duffy clattered out of the concrete dugout and sped down the right-field line toward the bull pen. *I'm fast as the muthafuckin' wind*, he said ... Bill could tell by the slurred roar of the Rowdies that Nick was off the bull pen bench.

"A hunch," said J.C. "I'll play a hunch."

"Good," said Bill.

"I played a hunch wida Browns once," he confided.

"Yeh?"

"Yeh ... In Detroit it was. Nineteen ... an' forty one ..." He continued to gaze out at left field as if the scene from forty years ago was unfolding just above the fence. " ... They was down by two. Nynt' innin'. Guy on firs'. No way he was gonna run. Nynt' innin'? Down by two? ... I'm behinda plate. Somethin' tells me this guy is gonna run. Don't figure, but I get a hunch this guy is gonna go. Somethin' tells me, Watch 'is guy. So we pitch out ... Bango! He goes and he's out by plen'y. Ten feet maybe. Just a hunch. Funny, eh?"

"Yeh ..."

The Dodgers failed to score in their half of the ninth. J.C. clapped his hands as the defense gathered their gloves and scampered out to the field.

"Let's *hol'* em," he said. "T'ree up, t'ree down."

"Play some *de*fense," said Sly, returning from the third-base coaching box and sitting next to J.C. "Suck it up out there."

Danny trotted out to the mound.

"Nesbitt?" said Sly.

"Yeh," said J.C. "He's due."

"And then some ... You know we got a shot at winnin' the first half, John. We sweep here and take three from the Oaks and we got a good shot. Put us in the play-offs for sure."

"I got a hunch," said J.C., grunting as he stood up.

Nesbitt's first warm-up pitch hit the dirt and skipped by Loony to the backstop.

"A hunch, eh?" said Sly.

"Re*lax*, Danny," yelled Bill.

Danny nodded without looking toward the dugout.

"Yeh," said J.C. "... You wanna kitty?"

"A what?" said Sly.

"A kitty-cat ... a baby. Waldo had kitties."

"Waldo-had-kitties," said Sly, staring at J.C.

"Six ..."

"Waldo had six kitties," said Sly.

"Yeh. Real tiny. No bigger'n that ... You want one?"

"Eh ... No. No place to keep it."

"Too bad. De're nice kitties. I got a neighbor who watches," said J.C., positioning himself at the corner of the dugout, one foot on the bottom step.

"Wonderful," said Sly, removing his cap and slumping back

on the bench. "Really wonderful."

The first Pioneer batter walked to the plate as the Dodgers fired the ball around the infield, Gunderson to Klinger to Ramirez to Tenor.

"Crush the invaders," said Tenor, tossing the ball to Nesbitt. Danny looked in to get the sign from Loony.

"You think Coleman's too shallow in right?" said Sly.

"No," said J.C. without looking.

The first pitch was a strike.

"Looks awful shallow," said Sly.

"He's okay," said J.C. "This guy ain't hit nothin' to the right side in a mont'. Pulls everything."

The batter lifted a lazy fly ball to left. Manny drifted to his right.

"Piece a cake," said Sly.

"Can a corn," said J.C.

"Easy money," said Sly.

"Routine," said J.C.

"In the bucket," said Sly.

Manny camped under it. Waited. And dropped it.

"*Jesus*," said Sly, running a hand through his thinning black hair. "I can't be*lieve* it. How can you drop a fly ball like that? Jesus ..."

"Okay, get two now," said J.C., seemingly unperturbed. "Double play."

"Jesus ... Suck it up out there," barked Sly.

"Get two now."

"And you know, the thing is, John," said Sly, "the guy don't speak *En*glish. I have to tell *Ped*ro to tell *Manny* what to do. Jesus ... What kinda shit is that? We never used to have this kinda problem."

"Things is diff'rent," said J.C.

"You bet your sweet ass they're different."

"Nobody hurt," yelled Bill. "Just relax out there, Danny."

"Relax," snorted Sly, pacing the dugout. "That kid relax any more he'd be a*sleep* ..."

Loony took his time getting ready behind the plate. Danny

fidgeted nervously on the mound. Manny wandered around in left field kicking at the grass and swearing in Spanish.

Danny dropped a good curveball in for a strike on the next batter. Then another. The last pitch was a sizzling fastball on the outside corner.

STEEEEEERIKE THREEEEEE!

One out. Loony called for a pitchout on the next batter and nailed the runner going to second by ten feet.

J.C. turned to Bill.

"... A hunch," he said, shaking his head in approval.

"Yeh," said Bill.

"Kid's gonna make it."

Sly mumbled under his breath at the far end of the dugout.

"A hunch ... six kitties ... guy in left field don't speak English. Jesus ..."

Danny proceeded to strike out the last batter on three successive curveballs. *Clunk ... Clunk ... Clunk ...* Just like they rolled off a table. There were high fives all over the infield as a jubilant Danny Nesbitt skipped off the mound.

Later that night, at the Highway Haven Motel, Gunner was fishing through his battered cigar box in search of some spare change. He was a tall, solidly built young man with long blond hair, a graduate of the University of Minnesota in his second year of professional baseball.

"You got a quarter, Bill?" he asked.

"Yeh," said Bill without looking up from his book.

" ... Well?"

"Well what?"

"Well, *gimme* a goddam quarter, willya?"

"You just asked if I *had* a quarter, Gunner. You didn't say you *wanted* one."

"You think I'm takin' a survey, Mahoney. Of guys who got quarters? I wanna *borrow* a goddam quarter."

"Why didn't you *say* that?"

"Just gimme a quarter, willya? I don't wanna get involved in a long discussion about semantics."

"Certainly ... In my pants over there. On the chair."

"It's true," said Gunner, shaking his head. " ... What they say about pitchers. It must be the strain." He walked over to the chair and picked up Bill's faded Levi's. "I'm takin' *two* quarters."

"I'll pretend I didn't notice," said Bill.

Gunner sat on the side of his bed and examined the small chrome box mounted on the headboard.

"Listen to this," he said. "... 'Magic Fingers Relaxation Service. It quickly carries you into a land of tingling relaxation and ease. Try it—You'll feel great! Home units available. Ask your helpful Innkeeper.' ... Sounds great, eh?"

"Yeh."

"It's not," said Gunner, slipping a quarter in the slot and stretching out on the bed. "They make it *sound* like it's gonna make you feel *great* ... like you could almost get off behind it. And actually ... it's a bummer. You wanna try yours? I got this extra quarter."

"I'll pass," said Bill. "Just makes my ass itch."

"Yeh," said Gunner. "*Yeh*... Mine too. Maybe if you could get three or four of 'em hooked up on the same bed. Might be worth somethin'. But this? .... *bzzzzzzzzz* ... It's nothin'."

"Why waste your money?"

Gunner thought for a moment before he answered.

"Hope," he said. "That's the key. Eternal hope ... And besides, it was *your* money."

"Clever."

"Maybe if I lay on my stomach," said Gunner, flopping over on the bed. "You know ... I always expect *more* from things like this. When it says I'm gonna feel great I really wanna feel great ... I wonder if that's a flaw in my character. You think?"

"A flaw? You? ... You can't be serious."

"All that glitters is not gold."

"Well said," said Bill.

"I had a philosophy teacher in college used to say that."

"Profound," said Bill.

"Yeh. You know what his name was?"

"Plato?"

"No ..."

"Socrates."

"No no ... His name was Wisdom. John Wisdom. Isn't that a

great name for a philosophy teacher?"

"Terrific."

"Hell of a guy. About five-feet tall. Smelled like mothballs ..."

He trailed off into silence for a few minutes.

"You think we got a shot at winnin' this year?"

Bill closed his book and put it on the nightstand.

"Yeh," he said. "We got as good a shot as anyone."

"... First half?"

"Well ... maybe not the first half. But we'll be in the play-offs."

"Wouldn't that be great?" said Gunner. "Win it all this year. Next year I'd be in San Antonio. Then Albuquerque ... then ... the big club. L.A. here I come. Maybe I can skip San Antonio and Albuquerque and go right to L.A."

"I don't know if you heard, Gunner, but they got this guy Garvey playing first base in L.A. now."

"So? ... He can't last forever. What is he now? Thirty-two? Thirty-three?"

"Either way, very old," said Bill.

"Yeh. And I don't have a whole lot of time to be fuckin' around in the minors. I'm already twenty-two. Be twenty-three soon."

"It happens that way."

"I'm runnin' out of time."

"There's always time."

"Huh," said Gunner. "I don't believe that for a minute. I don't even believe you believe it."

"I gotta believe it."

"Huh ... You don't make it the first couple of years, you're gone. So long, pal. Here's your bus ticket. Have a nice trip."

"Anyway, twenty-two is not exactly ancient," said Bill.

"Easy for you to say ... You know, Mahoney, when I first saw you, I thought you were a scout for the big club. I didn't think you were actually a player."

"Too old, eh?"

"Well, you'll have to admit, you're older than your average rookie."

"... Well-traveled. On the comeback trail ..."

"But why?"

"... At my age?"

"*Whew* ... I'm glad you said that."

"It's a long story."

"I got time."

"Too long for one season. I may write a book about it."

"Send me a copy."

"You'll be the first ... second maybe. But you'll be on the list."

"Thanks." He puffed up his pillow. "You know what I'd really like to do?" he said. "I'd like to make it to the big leagues next year ... *Maybe* the year after. At the latest. Haul down three or four hundred thou a year and settle down ... Get married even."

"Be serious, Gunner."

"Yeh ... I've considered that."

"Do you have some unfortunate girl in mind?"

"No. But I'll find one. I'm actually *tired* of chasin' pussy. Can you believe that?"

"No."

"It's true ... You ever married?"

"Yeh," said Bill.

"How was it?"

"It was ... okay."

"Just okay?"

"... Barely okay."

"What happened?"

"It ... just ended. All that glitters ..."

"Right," said Gunner. "I knew this guy once who had a formula for what it cost you to get laid if you were married. He called it the Price Per Piece. I forgot the formula but you gotta figure in house payments, car payments, clothes, food, laundry, Kotex, kids, everything. He said the highest he ever heard of was a hundred and eighty-three dollars. Can you believe it? A hundred and eighty-three dollars for every piece of ass." He groaned and lowered his face into the pillow. "Christ ... A hundred and eighty-three dollars."

"Sounds like a bargain," said Bill.

A hundred and eighty-three dollars, he mused. Per Piece. Going once ... Going twice ... *Sold* to the gentleman in the back row sucking his thumb and holding the brown teddy bear ... Would've been a bargain at a hundred and eighty-three dollars.

Total all the expenses and divide by the number of times you got laid. The little number into the big number. Easy division. The bigger the little number, the lower the Price Per Piece. Simple enough. But did it count if your wife was getting laid by someone else? By someone who had no real interest in reducing the big number? Did you add anything to the little number if only half the entry was getting laid? And what about sexual liaisons with persons of the same sex? Was that getting laid? Was that a Real Piece? Was it worth half a point? A full point? Or was it pointless? How do you figure in all the intangibles, the fractional reducers of marital bliss?

"A bargain," chuckled Gunner. "Some bargain."
"Yeh ... Some bargain."
"How about some sleep?" said Bill.
"What time is it?"
"Little after eleven," said Bill.
"I still got a few minutes of Magic Fingers."
"It'll put you to sleep."
"Actually, the goddam thing keeps me awake. It's like I keep expecting something to *hap*pen. You know? ... Something instead of the *bzzzzzzz* ..."
"But nothing ever does ..."
"... Not yet."
"All that glitters ..."
"Yeh."
"I got another one for you," said Bill.
"Shoot."
"There's a sucker born every minute."
Gunner looked over and grinned.
"Okay ... You win. Turn out the light."
"... And then there was darkness. Good night, Gunner."
"Good n ..."
The Motorized Magic Fingers Relaxation Service stopped its gentle massaging action.
"Shit," said Gunner.
"What's wrong?"
"It *stopped*," he said. "It just *stopped*."
"That's the way it is sometimes."

"... Maybe I should try another quarter."
"Tomorrow," said Bill.
"Yeh ... Tomorrow. And Bill?"
"Unhuh?"
"I'm gonna pay you back that quarter."
"Which one? The first one or the second one?"
"Both of 'em. When I get paid."
"I'll look forward to that ..."
"Good night ..."

Gunner banged lightly on the chrome box as if to scold it, then rolled over on his back and was breathing deeply in a few minutes.

Bill doubled up his pillow and stuffed it behind his head. He lit a cigarette. Highway lights flashed across the curtained window; mostly ghostly semis *who-o-o-osh*ing north to Eureka, south to San Francisco. A nearby neon liquor store light cast a garish glow across the counterfeit carpet. Shadow. Substance. What was real?

He glanced over at Gunner. Already asleep. Robert Spencer Gunderson. What would life bring the Boy Wonder from Minneapolis? Fame? Fortune? Headaches? ... A shot at the Bigs? ... He watched the smoke curl up toward the ceiling. What does it bring anyone? he wondered.

He snuffed out his cigarette in the bedside ashtray and turned over on his side. Two games tomorrow. Big day. If they were lucky, they might be able to take it all in the first half. But it didn't figure. The Giants had three in Stockton and three in Modesto: an easier schedule. The Dodgers would have to take the second half and win it in the play-offs.

It wouldn't be Yankee Stadium and world-wide coverage. It wouldn't even be Albuquerque and fifty thousand watts of Sun-Belt radio. It wouldn't be the dream he had when he was young. But he wouldn't trade the prospect of a Class A Play-off for anything in the world. Not for the World Series. Not for Yankee Stadium. Not for anything. The journey had been too difficult, the path too often treacherous. There were trolls disguised as dancing maidens, somber monks with toothless smiles, scenes that shifted in the twinkling of a thigh ... What victory there was he could savor. He had gained a certain wisdom, a sense of the world that only a survivor can have.

There were people he wanted to share it with, some already gone to whatever lay beyond the planed and louvered levels of reality that he knew, some who still seemed to hover nearby. His mother, her right side dead and gone long before she was, sending her love with half a mouth, stoically entrenched among the catheters and beeping monitors of the Evergreen Nursing Home. Others, passing names, lovers, some as closed as dying spinsters, some as moist as rotten plums, pilgrims touched and forgotten in the darkness of the journey ...

And there was his brother Christopher, whom he always saw as a friendly giant striding across the spindly strands of his memory.

The Peace Talks at Panmunjon droned on through the spring of 1953. The agonizing hill battles of Pork Chop, Triangle and Heartbreak were over, the shards of flesh long dried on the gutted slopes. Trenches—that's what Korea was in the spring of '53. Trenches and sandbagged, log-covered bunkers. Asian rats. Nighttime patrol. Recon.

Chris wrote three letters to Bill. Bill wrote back each time.

> ... I am fine. How is the War? You
> were right. I pitch beter the way you
> showd me. When are you coming
> home?

There were other newsworthy items such as his sixth-grade grades (not too good), a weather report (not too bad) and how he was doing fielding grounders with his Ducky Medwick mitt. Chris' last letter said that

> ...The war is fine ... I'll be home soon ...

He told Bill not to forget to follow through after each pitch. And keep his wrist loose. Get plenty of rotation on the ball— that's what made it move. Then he told him about rotation in Korea.

> ... Thirty six points and I get to come
> home. Four points a month at the
> front. Three points anywhere else in
> the combat zone ... But it'll be over
> before then, Buddy ...

Bill wrote and asked him if he'd killed anybody yet, but Chris never answered.

It was late in May when the letter arrived, only two months before the Peace Treaty was signed. It said that Corporal

Christopher W. Mahoney had been killed in action while on patrol.

Dorothy wept for days. Thomas showed few visible signs of emotion, though he did beat a balky chicken to death one day in the number four chicken house. He began to eat a lot; even put on some weight. Some nights he sat astride his horse on the small knoll overlooking the valley, slumped forward in the saddle, leaning on the pommel. He rode King hard, digging his heels into the sweaty sides as if the motion itself would tear away the memories. He retreated into a moody silence and began to drink heavily. He didn't talk about it ... No one did.

Bill was crushed. He read and reread Chris' last letter. *I'll be home soon ... I'll be home soon.* ... Then why don't you *come* home? he sobbed. He ran away and hid in the orange groves for three days. He punched himself in the stomach until he was sick. He beat on his thighs till they were black and blue. Sometimes he just cried. He read his favorite Pooh stories. Nothing seemed to help. He put his glove and the old taped baseball away in the closet. For good. He was never going to play again. He didn't even watch the World Series that year ... The Yankees and the Dodgers. Erskine struck out fourteen in the third game; Campanella homered in the eighth. Mantle hit a grand slam in the fifth game ... Thomas drank straight Heaven Hill Kentucky Bourbon from a small cheese glass and cheered his beloved Yankees.

Bill wanted the Dodgers to win; he hated the Yankees. The Yankees won it, 4-2.

But the following year, when the papers were full of stories about the Hollywood Stars and the L.A. Angels going to spring training, he dug into the back of his closet and got out his Ducky Medwick mitt. He rubbed it carefully with saddle soap and applied a light coat of neatsfoot oil. He nearly cried when he put it on. He decided then that he was going to be a major league pitcher. He'd practice until he was good enough. Chris told him he had a great arm. *All the tools, Buddy* ... That's what he said. *You've got what they can't teach ... A great arm.*

He trudged up the hill to the County Reservoir and threw against the concrete wall. Hour after hour. Day after day.

Slowly. Methodically. It was as if he took out all his pain smashing the baseball up against the wall ... Thomas told him if he didn't stop throwing across his body like that, he was going to hurt his arm, but Bill wouldn't listen.

For some months following Chris' death, Dorothy trailed her remaining son like a benevolent shadow. She urged him to eat more, to put on warmer clothes, to get more sleep, to be careful crossing streets. She listened for the sneeze, the telltale cough that would signal the onset of some fatal malady. He too would be taken. She was sure of it. She was being punished. And why not? All those years thinking that God wouldn't notice that she was practicing birth control, that she didn't go to Mass, that she committed sin after sin after sin. Perhaps worst of all, she hadn't insisted that Christopher be baptized. What would become of him? At best an eternity in the squalid confines of Limbo. At worst ... she couldn't bear to think about it. She was shut off from the sacramental life of Holy Mother Church. Banished. She, who used to sing in the choir at St. Polycarps, excommunicated.

She wrestled with the daemons of conscience for several weeks, prayerfully seeking guidance during unattended moments. Then she resolutely closed her thighs, sealing her beleaguered orifice from further abuse. No amount of pleading by Thomas could change her mind. She was adamant. No. Simply no. It was not negotiable. She returned her sexuality to God where it lay fallow, her cloistered cranny closed forever in a tight round fist, her gift to the Giver a simple denial.

She thrust upon Bill all manner of religious books—Bibles, catechisms, commentaries, Lives of the Saints illustrated with color plate pictures of newly minted saints fresh from the tortures of martyrdom, their faces wreathed with beatific smiles. There were boys, girls, men, women—raped, fried, crushed, stoned, drawn and quartered, butchered by the godless, slaughtered by the heathens, leaving this vale of tears with what-me-worry? smiles on their faces. Bill was both repelled and fascinated by the stories.

Against overwhelming odds, Dorothy learned to drive and began to take him to church every Sunday. She presented him to the priests like the wayward lamb he was. He began the indoctrination that would lead to his Baptism and First Holy Communion. Saturday mornings when it seemed that everybody, just everybody, was out playing baseball, Bill was confined to the rectory of Our Lady of Sorrows with three hundred pounds of Father Leroy Murgatroyd. Bill dreaded those rectory mornings with the stale odor of sacramental wine, the worn carpet seething with dust, the old brownish books on mahogany shelves, the uneasy flatulence of his mentor. Often they were alone. Occasionally another wayward lamb would appear, only to vanish the following week. But Bill stayed; his mother saw to that. Father Murgatroyd lurched about the rectory, a sea of flesh enclosed in a tight black suit. Mighty pink jowls blossomed like Grandiflora roses above the Roman collar that ringed his neck. Bill wondered if he didn't feel choked all the time, often nervously rubbing his own neck. Father Leroy tucked him under his sacerdotal wing and led him from In The Beginning to the intricacies of the Trinity in ten short weeks. He told him what evils he might expect from his maturing body.

> ... We must overcome these temptations,
> Billy, these *urg*ings of the flesh ...

wagging his sizable finger like a metronome, wheezing like an overfed walrus. There were anxious moments when information concerning certain practices that would lead to death and insanity was conveyed in the fetid air of the rectory.

Erections were mentioned in passing. Also nocturnal emissions. No explanations were provided. Bill nodded at what seemed like the appropriate times. When it was over, Father Murgatroyd seemed pleased. He had managed to get through it all without once saying masturbation.

It was not long before Bill discovered, quite by accident, the forbidden joys obliquely referred to by the ponderous priest. Guilt and the enormous ghost of Father Murgatroyd accompanied his first frantic struggles with his recently erect appendage. Insanity ... Sin ... Death ... Still, alone in the bed at night, his mind aclutter with visions of alabaster thighs spread like frog's legs beneath his quivering hips, his hand was drawn like a magnet to his teen-age tumescence.

huff huff huffhuffhuff ka-booooom. ...

In the aftermath of countless soiled socks (which he carefully washed in the upstairs bathroom), he was engulfed by remorse. He frequently examined his penis for signs of warts, his mental state for signs of deterioration. He found no warts.

He went to church with his mother each Sunday, watched sheepishly as she trooped to the communion rail, head bowed, parchment hands clasped at her breast. She never failed to ask if he was going to receive. His answer was always Oh, not today, Mom. As if next Sunday was a possibility. He looked at the wall or examined his fingernails when he said it though, not wishing to chance a direct encounter with those probing eyes.

> ... We're pilgrims, Billy, she had informed
> him. On trial. God is watching to see if
> we're *wor*thy, if we de*serve* to spend
> eternity with Him. God sees everything
> we do, Billy. Everything. Even what we're
> thinking ...

Was it possible that God was watching the day he tried to give himself a blow job; pretzled over, gasping for breath, his tongue a scant millimeter from the tip of his pulsating penis? He wondered if anyone else had ever tried it. In later years he would think how much grief he could have saved himself if he had only been a bit more limber.

At times, his sense of himself began to fade. For a while, he thought he had an exact twin somewhere and he was thinking his twin's thoughts. How else explain the strange notions that filled his head, the often bizarre behavior that followed? Who was it that urged him to rifle his mother's dresser drawers in search of silk unmentionables; that condoned the violation of three large chickens and one smelly pig? Who was it that he saw in the mirror?

There was a surplus of strong young arms in Rookie League in the summer of 1961; a glut of hummers from places Bill had never heard of—Schenectady, Chickasaw, Brownsville. Strong arms, live arms, arms that could bring it, arms that flailed like bullwhips from well-muscled shoulders, arms of destiny. Bill's arm, though still young, was no longer strong. A simple trick of Fate, like death. Tricks that Fate could play on an unsuspecting arm included Chronic Tendonitis, Hyperextension, Damage to The Rotator Cuff and the all-encompassing Elbow Problems (which included Bone Chips and Calcium Deposits). And there was no way of knowing when Fate would playfully squeeze a promising young arm. Just like that it would happen. Just like that. Willy nilly, Fate would strike. One day there was a future, a career, the next there was just another sore-armed young pitcher uselessly sticking to the surface of the earth. In some instances, the Arm would be given a chance to redeem itself. Surgery was a possibility for some (though in Bill's case, a second surgery was not considered financially sound). Advice ranged from More Rest to More Work to Soak It In Ice. In some cases a bus ticket awaited the damaged Arms and they would disconsolately pack their few things in a carryall jock bag and head home to Kinnebunkport or Mt. Kisco. They left, nonchalantly tossing good-byes like a peanut vendor at a double-header, with an I-don't-give-a-fuck smirk that belied the pain. Most never asked why. They knew. They had simply failed. The years of promise—years when coaches, peers, parents, scouts and fans lavished them with praise, did homage before the altar of Talent—the years of promise were gone. No gaggle of girls to vie for a smile from those MVP lips. No eager Prom Queen to unzip his Sears Best cords and examine his throbbing member in the dim dashboard lights. No back-slapping pals to herald his weekly performance, to enrich their impoverished lives by a friendship with Joe the Jock. On the bus home with his carryall bag he would look just like all the others: drifters, travelers, swallowed up in the vast veiny network of Greyhound bus routes.

Bill didn't have it anymore. He suspected it the year before when he struggled through his first dismal season fresh out of high school. He got some people out, won some ball games, but he knew he didn't have it anymore. The fastball was gone. The Bread and Butter. The Heater. Gone. Absent. No mustard. No zip ... It wasn't from lack of effort; if gritting his teeth and pushing himself through the pain would have done it, they'd have given him a contract instead of a bus ticket. There was only the struggle each time he went to the mound. Would the high fastball, red cotton stitches biting the wind, rise as it approached the batter? Or would it be flat, stiff, striking each bat and leaping to the power alleys in left- and right-center? Desperation sucked at his mind. He discovered that the difference between a ninety-mile-an-hour fastball and one traveling in the vicinity of eighty miles an hour was about six points on his earned run average. A mistake that might sneak by a high school senior now went for extra bases. He was meat. Batting practice. He tried to spot the ball; in and tight, down and away. But he made too many mistakes. At first they were patient ... "Jes take it easy, Mahoney." ...

They adjusted his motion, his delivery, tinkered with him like a defective toy.

> ... You're rushin' ... Comin' off the
> mound too quick ... openin' up too
> soon ... Come over the top more ...

They tinkered and adjusted and counseled until his mind was a logjam of conflicting advice each time he went into his windup. Their patience soon ripened into cleat-shuffling, tobacco-spewing disgust ...

> ... Shee-it, Mahoney. Put somethin' *on*
> it ... Shee-it ... Somethin' 'side your
> hand ...

He felt the uneasy tremors of failure and despair.

In the afterglow of cheap red wine shared with his roommate Luke Braken, a blue-chip, can't-miss prospect from Prescott, Arizona, he sometimes ventured into elementary prayers of petition. Ask and you shall receive; he remembered that. Would a loving Father give a stone when bread was the item needed? God's will, his mother always said, an inflexible glare in her cast gray eyes. That's all we pray for, Billy. God's will ... (surely God would want him to have a healthy arm) ... Yet even in the asking, Bill felt a certain sense of guilt. He recalled the Lives of the Saints. ... Would St. John, his frail body encircled by flaming fagots, have asked for respite? Would St. Felicitas, her chaste thigh in the toothy grip of a ravenous lion, have prayed for mercy? St. Isaac Jogues watched stoically as Native American barbarians feasted on various parts of his anatomy while he was still alive, his sad round eyes already fixed on the portals of heaven. They had not prayed for mercy. Or deliverance. Or a return of the old fastball ... (He wondered if St. John had ever tried to give himself a blow job.)

"Luke, they're gonna wash me out," he said helplessly.
"Hang in there, Ace," said Luke.
"... Soon."
"Hang in there, Ace."
Hang in there ... Luke Braken was bulletproof. Bill could see that. Luke's joints and hinges were made of the finest bone and sinew available. Bill's were junk. Great arm, bad elbow. The weak link.
"Your arm ever hurt, Luke?"
"Nope."
"Never?"
"Nope."

God's will, his mother said, her eyes aflame with virtue, alive with grainy insights gathered in the wake of Christopher's death, her shoulders bowed under the weight of Worldwide Sin. God's will ... Amen ...
Was he being punished? Was that it? Had Father Murgatroyd been right?

Our Father Who art in The Bigs
hallowed be Thy Arm ...

He could not remember what it was like to pitch without
pain.

In a few weeks he was ticketed home. An amicable parting.
No hard feelings, kid. Just business. You understand. ... Got a
ticket to Tacoma. Or L.A.

... California here I come ...

He could have lived with the pain, the physical pain. In spite
of everything he could have lived with that. It was the crushing
sense of failure, the realization that the Dream had been
shattered, sabotaged by a simple trick of Fate.

... right back where ...

His baseball career was over. Over ... Small fissures in his soul
erupted and filled with dread. He began to view life through
splintered lenses, the images shifting, unstable ...

... I started from ...

He felt compelled to go to the men's room and wash his hands
each time the bus stopped. A film grew over his eyes. All the
towns looked the same.

The first half ended with the Dodgers in second place. No discernible miracle had occurred. They dropped the last game to the Pioneers, went to Visalia and split the four games with the Oaks. It wasn't enough. They needed help from the A's in their final series with the Giants in Modesto. But the A's, pitching staff riddled with sore arms, hitters afflicted with timid bats, provided no help.

Second place and ten cents, you can get a cup of coffee, said Sly, fingering the lingering strands of his thinning black hair, revealing how long it had been since he'd bought a cup of coffee.

J.C. held a meeting in the clubhouse after the final game of the first half.

"Secun' place. Not good ... not bad," he said. "Ya done a good job mostly. A few mistakes. Dat's humanly. It's not a big t'ing. The mistakes. Baseball is like dat." He talked with the meaty syllables of his crooked hands, shaping the words like a baker kneading dough. "Ya make a air-or ... and it's done. Over. Ya go on. But ya learn, see? Ya learn from dat air-or. In ya head ya know what to do nex' time. Don' dwell in the past. Only to remember and learn from. It's like life, baseball is. Dat's why it's the great American pastime. Always another play. Always another game ... Everything is not forever. Now ... The secun' half is comin' up. It's here ... We can win it." He stopped abruptly and walked out of the clubhouse.

Coach Sly cleared his throat and held up his hand for quiet. "What he means," said Sly, "is that you pricks better start playin' some goddam *base*ball out there instead of standin' around with your finger up your ass. I mean we lost some games there was no *way* we shoulda lost. Jesus ... I see guys droppin' fly *balls*, throwin' to the wrong *base*. Jesus. Keep your head in the game out there. Some of you are more interested in your *radios* than in what's goin' on out there. We could use a little less *mu*sic and a little more *base*ball. It's very simple ... We are not asking a whole lot. Just your undivided attention for two or three hours a day. We'd like you to know what the signs are, what the score is, who's ahead. Simple things like that. Be nice if you knew how many *outs* there were when you're out in the field. In case the ball comes to you and you manage to *catch* it, you'll have some idea of what to *do* with it. Now this year, Klinger, there are three outs an inning. No more, no less. Each side gets three outs. That rule has been in effect for some time now ... And it's *three* strikes, Coleman. Just three and you're out. Try to remember the song ... one, two, three strikes you're out ... There is no need to stand at the plate and wait for another pitch after the third strike has been called. Jesus ... Now the second half is comin' up," he said ominously. "Second half. Sixty-some games. I don't even wanna *think* about the Giants winnin' it. I suggest you get your shit together and get ready to play some baseball. Second half starts Friday ... But we're gonna have workouts tomorrow and Thursday so's you guys don't forget what a baseball *looks* like."

Assorted groans greeted the news.

"I know, I know," said Sly, waving away the objections. "Most of you guys would rather be out chasin' pussy. But we have this little business here where we're tryin' to produce ballplayers for the big club. Pussy chasers are not a hot item on the baseball market these days. I mean Al Campanis does not drop by and ask have we got any real good humpers might be able to move up to the big club. No ... He wants to know have we got some guys can *hit* ... maybe field a little. Guys that know how many *outs* there are. Fundamentals ... And that's what we're gonna work on. Fundamentals. We got guys still don't know what base to throw to, pitchers that don't know when to cover first base, stuff you shoulda learned in *Little* League ... What do you do on a ball hit to the right side, Keane?"

Keane sat staring at the floor, reviewing his lecherous relationship with Gerta Verbaik, the matronly Dutch lady from Upper Darby.

"Keane?" said Sly.

"Uh ... here," said Keane.

"I know you're here, Keane. I can see you ... What do you do on a ball hit to the right side?"

"Ball hit to the right side ... uh ... I cover."

"Cover what?"

"... Firs'."

"Right, Keane. Absolutely right. And I'd like you to *do* that next time. Run right over and cover first when the ball's hit to the right side. Last time that happened you stood on the mound and *watched*. Gunner makes the play, turns to toss to the pitcher coverin' first and ... *hey*, nobody's *there* ... Pitcher *al*ways covers first on a ball hit to the right side. *Al*ways. But where's Keane? Yoo-hoo ... Oh, *there* he is. *There's* Keane. Standin' on the goddam mound *watchin'*. Like a *spec*tator. You wanna watch the game, Keane, you should buy a ticket and sit in the *stands*. You wanna *play*, you better get your shit together."

"Jeez," said Keane.

"That's why we're gonna work out the next couple of days. Fundamentals. It's gotta be second nature. *Bam bam bam*, you're there. Reflex. Got it? ... Okay. See you tomorrow. Ten o'clock. Sharp."

He left the room to a muted chorus of grumbles.

"Jeez," said Keane. "How come that fuckin' guy always picks on me?"

"Cuz he loves you," said Gunner.

"Shit. That guy don't love *no*body. Old Tightass."

"I knew a guy once," said Gunner, "got all his shit together and it was so heavy he couldn't pick it up."

"That'll teach him," said Bill.

The second half of the season started officially on Friday, June 19. The Dodgers traveled to Euless Park in Fresno for three games with the Giants. Despite Sly's reference to sixty-some games left to play, there were actually seventy-four. The season would end for the Dodgers on August 30, the last four games at home against the Giants.

The Dodger-Giant rivalry was an ancient feud, originally

fueled on the city fields of Gotham and Flatbush, later transferred intact to the West Coast. It was the stuff of myths nurtured in the chronic mists of Candlestick Park and the balmy confines of Chavez Ravine; fed by the arrogant invincibility of Juan Marichal and the stubborn malice of Don Drysdale who stalked Giant hitters with the eagerness of a young bounty hunter. The mutual hatred carried through all levels of professional baseball—San Antonio and Shreveport in the Texas League, Phoenix and Albuquerque in the Pacific Coast League, and Fresno and Lodi in the California League.

It was not an auspicious second-half start for the fledgling Dodgers. Through a careful combination of poor fielding, untimely hitting and spotty pitching, they managed to drop all three games to the Giants. Gunner went hitless through fourteen times at bat, drawing the well-known collar, the oh-fer. Country continued to field his position with the grace of a baby rhino, the slowest ground balls thudding noisily off his bony hands. The normally adequate outfield of Coleman, Guttierez and Sosa combined for a total of seven errors, often throwing to the wrong base in their haste to atone for a miscue.

The short trip to Visalia through the flyspeck towns of Traver and Goshen was unusually quiet. Larry Duffy cradled his radio/tape deck and crooned softly into the silent speaker. He had been picked off first base in the crucial eighth inning of the final game when the Dodgers had a chance to get back into it. He had gone in to run for Gunner who was aboard on an error, did his usual frog jumps and limbering-up exercises, adjusted his cap over his bushy Afro, then signaled the ump that he was ready. The last thing Sly said to him was—Don't get picked off, Duffy. We need this run. ... *Plate!* barked the ump, pointing to the pitcher. Swift Larry Duffy took his lead. The pitcher came set. Larry leaned toward second. The pitcher fired to first. Larry fell down trying to get back to the bag. *Out!* yelled the base umpire, signifying with an upraised thumb. Easy call.
"Quick feet, slow brain," said Sly, turning his face to an unfriendly sky.

Chumley wheeled the old silver-and-blue huffnpuff bus down

the highway like a man possessed.

"The strike still on?" said Loony.

"You ever read the goddam paper?" said Gunner, angry because his batting average had slipped below .300 for the first time that season.

"What paper?"

"The *news*paper, Lanoski. The *news*paper."

"That's why they got TV, dummy. So's you don't *have*ta read the newspaper."

"Jesus," said Gunner. "Can you believe it?"

"And don't take it out on me cuz you didn't get no hits," said Loony. "It's not my fault you can't hit."

"Oh, I can hit, Lanoski. I can hit. As a matter of fact, I'd guess my batting average is probably seventy or eighty points higher than yours ... eh?"

Loony looked out the window.

"Catcher's a defensive position," he said. "Ask the Skipper. I don't get paid to hit."

"Good thing," said Gunner. "You'd starve to death."

"And first base is supposed to be where all the hot shot *power* hitters pl ..."

"What *is* your batting average?" said Gunner.

"None of your business."

".200? ... .210?"

"Never mind ..."

"You know my grandmother has a *bowl*ing average higher than that. She ..."

"I don't care about your fuckin' *grand*mother ..."

"I think *you* guys are on strike," said Sly, listening from several seats away. "The way you been playin' ... Like a bunch of *crum*bums. Three games into the second half and we're already three games out. Jesus."

"Crumbums?" Chewy said quietly.

Tenor just shrugged.

J.C. sat next to Sly reading his Barbara Cartland novel:

> "... Time has never counted in love,"
> Rex answered seriously, as if a million
> men had not voiced the same sentiment

before him. "Love either happens or it doesn't; you can't force it, you can't create it. Heaven knows what it is in reality!"

"Isn't it wanting to give oneself completely to someone else?"

"Will you give yourself to me?"

"I am yours."

Their lips met and time for both of them stood still ...

He sighed, closed the book and looked out the window. Pink and red and white oleanders whizzed by at an alarming rate.

"How fas' we goin'?" he said.

"What's top speed for this thing?" said Bill.

"Oh, prob'ly about eighty," said Tenor.

"... That's how fast we're goin'," said Bill.

"Hey, Chum," J.C. yelled above the whine and vibration of the old huffnpuff. "We don't haveta be dere till two."

Chumley gave no indication that he heard. He leaned forward over the large steering wheel, elbows out, his knobby back pauper-thin under the threadbare shroud of a pale blue shirt that flapped like a cape in the wind, all his attention devoted to the shifting world of the trifocal road. He wore a stylish gray tam tilted rakishly low on his forehead. Sometimes he closed his eyes and imagined that he could see the road. Nervous Doc Hardin, sweating profusely, always sat in the front seat and spoke softly to him during the trip. Chumley never answered.

"You know, what I don't understand," said Loony, "is how come we never get a ticket for speedin'?"

"I think it's Soapy," said Tenor, jerking a thumb toward the back of the bus where Charley Soprano sat quietly reading his Bible. "Maybe we got God on our side."

Sly grunted.

"That's what we need," he said. "God and a couple of base hits."

"Plen'y a time," said J.C. "We'll win it."

Sly grunted again.

"The strike still on, Skip?" said Loony.

"Yeh."

"When you think it'll be over?"

"Soon."

"... This week?"

"... In time for the Series."

"You really think so, Skip?"

"Yeh ... Big bi'ness," J.C. said slowly. "Too much money. It'll be over soon."

"Great," said Loony, greeting the news as a gospel guarantee. "That's great, Skip."

"..... August ninth," said Bill. "It'll be over on August ninth."

"Yeah?" said Loony. "August ninth?"

"Come on, Mahoney," said Gunner. "How do *you* know when it's gonna be over?"

"It just came to me."

"A vision, Mahoney?"

"August nynt'?" said J.C.

"That's what I get," said Bill. He felt strangely elated.

"Christ, Mahoney," said Gunner.

"Really?" said Loony.

"... Really," said Bill.

"Can I quote you on that?" said Gunner.

Bill closed his eyes. A small pink mouth sped toward his face. *Wanna kiss? Wanna kiss?* ... He forced his eyes open.

"You havin' stomach cramps?" said Gunner. "Your period due soon?"

Bill took a deep breath.

"I was trying to contact the Higher Planes and get some information on your batting slump," he said.

"Beautiful ... Any luck?"

"No ... Nobody up there ever heard of you."

"You don't happen to have a couple of stone tablets stashed away someplace do you?" said Gunner.

"No." He noticed that his hands were shaking. "Stop it," he said quietly.

"Tell you what," said Gunner. "If that strike is over on August ninth, I'll kiss your ass at high noon. At Lawrence Park. On the mound."

"Won't be anybody there at noon," said Bill. "Can we do it later? Just before the game?"

"Anytime," said Gunner.

"Can I take my pants off?"

"Pants on. Pants off. Whatever turns you on."

"Write that down," said Bill. "So you don't forget."

"Can I watch?" said Loony.

"Jesus," said Gunner. "I am surrounded by sickness."

They split the four games with the Oaks, not playing well, but managing the two wins with a little luck and some bad baserunning by the Oaks. Gunner continued his hitting slump, garnering only two hits in the series, and those the scratch variety that dribbled cautiously through the Oaks' porous infield. Soapy returned to the lineup for the final game, hitless at the plate but flawless in the field.

"Like a cat, ain't he?" said J.C.

"Pretty," said Sly. "Real pretty."

After the split with the Oaks, the Dodgers returned to Lodi for a nine-game home stand. The second half was only a little over a week old and they were already four games off the pace. The Giants, continuing their hot streak, took three out of four from the Stockton Pilots and led the pack by two full games. Sly threatened afternoon practices if things didn't improve.

> You guys gotta suck it up out there,
> he growled. When the goin' gets
> tough, the tough get goin'.
> Can you believe it? said Gunner. Can
> you believe he actually said that?
> Holy fuck, said Kaz.

Bill arrived home shortly after his mother suffered the stroke that would confine her to the Evergreen Nursing Home for the rest of her days. A hemorrhage, said the doctor, cerebral in nature; though thrombosis or an errant embolism was not to be ruled out. She was rushed to Good Samaritan Hospital.

A cerebrovascular accident, explained Dr. Ingleman, tidy as a Friday night date, a mischievous twinkle in his magnified eyes. High blood pressure perhaps; a diminished supply of blood to certain portions of the brain. Some dead cells.

> ... The prognosis is not favorable (he
> said), though I believe she will live. ...
> In all likelihood she will not regain
> full motor control of her right side ...
> Some perhaps, but ...

He went to see her as soon as he could. She lay flat in bed, thermometer thin, her head slightly pillow-propped, one El Greco-eye open, the other hooded, drooping anonymously, following the downward slant of her mouth. One side of her face made an effort to smile, the other remained passive, sagging like melted cheese. A pale white arm rose weakly from the blanket and began to trace circles in the air. Small waves of expression rippled over the working half of her face.

A bottle of clear liquid hung from a metal tree at bedside. A thin vein of opaque tubing snaked from its inverted mouth and disappeared beneath the blankets. To her arm? Her thigh? Her navel? A bedside monitor with a small screen beeped rhythmically.

Dorothy Mahoney struggled to speak. Her breathing came in short bursts. The bedside monitor beeped accordingly, increasing its tempo as the effort mounted. Like an ancient Victrola being cranked to life, she filled her lungs in tiny increments until she had enough breath to speak.

".... Vuvuvuvuvuvuvu ... vuvu ..."

The beeping slowed as she finished. She looked at him inquisitively, one eyebrow arched like a rainbow, the other inscrutably still.

Bill smiled and nodded.

She tried again, laboring up to speed.

"... Vuvuvuvuvuvuvu ... vu vu ..."

He stood by the bed and nodded. He put his hand in his pocket and jiggled his keys.

"Sure, Mom," he said. "Sure ..."

Her one bright eye fixed him with a baleful stare. He felt awkward, uncomfortable. He didn't know what to say. And he had no idea what *she* had said. He took a cloth from the bedside tray and wiped the saliva from her chin. He noticed the dark hair on her upper lip. Had it always been there? Her skin was dry and leathery. It didn't seem like his mother, this shriveled gnome glaring at him with one owlish eye, drooling from the side of a prolapsed mouth.

"You feelin' okay, Mom?"

... beep ... beep .. beep . beepbeepbeepbeepbeep ...

"......... Vuvuvuvuvuvuvu ... vuvu ..."

"Unhuh ... Well, you'll probably be up and around in no time."

Layers of antiseptic odors filled the room. The bed itself smelled dank and foul. Miasmic fumes from some hidden funeral pyre seemed to rise from the floor and cloud around his nose with messages of death and dismemberment. His mother's room partner, a similar lady with matted red hair, lay perfectly flat and perfectly still, her eyes fixed on her own bedside monitor, following the whitish dot as it traced across the darkened screen making small heartbeat pyramids, beeping triumphantly. Sometimes the monitors would beat in unison, more often they were spaced in a strange counterpoint of one trying to catch the other. He tried to guess which one was going faster, but he couldn't tell.

He looked at the floor. Was she in pain? Was she going to die?

"I just got back from camp," he said conversationally. "Base-ball camp. You remember when I signed with the Cubs? ... I didn't quite make it." He flexed his elbow. "Arm trouble ... bone chips ..."

".... Vuvuvuvuvuvu ... vuvuvu ..."

"It's okay," he said. "No big thing. Baseball's not everything."

.... Beep .... beep ... beep .. beep . beepbeep ...

He held up his hand to stop her from speaking.

"It's okay. There's lots of things I can do." Though at the time he could think of none. "I'll be okay ... I could go back into the gopher business. Remember? ... I was good at that ..."

Dorothy Mahoney, his staunchest supporter. Through thick and thin, gravy and gruel, no-hitters and ten-hitters, she had always been there. Tuck-and-roll nylons knotted at her spindly knees, spidery hands massaging the flowers on her apron, eyes a little too large for her face, she had always been there. Even Prissy had gone the way of all flesh, bearing their separation until the next long-limbed giant hove into view, stuffing her thighs with mechanical sighs, forgetting the pledges of summer. Her last letter said that she was regretful that it didn't work out ... Regretful. He wondered if she had learned that in Mr. Tawallaby's senior English class. And sorry. She still liked him a lot and hoped they could be friends. Sorry and regretful. And friendly. Jesus ... He wrote her a letter and called her a worthless cunt, but he never mailed it.

"... Vuvuvuvuvu ... vuvu ... vu," said his mother.

"I know, I know," he said. "But I could go to college. There's lots of things I could do ..."

He stopped, surprised at his comments. What had she said that prompted his reply? Were there words hidden in the monotonous *vuvuvu*'s that tumbled stillborn from those pale gray lips? Without realizing it, had he actually understood what she'd said? He looked at the face poised above the sterile sheets. It was no help; merely a cleft rendition of a once lively countenance, a sorrowful reminder of life's disparities. For a moment, he thought he would be sick. His heart seemed to thump in unison with the monitor. His mother's left eye appeared to grow larger and larger, as if to compensate for its frozen twin. He felt himself drifting.

"Well, well ..." boomed a portly nurse who seemed to just materialize at bedside. "How *are* we today, Mrs. Mahoney? ... Uh? ... I can see we're doing just fine ... just fine and dandy." She hummed a random tune.

Bill was startled by her sudden presence. She fussed with the sheets and checked the level of liquid that hung in the metal tree. She stopped momentarily and looked at the beeping monitor. She gathered Dorothy's limp wrist between a meaty thumb and forefinger and held it for several seconds, though she could have just as easily counted beeps. She looked at Bill's shoulder without blinking. And without acknowledging his presence.

"U-huh," she said, letting the arm drop to the bed.

Dorothy followed every move with her good left eye.

"You'll have to go now," she said, addressing Bill without looking at him. "We're going to wash her."

"Yeh ... sure," he said. He kissed his mother on the forehead. "I'm really sorry you're sick. I ... I'll say a prayer for you."

He looked at the woman in the adjacent bed on his way out. Both hands were clutching the sheet just under her chin. Only they didn't look like hands; they looked more like tiny raccoon claws, brown and discolored against the white sheet. They didn't even look like live things. She continued to stare with unwavering reverence at the monitor. Would she get washed, too? Did everyone get washed; all the wasted old bodies tucked neatly between the sheets? Row upon row, clean and sparkling. The doctor will be in soon ...

Well ... Well ... Well .....

He examined the decaying forms with fingers like fuzzy pink caterpillars. Eyes on hollow faces grew round in expectation; eyes like shattered glass ...

In a voice as clear as ice, a voice so hard you could chisel it, he told them they were doing just fi-i-i-i-ne ...

"Somebody gave me a BM," said a lady two doors down from Dorothy.

"Is that *so*?" said the Nurse, wiping the evidence from between

those withered thighs. "Was it a *present*? Like at Christmas?"
The lady smiled and tried to retain her stately dignity.
"I have a son who's a state senator," she said.
"My my my," said the Nurse. "How really *nice* for you."

All that remained of the chicken ranch was a quarter of an acre of land and the two-story house. The Mahoney flock had been decimated by the twin plagues of coccidiosis and new zoning laws. The surviving chickens were sold. The horses went to a commuter who lived in the Simi Valley where zoning laws were still liberal. Most of the land went to a developer who leveled, graded and planted it with Country Classic Homes, six to an acre, only the addresses different.

Thomas roamed the house like a derelict adrift on a sea of memories, sipping whiskey from a small cheese glass, clenching and unclenching his fists. He rose early as he always had, but now there was nothing to do; no clarion call of five thousand white leghorn laying hens, ready for a breakfast of barley and mash, primed to lay an egg. He sat at the kitchen table and gazed out the back window where the chicken houses had been, the morning paper, unopened, next to his coffee. He listened to the din of progress, the march of suburbia, the slamming of a hundred car doors at exactly seven-fifteen, the voices of children, the dissonant hum of gas-driven chain saws toppling tall eucalyptus trees.

He approached his mid-fifties with the harrowing skill of a lifetime pessimist. He recalled his own family, the Brooklyn Mahoneys, Irish to the nub—a banker, a minor clerk, a bitter cleric disenchanted with the weighty cross of celibacy—trudging through life with heavy, Irish burdens. They could all tell a grand story; he remembered that. They gathered at parties to celebrate marriages, baptisms, departures, deaths, all with the same drunken solemnity, cursing the lousy Brits and the sad state of their own adopted nation. Uncle Gene always told his story about the Black and Tans; his hatred would last to the grave and beyond. They learned to be unforgiving at an early age.

There were dowager aunts, crusty uncles, relatives by marriage and mistake. Irish by adoption and injestion, all deeply committed to Time and Decay. Boyhood bellies grew round and unwieldy, pouches of prosperity supported by drooping belts, bisected by midriff ties that only pointed to the source of the problem. The women simply spread, thighs and waists expanding to fill the available space. Their hope was always the children, their sighs of discontent marbled with yearning that the young would live in the dreams that they were busily discarding.

Time had changed only the cast of characters.

He had wanted better things for his family, for his boys. But the ranch had been sacrificed to the scythe of progress; his oldest son killed on foreign soil; his wife, frigid, unsparing, felled by a near fatal stroke. Only Billy was left. A stubborn child, he thought ... They had never been close. Civil most of the time, but not close.

They prowled the grounds like orphaned children, each seeking an interlude, a space, a moment in time to knot the present. Neither found it; there were only relic reminders of remembered days, trinkets that crumbled at the touch ... Time. And the killing present.

They seldom spoke. Thomas sometimes asked about his arm. Bill sometimes answered. What little common ground they had was gone, their meeting place on the diamond of possibilities, of squeeze bunts and strategy, vanished with the fading fastball and the failing elbow. They were strangers, always had been. They met on occasion at the small RCA television, but the dialogue was spare, more truce than friendship.

Bill ran his hands along the heavy, wood mantlepiece above the fireplace, remembering the Christmas stockings, touching the tortured old clock that he and Chris bought for Dorothy on Mother's Day in 1952. The clock no longer ticked, its springs and sprockets stilled forever in a February fall, its hands frozen at 9:23 behind the cracked glass face. He went to Christopher's room, sat on the bed and fingered the dust from the only trophy:

MOST INSPIRATIONAL PLAYER
CHRISTOPHER MAHONEY
CLINTON HIGH SCHOOL
1952

The old Chippewa boots still waited patiently by the bed to be occupied by the familiar size-thirteen feet.

Bill contemplated his twentieth year without relish. In his dreams he could no longer see the Rainbow, the Pot of Gold, the Path that ran straight through the center of his life to a Big League Career. He was free to do anything he wanted; anything but play baseball. It had been different when he carried a Career and Purpose around in his pocket free and easy, the way some people carry loose change. Everybody knew what Bill Mahoney was going to do. The Kid from Clinton. Everybody knew. Some basked in the long shadow of his success, saving for future generations tales of close friendship that began with I-knew-him-when ... (Did he just imagine that people were secretly glad that he failed? That he was mortal? That he was, after all, just like them?) ... In those days, tomorrow was a day to work on the curveball, to perfect the change. September was a month to get ready for March. Now, tomorrow was a jelly day, soft and suspicious as a beanbag chair.

He tested his arm every few days, hoping that some miracle of healing had occurred. He tried to teach himself how to throw left-handed, but after three weeks all he could manage was a girlish lollipop toss that traveled less than the required sixty feet, six inches. He nipped at the Straight Kentucky Bourbon that Thomas kept in the cupboard. He took off his pants in the upstairs bathroom, stroked his vision of Anita Ekberg and spiraled the remnants down the washbasin with a blast of hot water. He wondered if all that stuff would eventually plug up the sink. The cloudy mirror returned a picture of a narrow face, the eyes deep set, the forehead rippled with frowns.

He bought a green 1948 Ford with the last of his bonus

money, drove the crisscross streets and visited old school chums. They drank grownup drinks and smoked with the angular disdain of the young. They reminisced until the memories were tortured and useless. Sluggo Larsen was married, working at Rocketdyne, a porky replica of the elder Larsen, his bulky bride a young balloon with a vacant smile. And he owned his own home, thanks to the generosity of his ailing father. Sluggo was twenty, his wife a burgeoning seventeen.

Bill joined them for dinner one night and sat through an endless evening of grayish casserole and forced conversation. Laurel Larsen, blonde ringlets stuck to her sweaty cheeks, made trip after trip to the kitchen for forgotten items: salt, napkins, spoons for the rubbery chocolate pudding. Sluggo sat in a big easy chair and put his feet up on the imitation leather ottoman. He recalled the old days as if they were centuries ago. He lit a cigar, sighed heavily and gained two more pounds. Bill left as soon as he could.

He began to spend much of his time alone in his bedroom reading thick gray books culled from the shelves of the Third Eye Metaphysical Bookstore. St. Francis and Theresa Neumann performed saintly feats in a virtual bloodbath of spirituality. Swedenborg drifted effortlessly into the Paradiddles of Pantagruel. Madame Blavatsky blended with Aleister Crowley in an awkward, though substantial, union. They only deepened the gloom.

He closed his eyes, opened *The House at Pooh Corner* and read where his finger touched:

> Pooh said, "Oh!" and "I didn't know,"
> and thought how wonderful it would
> be to have a Real Brain which could
> tell you things.

The Encyclopedia of American Sexuality, 2d Edition, furnished him with the startling fact that the average erect American penis was seven and five-eighths inches long. He read the sentence several times. A schoolroom ruler confirmed his suspicions; he was short by nearly two inches. With the aid of a jockstrap, a wide rubber band and two short pieces of string, he devised an ingenious method of suspending weights in the elastic pouch to lengthen and strengthen his diminutive dong. He sat on the edge of a wooden chair, gritting his teeth, while his future stretched painfully between his legs. He exercised it frequently, sometimes massaged it with Madame DuBarry's Skin Conditioner and Toner. He read of Indian fakirs who could lift twenty-pound weights with that slender appendage. Daily evaluations indicated that he was not measuring up.

One night he walked north on Desoto toward Oat Mountain, up beyond the fringe of houses that crept relentlessly up the slopes, shed his clothes amid the clump grass and midget sage and yelled at the moon.

"See me pull my wagon?" he shouted.

"You don't have a wagon," said the moon.

"Tiggers can do anything," he said, but he said it quietly.

He gave the finger to an indifferent sky and trudged back down the hill. He felt separated from himself.

In August, his mother was moved from Good Samaritan to the Evergreen Nursing Home, where aged and infirm residents howled and whimpered long into the nights. On Sunday afternoons the occupants, strapped in their wheelchairs, lined the hallways cooing to fuzzy stuffed animals, talking to imaginary friends, rocking back and forth in a cradle of memory. Relatives came to visit, to stroll among trolls no longer fully present; husbands, wives, sons and daughters, trying to pry from dwindling cells some preposthumous memory of years gone by.

Like a dutiful son, Bill went to see his mother each Sunday. He didn't want to; he felt bad about going and bad when he left, but a legacy of guilt sped him on his way each week. The rooms and halls were filled with rotting carcasses cradling soft cuddly dolls, the attendant nurses numbingly cheerful amid the carnage, like so many ghouls in a cemetery.

Dorothy improved slowly, though Dr. Ingleman was frankly wary about predicting any meaningful progress. By the end of summer she could be propped up in bed without falling over. She could clutch a pencil in her left hand, though she couldn't write. Her vocabulary was confined to the usual *vuvuvu*'s with an occasional *wawa*. She was locked in her disconnected body, unable to get out.

In the fall, Thomas began to frequent the Chatterbox, a local cocktail lounge for the semiaffluent in nearby Woodland Hills. Affecting a steely crewcut and a frown beneath his white Panama hat, he looked out of place among the younger, white buck crowd who came to rub elbows and other bones over Scotch and small talk. Periodically he came reeling home at 2 A.M. with a high-heeled sprite in tow. Barging through the downstairs house, they disrupted the morning hours with loud, lascivious sounds. Bill listened in his upstairs bedroom, sometimes at the door, practicing his solitary beat to the counterpoint below. He thought of his father in bed with a woman. The idea made him uneasy.

In October, Betty arrived. Red hair, two red suitcases, driving an old red Pontiac. Thomas introduced them ... Betty, this is Bill. Bill ... Betty. They shook hands. Just Betty. And just plain Bill. She looked to be a well-traveled forty, sandstone complexion, let's-pretend eyes and a flashy red mouth. They didn't get along. The first time she made his bed, he told her he'd rather do it himself, though he never did.

Two weeks later he got a job as a hod carrier with the Fiesta Pool Company. They just said good-bye. Thomas didn't ask where he was going and Bill didn't volunteer the information. No handshake. Just good-bye. Like strangers.

Bill had been thinking about asking Alice Poole for a date ever since he first saw her peddling Sno Cones and Cokes behind the counter at the Lawrence Park Snack Bar. She was a beautiful strawberry blonde with a faint purple birthmark on her right cheek, high cheekbones and pale blue eyes that glistened like wet marbles. He knew that she wasn't married, though she had a daughter named Carla who sometimes helped out at the snack bar. He didn't think that she dated any of the ballplayers. Gunner had tried and failed. Twice.

> She actually turned me down, he said.
> Foolish girl, said Bill.
> Can you believe it?
> Absolutely not.
> It's true ... Maybe she doesn't know who I am.
> Unlikely, said Bill. Unlikely.
> What tits ... Jesus ...

Brushing aside the numerous excuses he had fabricated, he approached the snack bar with an anxious heart.
"Hello, Alice."
"Oh ... Hi, Bill."
Lub-*dub*, lub-*dub* went the valve-and-piston clatter of his fearful heart.
Her smile was radiant.
"Would you like to go to a movie Sunday?" he said.
He hoped his nervousness did not show. She delivered a purple Sno Cone into the unfurled fingers of a small sooty hand that barely reached the countertop.
"Pardon me?" she said sweetly, cupping the two dimes that were dropped from the dirty hand.

"A movie," he said. "Would you like to go to a movie Sunday?"

"Oh."

"Gimme two hot dogs, two Cokes an' a big popcorn," said the man who had been standing in line behind the grimy child. He smiled faintly at Bill, showing his friendliness, but not wanting to be friendly enough to let Bill in line in front of him. Bill smiled that he understood. He waited while the two hot dogs, two Cokes and big popcorn were delivered and paid for.

"I thought maybe that would be fun," he said quickly before the next patron, a tall pimply teen, could place his order.

Alice nibbled on her lower lip and stared at the mustard jar.

"Sure," she said. "I'd love to."

"Great," he said. "That's really great."

The teenager wrinkled his cratered face into a knowing smirk.

"That's great," said Bill. He stood at the counter and stared at her.

"Do you want something?" she asked.

"Want something?"

"A hot dog? Coke?"

"Oh ... Oh. No ... Thanks."

"Kin I have a fifty-cent Coke?" whined the tall teen.

"I'll call you," said Bill, dashing away from the snack bar, not realizing till later that he didn't know her phone number. He returned after the game and she wrote her phone number and address on a napkin.

"I'll call you," he said, carefully folding it in fourths and putting it in his back pocket.

"I'd like that," she said.

"Great ... That's great. Me too."

They drove the twenty-nine miles to Stockton to see *Fat City*, one of his favorite movies. She smelled faintly of fresh pine. He bought a two-dollar bucket of popcorn in the littered lobby of Guild Theater. Her purple birthmark was barely visible in the darkened theater. He felt a certain electricity between them, a faint responding pressure when their knees or elbows touched. A thousand nervous feet danced in his stomach.

After the movie they drove back to Lodi and went to the New York Cafe for coffee and pie. She lo-o-o-ved the movie ... Who was the girl? Susan? Susan Tyrell? Wasn't she great? Boy ... The way she played those drunk scenes ... Peach pie's my favorite, too. With ice cream ...

Two large flies dueled over a sticky spot on the back of the vinyl booth on Bill's side. She said Shoo! several times, but they paid her no mind.

"I work at Palmer's Beauty Salon," she volunteered during a blank space in the conversation. "Doing hair ... I mean besides the snack bar ..."

"Yeh?"

"Just three days a week, though."

"Oh."

"Yeh ... Actually, I'd rather do faces. Instead of hair. But there's not many people here get their faces done. In L.A. now ... Boy ... There's some people get their faces done every day. Every single day. Beverly Hills types."

"What is it you do? ... To faces?"

"Oh, I do makeup. Eye shadow and liner and rouge. Lipstick."

"... You like it?"

"Yeh ... It's fun. You can change a person's whole appearance that way. I mean they actually *act* different ..."

"... Huh ..."

He looked out the smudged plate-glass window at the sparse traffic on Highway 99. What am I doing here? he wondered. What am I doing anywhere? .... He could see her image reflected in the glass. She seemed to be looking at him, at his reflection. He blinked. Her face began to splinter. He thought for a moment that the glass had broken ... Not now, he thought. Please not now ... When he looked back she was drinking her coffee.

"It's really weird," she said.

"What is?"

"The way some people act ... when you do their faces."

She dabbed at the corner of her mouth with a napkin. He looked at his hands.

"What'd you do," she asked, "before you played baseball?"

"Oh ... Worked construction mostly."

"... Did you like it?"

The conversation seemed in danger of sinking.

"It was okay," he said.

"Were you ... married? Ever?"

"For a while ... It didn't work out."

"Mine neither. Almost eight years. Boy, how the time flies, eh?"

"Yeh."

She picked at the crust of her pie.

"I was married to a cop. Frank ... Frank the Cop. He used to call me Pickle Puss." She touched her birthmark.

"You're very pretty," he said.

"Thanks." She looked down at her plate.

"I mean it." He felt short of breath.

"Thanks a lot, Bill."

"You're welcome."

"When I was little my mother told me that God put a stamp on me so's he'd always know who I was."

"Huh ..."

"She said it made me really special ... Can you imagine God running around putting purple stamps on babies?"

"No."

"Boy ... The things parents tell their kids." She tore a napkin in half and blew her nose. "I don't believe any of that any more."

"... Of what?"

"That stuff about God ... Do you?"

"I ... don't know. I don't think so."

"My great-grandfather was an Indian. Indians believe that everything is sacred; part of the Great Spirit ... The earth. The sky. The trees. ... everything." She concealed a delicate burp with her napkin.

"Huh ..."

"They believe in Life ... in Nature. That's what I believe in."

"Huh."

He didn't know what he believed in. If anything.

"More coffee?" she said.

He glanced at his watch.

"We'd better be goin'. Curfew ..."

They drove the few short blocks to her apartment in his 1971

Ford Mustang. He walked her to the door of her duplex apartment.

She smiled up at him, her face transfigured in the yellow glow of the porch light. Her lower lip looked like a soft red pillow. Mysterious shadows gathered at the dark cleavage in the center of her peasant blouse. He stood with his hands in his pockets, mute, indecisive.

"Uh ..."

"Yes?" she said, her face like a flower in the moonlight.

"Uh ... We'll do it again, eh? Go out?"

"Yes. I hope so. I loved the movie ... And I really had a good time."

"Yeh ... Me too."

"... You know I really identified a lot with the guy in the movie ... It's really hard to get goin' once you've been down."

"Yeh ..."

She reached up, gathered his face in her hands and gazed at him.

"You're a warrior," she said.

"A what?"

"A warrior ... Your destiny is favored."

He felt himself blush.

"Huh ... How do you know?" he said.

"Women know," she said.

She pulled his face to hers and kissed him. A quick wave, a "ciao" and she was gone before he could get his hands out of his pockets.

She went inside, turned the living room lights out and sat in the dark for a long time.

He walked slowly to his car, his pace belying the quickening pace of his lub-a-dub heart. He tasted the tacky imprint of her lips with a curious tongue. He squeezed the steering wheel and shook his head.

"Jesus," he said.

He started the Mustang, checked the side-view mirror and pulled out into the street. He rolled the window down and felt the warm breeze against his face. His stomach churned. He stopped at the light on Logan. ... We'll do it again, eh? Go out?

... The noble warrior ... We'll do it again, eh? Oh, I hope so. I hope so ... His hand, eager as a cat's paw, reached out to touch an absent breast ... His breathing became labored.

A honking horn startled him out of his reverie. He accelerated through the intersection. Halfway down the block, a blue pickup whizzed by.

"Green means *go*, Pops!" yelled a scraggly youth from the passenger side of the pickup.

"Right on," said Bill. "Right on."

A few minutes later he pulled into the Emerson Courts on East Wayne. He turned off the lights but left the motor running. Doubts as pervasive as sand fleas nagged at his mind. What if they did go out again? What if they lay abed, progressed to the point of penetration? ... What if his lingam, limp as linguini, his fractional, foot-long Dodger Dog, failed to rise to the occasion? ... Dare he risk it? What then of the mighty warrior?

He was afraid; he recognized that much. To risk was to hope again. Yet (he asked himself) wasn't that what this was all about? The return to baseball. Wasn't it about learning how to play? How to have fun? How to live?

And maybe he knew more about life than he thought. Just maybe. Maybe he knew everything. He shook his head. Be a lot easier if someone would just tell me, he thought.

"You gonna sit out there all night with the motor runnin'?"

It was Gunner at the door of number seventeen.

Bill turned the key off and went inside.

"Well?" said Gunner. "How'd it go?"

"Great ..."

"Didja fuck her?"

"Does a bear shit in the woods?"

"Come on, Bill ... That's no answer."

"Let's see ... Twice before the movie. Once on the way home ... Then a quicky on the sidewalk."

"No, really," said Gunner.

"Really?"

"Yeh."

"No," said Bill.

"Next time?"

"Yeh ... Next time."

"You know she wouldn't even go out with me."

"I heard that."

"I can't figure it ..."

"She's too old for you, Gunner."

"You think?"

"Yeh."

"What is she ... thirty or so?"

"... Close to it."

"Great lookin' chick, though," Gunner said wistfully. "Great tits."

"Yeh ... Great tits."

"... And a great ass."

"Fantastic," said Bill.

"Face is ... average."

"Ummm. ... I'd give it a little better than average."

"Okay," he conceded. "But not much. That purple spot doesn't help. Looks like a catcher's mitt."

"... Gives her face some character. How many people you know have purple birthmarks? That look like catcher's mitts?"

"Nobody."

"See?"

"... Maybe. ... Think you'll get her next time?"

"Easy ... Bet the farm on it," said Bill.

He sat on one of the twin beds, took his shirt off, tossed it toward the chair in the corner, then lay back and lit a cigarette.

"You missed," said Gunner, pointing to the shirt on the floor.

"Waste pitch," said Bill. "Didn't want to give the chair anything too good to hit."

"Looks like somethin' *I* mighta swung at ... You know I haven't been hittin' worth a shit lately."

"I noticed," said Bill. "... And I'm not the only one."

"Fuckin' terrible."

"Unhuh."

"I gotta start doin' better."

"You will."

"You think?"

"Yeh."

"When?"

"... Soon," said Bill.

"I hope," said Gunner. "Christ ..."

"It's not the end of the world."

"It's not the goddam beginning either." He slumped down on his bed. "You think I got my back shoulder down too much?"

"No."

"That's what Sly thinks. He says I'm swingin' up. Goin' for the fences. He wants me to shorten my stride and punch the ball more. Says that'll help level out my swing."

"No," said Bill.

"No what?"

"No, you're not swingin' up. No, you shouldn't shorten your stride and punch the ball more. You're not that kind of hitter. There's nothing wrong with your swing."

"Then how come I'm not hittin'?"

"You ever heard of a major leaguer going through a season without a little slump?"

"Well, I ..."

"Worst thing you can do is start changing things ... What'd you hit last year?"

"Eh ... .363."

"And what'd you hit the first half this year?"

".317."

"Pretty close to the best in the league, eh?"

"Fourth best, I think."

"So you have a few bad days at the plate and you want to change things ... There's absolutely nothing wrong with your swing, Gunner. Believe me ... Let it be."

"I don't know," said Gunner.

Bill lit another cigarette.

"We're all in the dumps," he said, "for diamonds are trumps; the kittens have gone to St. Paul's ..."

Gunner stared at him.

"What's that mean?" he said.

"I don't know," said Bill, rubbing his temples. "It was something my mother used to say ... You know what the rest of it is?"

"The rest of what?"

"That nursery rhyme."

"No."

"... The babies are bit, the moon's in a fit, and the houses are built without walls."

".... houses are built without walls, eh? Whew ... Heavy duty, Mahoney," said Gunner. He puffed up the two pillows and picked up his book. "But I'm still gonna shorten my stride and punch the ball."

"Good luck."

"All that glitters is not gold."

"Wise words," said Bill. He was silent for a moment. "Gunner ... What would you do if you couldn't play baseball? Say something happened and you couldn't play any more."

"... Kill myself."

"Yeh?"

"Mahoney ... People don't kill themselves because they can't play baseball anymore ... I'd probably be a ... a male prostitute."

"Good choice," said Bill. "But I thought you were tired of that stuff."

"If the money was right, I could make an exception."

"Spoken like a true whore." He took a drag off his cigarette. "Worth thinkin' about."

"You're too old," said Gunner.

"Huh ... Tiggers can do anything."

"... What?"

"Nothin' ... Just thinkin' out loud."

Bill had rented a small apartment in Van Nuys and begun his apprenticeship in the construction trade. He pushed a wheelbarrow. Everywhere. Up driveways. Around corners. Across streets. Over treacherous planks. His cargo: Portland Cement and pure white sand mixed to perfection in an old paddlewheel cement mixer. He was a Wheelbarrow Man. Oklahoma Diesel Driver. You got a license for that thing, kid? Soon he was in the swimming pools learning to be a finisher. His right hand cramped at night while he slept, protesting the long hours wrapped around the handle of a trowel. He awoke in pain and had to pry each finger loose from its cramped curl. But it passed; his hand became accustomed to the wooden grip. In a few months he could put a cigarette out in the palm of his callused right hand—an old pool plasterer's parlor trick.

The months passed at varying speeds. Life seemed to be a time track sequence of random events. It made him uneasy. He grappled with its inconsistencies, but came to no conclusions. He had vague premonitions in his dreams. Some days were filled with strange sense of déjà vu, as if the time track had suddenly reversed itself ... He was five years old. He was eight years old. He wet the bed. His father slapped him across the face. I'm twenty-two years old, he thought. How can I wet the bed?

The dreamy scribe of routine etched his days. He bought a guitar and learned "When Irish Eyes Are Smiling." The songs he planned to write stopped after the first one. He was up for work at 5 A.M., sometimes with a sense of renewal, though it seldom lasted; the day wore down his sharp resolve. Most nights he went to Sleeveless John's with the boys. A few beers. Some bumper pool. He belonged—embraced by the broadcloth feel of working men, the strident sounds of broken dreams ... A few beers. Shuffleboard. A few more beers. Some pills. A search of the honky-tonks.

Brief nocturnal alliances were more like collisions than relationships, basic deficiencies magnified in the long grim nights. After two dates, Della informed him that he was a very weird person. He scrambled to explain the wetness of the bed, but could come up with nothing rational. Tiny Nurse Nora urged him on to repeated entries while relating her latest libidinous adventures with the terminally ill. She couldn't get enough. He was sure he didn't have enough to give. He went to sleep listening to the rhythmic slush of her self-stimulation. Ruthy left after the first night, tearfully wiping sperm from unlikely places. Beer Bar Belles turned surly in the early morning. Aimless couplings brought neither respite nor peace. He didn't know if they should. Others seemed to place great store in them. Was there something hidden, he wondered, some ancient mystery—concealed between those soft vaginal folds—that escaped his search? Was his probe too short to plumb the depths?

He bought a loosely hinged mannequin at a rummage sale, equipped it with a suitably soft slot and stored it in his closet. A blonde wig and female attire followed. He called her Rover. She was the subject of the only song he ever wrote. It began:

> .... Roll over, Rover,
>
> My search is over ...

He twisted her into seductive poses and used her when the nights were very dark. He seemed to do better with inanimate objects. He despaired of finding anyone ... And then he met Gloria ...

"Hey, Flaco, you gonna get *marry*?" said Toasty, sliding his trowel up the short wall near the shallow end of the swimming pool.

"Yeh," said Bill, flicking some water on the wall with his brush and troweling out a rough spot.

Toasty grunted.

"I been marry four times, man."

"So?"

"... So I been marry four times."

"Oh."

"Seven kids ... Jesus."

"Well ..." said Bill. "I don't figure on gettin' married four times."

"*Ha* ..." said Toasty. He was a small swarthy Mexican with numerous homemade tattoos gracing his upper body. He straightened to his full five-feet, four-inch height. "*Ha* ... Better jus' fuck her and forget her, man ..."

"Oh, marriage ain't so bad," said Big Al.

"Ain't so good neither," grumbled Toasty.

"... If you got a good old lady."

"You got a good old lady?" said Lushwell, sweating profusely, troweling under the scaffolding at the deep end of the pool.

"She's okay," said Big Al.

"She suck your dick?" said Lushwell.

Al made a sour face.

"You are without a doubt the most foulest-mouth son of a bitch I have ever met."

"Thanks," said Lushwell. "Now will you guys get these goddam planks and jacks outta here before we have to finish this thing with a jackhammer."

"Raymond!" yelled Bill from the shallow end.

Raymond came running from the street, his face and shirt flecked with white cement, pants wet from the knees down, old brown fishing hat squashed down on his head.

"Planks out."

"Okay okay okay," said Raymond, his gravelly voice several octaves too low for his size. He was the only man on the crew shorter than Toasty.

The planks and jacks were lifted out and the serious work of finishing the pool began; one pass down the bottom and both sides with knee boards, then the final pass with special finishing shoes. It was too hot to talk much. Ninety-degree California heat increased some forty degrees in the bone-white bottom of the pool. Perspiration stung the eyes. Hair and eyebrows bleached white in the summer sun. Boots sloshed with sweat. Only Toasty, still feeling the effects of a lunch of Budweiser and bennies, mumbled curses about his four wives and his worthless children. They troweled their way down the center, then back up the sides; the last man out leaned over the side at the shallow end to trowel away the remaining footprint.

Lushwell threw up in the gutter out by the street and leaned weakly against the truck.

"Taste good?" said Raymond, hosing down the driveway.

"Great ... Always tastes better comin' up."

"What you need is a nice cool one at John's."

"You buyin'?"

"The second one," said Raymond.

"Tight fucker," said Lushwell. "See you back at the yard."

Raymond finished cleaning up, crawled into the cab of the two-ton truck, jammed it into low gear and whined away toward South Gate. He sat on two small pillows so he could see over the dashboard. The others piled into the two pickup trucks and headed for the yard. Another pool, another thirty dollars. Two pools a day most days. Not bad ... Lushwell rode with Bill. Both battered trucks stopped at the first liquor store. Bill bought a tall Oly and Lushwell a half pint of Jim Beam. Toasty and Big Al were still arguing about who was going to pay when they left the store. Lushwell opened the half pint, tossed the cap out the window and took a long gulp. Bill waited till Lushwell opened the door and threw up before he pulled out of the parking lot.

"Ahhhh," said Lushwell. "Smo-o-o-o-th ..."

Lushwell, alias Jimmy Ferguson, ex-Golden Glover, current barroom brawler. At thirty-six he looked like he could still step in the ring and hold his own. Fightin' Fergy, his ring career washed away by too many half pints, his training too often confined to a romp in the sheets instead of a run through the park. Hell of a man. Everybody said that. Like Toasty. Hell of a cement finisher, that Toasty. None better. When you could find him, get him to the pool. Half a roll of whites and a bottle of Bud, Toasty could set a pool on fire.

Bill turned west on Leffingwell.

"You gonna stop for a cool one?" said Lushwell.

"Yeh."

"Could I interest you in a game of shuffleboard?"

"How many you gonna spot me?"

"Spot you? You almost beat me last time."

"Yeh, sure," said Bill. "I need seven. At least."

"*Seven* ... *Jesus*, Bill. If you need a beer that bad, why don't you just ask?"

"Okay ... Buy me a beer."

"Fuck you."

"Then I need six. Minimum."

"I'll give you five," said Lushwell. "And that's too many."

"Deal," said Bill.

But he knew that even with the five points, his chances of winning were slim. Dead drunk, Lushwell was good. Either hand.

"You really gonna get married?"

"Yeh," said Bill. "Couple of weeks."

"Want some advice?"

"No."

"Don't do it."

"Thanks."

"Well," said Lushwell, "I suppose everybody ought to try it once." He laughed dryly. "Shit, I did it three times."

"Slow learner?"

"I guess." He wiped the top of the bottle with the palm of his hand and took a drink. "Women ..." He shook his head. "Worthless ..."

"Sour grapes," said Bill.

"... Just wait."

Bill veered right onto Imperial Boulevard. Not Gloria, he thought. Some of the others maybe, but not Gloria. She was different.

They had met that spring at Jose's Number Two, a decomposing diner on the west side of town. She was the young, willow blonde with air-brush features and warm brown eyes. Frank's date. Their eyes met and for several seconds neither could look away. A week later he casually asked Frank if he had the hots for that what's-her-name he was out with last week? Gloria? Yeh ... No ... Mind if I ask her out? ... No ... From the beginning it was magic. Though she would allow him to fondle her, she drew the line at intercourse ... I don't want to lose my status as a practicing virgin, she said ... When he got especially frantic, she would remove a scented hanky from her embroidered Guatemalan purse, drape it over his quivering organ, wrap her two small hands around it and furiously pump up and down till he shuddered, made those funny noises and slumped back in the seat. He always found it odd that she folded the hankies in neat little squares and put them back in her purse. He wondered if she saved them. Five weeks after they met, he asked her to marry him. She readily agreed, obliquely promising sexual delights after the nuptials.

"My first lady just walked out," said Lushwell.

"Musta been crazy to leave a prince like you," said Bill.

"Yeh." He finished the half pint and tossed the empty on the floor. "If I ever find her, I'll break her fuckin' neck."

"Great idea," said Bill, draining the last of his Oly. "That's what I'd do."

He turned right on Atlantic, drove the block and a half to the yard and parked on the street. They jogged across the four lanes of intermittent traffic to Sleeveless John's.

John Jenkins, the sleeveless one, was banging the dice cup on the bar when they entered.

"Fi-i-i-i-ive fives," he bellowed. "Beat that, chump."

Mambo Pruitt frowned as he shook the dice cup, lifted it over his head and slammed it down on the bar as hard as he could.

"Come *on*, motha*fuck*er ... Give old Mambo some *sixes*."

They surveyed the dice: one six, three fives and a three.

"Better take the fives," said John.

"Hah!" snorted Mambo, leaving the six and shaking again. "Mambo's mommy didn't raise no mothafuckin' *fool*."

"How about a beer, John?" said Lushwell.

"... Lushwell," said John. "And his faithful companion, Billy the Kid."

"*Four* mothafuckin' sixes," said Mambo.

"Hi, J.J.," said Bill.

Mambo flipped the remaining die until it turned up six, then slammed the cup down on the bar.

"*Five* mothafuckin' sixes," he said.

"Put the dice in the cup, Mambo. I didn't hear no rattle."

"I did, man. I did."

Chapter 12

"Jesus ..."

"You owe me," said Mambo, smiling wickedly.

They drank through the afternoon. The bar gradually filled
with men from other construction crews, a few women from
the Packaging Corporation of America down the street. The
juke box cranked out Petula Clark and Sam the Sham and the
Pharaohs. Only three, Bill promised himself when he went in.
After he drank the three, he decided five would be okay. What
the fuck, he thought. What's five beers? Mouse nuts. ... Gloria
didn't approve of his drinking. And she didn't even know about
the pills. But Jesus, five beers. Or six even. ...

Daylight faded to a back-bar glow. John turned the outside
lights on. The newly erected neon sign depicted a sleeveless
arm in constant motion.

"Cost a grand," John said proudly.

"Looks like he's jackin' off," said Lushwell.

"... Only you would think of that ..."

Bill stared at his reflection till his face began to fragment. He
poked a finger at his eye.

"Another beer, J.J.," he said.

"Comin' up, kid."

He lifted his glass and toasted the face in the mirror.

"... Vuvuvuvu ..."

But he knew she was gone. He remembered the funeral.
Precious Blood Cemetery; the plastic crucifix on the hump-
backed coffin. She never spoke again after the stroke, only the
slurred *vuvuvu*'s that seemed to get clearer but never seemed
to make words. She progressed to a wheelchair, even made
some halting progress in a chrome-plated Winston Walker,
vuvuvu-ing excitedly as she lurched down the tightly carpeted
hallways of the Evergreen Nursing Home. But a series of
setbacks secured her forever to the white linen rack where she
lingered unto death. Into Father Murgatroyd's jumbo hand she
squeezed her last mute confession. He absolved her with a
weary blessing, passing her sins to Jesus without comment.

Near the end, it seemed to Bill that she began to decompose
before his eyes. The cellophane hand that once traced mystic

circles in the air lay still as stone on the woolly blanket. A leg that always twitched when she got excited moved no more. One day both eyes were closed, her cheeks collapsed. Only the shallow breathing and the rhythmic beat of the bedside monitor gave evidence of life. Two weeks later, the monitor simply *bee-e-e-eped*, its electric fingers connected to a body growing cold and stiff.

Thomas was present at the funeral, somber and alone. Bill was surprised that he looked so old; his crew-cut hair was nearly white beneath the white Panama hat he removed only when the coffin was lowered into the ground. Father Murgatroyd sprinkled holy water like a man possessed, mumbling mixed metaphors about deliverance and resurrection as the earthly maw claimed the wrinkled remains of Dorothy Krueger Mahoney.

After the funeral, Bill shook hands with Thomas, who shuffled his feet and looked as if he wanted to say something. But Bill was gone before he could speak, masking his tears with a manufactured cough.

"You don't quit talkin' to yourself," said Lushwell, "they're gonna come get you with a fuckin' net."

"Who?" said Bill.

"You."

Bill rubbed his hand across his forehead. He wondered what time it was. Jesus ... He had things to do ... He'd have to remember to get rid of the mannequin he kept hidden in his closet. That was important. Gloria would never understand.

"How 'bout a beer, J.J."

"Comin' up, kid."

His head felt like it was full of spiders.

The Dodgers struggled through late June and early July. Gunner's batting average continued to drop like an Arctic thermometer.

"Ten for sixty-two," Gunner moaned. "Can you believe it?"

"No," said Bill.

"It's true."

"I absolutely refuse to believe it."

"It's fuckin' true."

"Well ... don't give up the ship."

"Don't give up the ship," he mimicked. "That's great, Mahoney. Wish I'd said that."

"You just did."

"Christ ..."

Charley Soprano appeared to be regaining his form in the field, but still seemed hesitant and fearful at the plate. Opponents pitched him inside. Charley inched off the plate in anticipation of the inside pitch. Then they pitched him outside. Everything seemed to be in on the hands or out off the end of the bat. J.C. took him aside in the corner of the dugout after a particularly tough game.

"How is it wid ya, Cha'ley?"

"Pretty good, Mr. Christianson. I'm not hittin' real well yet, but ..."

"No hurry," said J.C. "It'll come aroun'."

"Oh, I know it will," he said quickly. "It's just that ... I feel like I'm letting everybody down. I'm not ..."

"No let down," said J.C. "I jus' wanna let ya know ... to jus' take ya time. Time is plen'y. I un'erstan' how it is ... I was hit once. In Triple A. In a head."

"Gee ..."

"Yeh ..." He touched a spot just below his left ear. "Before helmets."

"... Gee ..."

"Yeh ... An' I was scared." He looked at Soapy and held his gaze. "Scared ... I di'n even know if I wan'ed to play. Every time I went to the plate. Scared ... My knees would shake. Like dis ..." He straightened his legs and gave them an exaggerated shake. "I thought everybody could see ... Dis one guy ... Burgett. He'd say, Come on, Sissy. Quit bailin' out dere ... Dat was Burgett. Big guy. Played firs' base. Never forget 'im. But I di'n quit. I just kept goin' to the plate. Scared. One day I was more scared dat I *wou'n* play than I was a gettin hit. ... Ya see?"

Soapy nodded.

"Yes, sir. It's not so much that I'm afraid ... It's ..."

"Everybody's scared ... sometimes ..."

"I ask ... the Lord to help me."

"U-huh ..."

"I pray."

"U-huh ..."

"To Jesus ..."

"Prayin' might help," said J.C.

"The Lord always helps me."

J.C. grunted, leaned forward and spat some Red Man on the dugout floor.

"U-huh ... Ya do whatever helps. I jus' wan'ed to tell ya we're behin' ya. One hunnert percent. No pressure ... We know ya can do it."

"Thanks, Mr. Christianson."

"Don' mention it."

"I'll do better."

"No pressure."

J.C. watched him walk out of the dugout. Nice kid, he thought. Maybe too nice. Kids like that just disappeared with that same vague smile on their faces. He sometimes wondered what became of them. Kids that kicked the bat rack and threw batting helmets seemed to be able to handle the setbacks better.

He sat alone in the dugout. A late Sunday afternoon. The field empty, the last of the fans gone home, the blue stands littered with empty cups and candy wrappers ...

Pilots 13
Dodgers 2

What a day. The groundskeeper would be out soon to rake the infield and set up the rainbird sprinklers. The outfield walls were covered with the madcap murals of local advertisers. ... Hit the yellow bull's-eye and get a free lube and oil change at Jacobson's Garage ... Colorful. Didn't have things like that in the big leagues anymore. Just plain green walls. No more Dizzy Deans or Pepper Martins. Big bi'ness, he thought. Only they wore baseball uniforms instead of three-piece suits. Same t'ing ... But not much fun. Not any more. ... He pulled the paperback from his back pocket and opened it where the page was turned down.

> She gripped her fingers together and
> knew already that Rex's power over her
> was strong. She ached now for the touch
> of his lips and the strength of his arms
> holding her. She longed to hear his
> voice, low and broken, calling her name.
> She gave a little sigh and realized that
> the kettle was boiling.
> As she made the tea she found herself
> whispering his name aloud: "Rex! Rex!"

He read for a few minutes and closed the book. He put his hands on his knees, rocked forward and got to his feet. A sharp pain tugged at his chest. He massaged the left side of his chest with both hands until the pain went away. "Ahhhhh," he said. That pain ... A bother. He took a deep breath and trudged up the dugout steps.

"Hi, Fred," he said to an old man raking the dirt around third base.

"Hi, John. Tough day, eh?"

"We have played better, Fred. Much better."

"You'll get 'em tomorrow."

"I hope. .... Ya ever pray, Fred?"

"I ever what?"

"Pray ... Like in church."

"Sometimes."

"It help?"

"Sometimes."

J.C. nodded and kept walking, hands deep in his back pockets.

Chumley wheeled the old huffnpuff down Highway 5 like a man fleeing the plague. His gray tam pulled low over his eyes, touching the top of his trifocals, a grim smile twisting his mouth, he studiously avoided all efforts by Doc Hardin to engage him in conversation. He closed his eyes near the 205 cutoff in Manteca and envisioned an eight-lane highway that ran straight to the sun. When he opened them he was almost on top of an Econoline van that was struggling to stay above 50 mph in the headwind. Chumley slammed his palm down on the horn like he was squashing a bug, whipped the bus to the left and passed without taking his hand off the horn.

"Turd," he snarled.

Larry Duffy's stereo clattered to the floor.

"Pretty close," said Doc, wiping his forehead with a handkerchief. "Pretty close there."

"Turd," said Chumley.

Doc couldn't tell whether he meant him or the guy driving the van.

"My muthafuckin' *stereo* broke, you got trouble, old man," groused Duffy. He picked it up like a fallen child, hoisted it to his shoulder and tenderly turned it on. A small smile cracked his scowl. "Lucky you," he mumbled, staring at the knobby back hunched over the wheel.

"Brakes?" said Gunner. "This thing got brakes? What about my career?"

"Got a good horn, man, you don't need brakes," said Chewy.

"You must be from Mexico, sir," said Gunner.

"I fucked your sister," said Chewy.

"I don't *have* a sister."

"No wonder," said Chewy. "No fuckin' wonder."

Aside from a few pointed exchanges, the ride was unusually

subdued. The season was creeping into the dog days of July when the bus rides seemed interminable, when the eager friendships of April and May turned sour in the summer heat. The Bigs seemed further away as batting averages fell and earned run averages climbed.

The Dodger ship foundered in seas of inconsistency. When the pitching was effective, the hitters took the night off. When both were acceptable, gloves developed holes that allowed routine ground balls to skip through and pop flies to drop untouched. They developed new and ingenious ways of losing. Coach Sly became surly, communicating in grunts and four-letter epithets. He saw his chances of managing in the big leagues diminish with each passing day. He took to throwing his cap against the dugout wall in times of stress.

The Skipper remained calm, a rock of reassurance. Though he juggled the lineup and changed the pitching rotation, he refused to panic. Lanoski seemed to catch fire in the second half, raising his batting average to a healthy .270, beginning to hit with power. J.C. moved him up to the number five spot in the lineup. He shifted the slumping Gunner to number eight. Tom Coleman in right field was benched and Nick Malducci was given a shot at the outfield. He performed adequately in the field and was beginning to find his eye at the plate. He had a disturbing tendency to run into outfield fences, but if he stayed healthy, J.C. knew he would help the team. Charley Soprano, once an excellent leadoff man, was relegated to hitting ninth. Little League coaches told their tiny charges that the number nine hitter was their second leadoff man, thus trying to soften the blow of hitting last. Bigger boys knew better. On the rare occasions when he made contact, he was so far back on his heels that he couldn't hit with power. Opposing infielders crept closer, negating his speed down the line. Soapy continued to pray.

"You know, Mahoney," said Gunner, "I heard about this guy in the majors that dyed his hair orange."

"Yeh?"

"Yep ... Pulled him right out of a batting slump."

"Yeh?"

"Yep ... Started hittin' a ton."

"Orange?" said Bill.

"Orange. A Jewish guy. Blomberg ... Mike Blomberg. With the Mets I think."

"Orange hair ..."

"Started hittin' a ton ... One absolute fuckin' ton."

"You think that did it? Dyin' his hair orange?"

"I don't know ... Blomberg thought so. Said he could see the ball better."

"Huh ... See the ball better. ... Hardly makes any sense at all, does it?"

"... Not much."

"Well ... takes all kinds I guess."

"... I guess."

Gunner went back to clipping his fingernails.

Southbound on 680 through Fremont and Milpitas ... huffnpuff ... huffnpuff ... huffnpufffff. ...

Daniel Lanoski, sitting across the aisle from Nick Malducci, was demonstrating his new and devastating swing.

"Like this, Nick," he said, swinging an imaginary bat in the aisle. He brought his arms forward slowly. "The chin has to be down." He tucked his chin into his chest. "That way you *can't* pull your head. It's not your *eyes* you have to keep on the ball. It's your *chin* ... You can still pull your head and try to look at the ball. Like this ..." He turned his head to the left and gave an improbable demonstration. "Ever see Steve Garvey hit?"

Nick nodded.

"Like that. Even after he follows through, his head's still down. Like a golfer's. Ever see a golfer swing?"

Nick nodded.

"Like that. And keep your weight back. Hit off the back foot. All power hitters ..."

"Can you believe it?" muttered Gunner. "Fuckin' Loony givin' batting instructions. Christ ..."

"Whatever happened to this Blomberg?" said Bill.

"I don't know."

"Maybe he joined the circus."

Gunner ignored the comment.

"Stayed up a couple of years, I think. There's not a lot of

Jewish guys in the majors." He leaned forward so that Chewy would be sure to hear. "... Jewish guys or *Mex*icans ..."

Chewy gave him the finger without turning around.

"Up yours," he said.

Gunner smiled and settled back in his seat.

J.C. mulled over his pitching rotation for the four-game series with the San Jose Missions. He doodled on the inside back of his Barbara Cartland novel. Kaz ... Keane ... Nesbitt ... Maybe give Mahoney a spot start. Didn't see many guys his age in Single A ball. A few, on their way down, might play Triple A for a while. ... But he was good with the younger pitchers and .... hell, he had the third best ERA on the staff.

The hitters were a mixed bag. Lanoski, after a disappointing first half, was on a tear. Soprano continued to be timid at the plate. J.C. decided to stick with him, though he wasn't sure that Klinger, for all his errors, might not be more help. Gunner was a puzzle. A proven left-handed power hitter, he was mired in the midst of a terrible slump. J.C. penciled him in at the cleanup spot. Maybe that'll help, he thought; give him some confidence.

The rest were all having average years, about what you'd expect in Class A. The trouble was, they could never all get average together. A few would sparkle, the rest would be awful. They had enough talent to win it; he was sure of that. Maybe only the Giants had as much. But the Giants were well out in front; four up on the Oaks, six-and-a-half in front of the Pilots, seven up on the Missions and an incredible nine games in front of the Dodgers. The Pioneers and A's wallowed far back. Only forty-three games left to play. Nine games to make up. The Dodgers would have to win maybe eight out of ten to make a run at it. Unless the Giants hit the skids. Not likely. Snake Simpson was having an outstanding year; J.C. was surprised he hadn't been called up. Bobby Elford was hitting over .350 ... No, it didn't seem likely that the Giants would fold. The Dodgers would have to do it themselves. J.C. opened his book ...

> ... He spoke the last words in such a
> lover-like way that Fenella glanced up
> apprehensively. Elaine, fortunately,

was not in the room, having gone
upstairs after dinner.

Sir Nicholas and Moo were in the
corner playing Corinthian bagatelle
which Rex had brought back that
afternoon from his home and not yet
taken down to camp.

This intimacy with Rex was too dangerous, she was afraid it would betray
them. And yet she found it hard to
ignore him even for a moment when
he was in the room with her.

"Okay, crumbums," said Sly, as Chumley jammed the brakes
on in the parking lot outside the San Jose Municipal Stadium.
"Let's see if we can't win a ballgame or two here ... for a
change."

"I'm gonna dye my hair orange," Gunner whispered as they
left the bus.

"... Is that a threat?"

"No. I just wanted you to know so's ..."

"I won't tell," said Bill. "But someone else may notice ..."

"I know that ... Christ, Mahoney. I know ..."

Bill put his hand on Gunner's shoulder.

"Just kiddin'," he said. "But after you dye your hair, do me a
favor and stop tryin' to shorten up and punch the ball, willya?
Just swing at the goddam thing. You've got one of the smooth-
est swings I've ever seen and you're up at the plate tryin' to
punch the ball. I can hardly stand to watch. Most times I just
close my eyes. You look like some old *la*dy up there tryin'
to ..."

"All right all *right* ..."

"Bring some joy to Mudville, Mister ... swing the goddam bat
..."

"All *right*, Mahoney. I *hear* you ... Christ ..."

The United Presbyterian Church in
Canoga Park was the setting for the
wedding of Gloria Alsop, daughter of
Mr. and Mrs. Bruce Alsop and William
Mahoney. Mr. and Mrs. (deceased)
Thomas Mahoney are the bridegroom's
parents. The Rev. Bertram Mueller
officiated. Miss Kandy Karol and Mr.
Harold Larsen Jr. attended the couple.
The newlyweds will reside in Van
Nuys.

Valley News & Greensheet

June 20, 1965

The reception at the Alsops was a blustery affair; four-layer
wedding cake with a tiny bride and groom revolving slowly on
the top tier (Don't eat the bride and groom, confided Mrs. Alsop
... They're plastic), cases of California Sparkling Burgundy, a
generous supply of Scotch, finger sandwiches from Linda's
Catering, a crush of well-wishers clogging the smallish house
like an obstructed drain. Bruce Alsop's ruddy face beamed
behind a glass of bubbly, his demeanor that of a generous king.
Though no one asked, they wondered how he felt about this
young man bedding his oldest daughter. Many would gladly
have traded places with the groom. Mrs. Alsop flitted around
like a blue darter, present everywhere at once, greeting a
newcomer, farewelling an early leaver, producing more sandwich fingers with a snap on her own. Ordinarily a pleasant
woman (trying to adjust to recently prescribed bifocals), she
was a dervish that sweltering June afternoon. Dawn, Gloria's
little sister, watched disdainfully through thick, owlish glasses,
grimly refusing to enjoy herself.

In midafternoon, Eddy Nelson launched into the "Anniversary Waltz" on his accordion. Bill and Gloria danced. She was luminous, a vision of innocence. Her high-school chums watched, breathless and teary, conjuring images of weddings to be. Bill squirmed in his tuxedo, flushed and uncomfortable. They cut the cake, posed for pictures and mixed with small clusters of guests. Bill awkwardly accepted congratulations from middle-aged matrons. Only a few of his friends were there, those from his high-school days. He knew enough not to ask Toasty or Lushwell or Sleeveless John. Sluggo Larsen, whom he did not view as a close friend, was the only one he could think of to be best man. When he made up his wedding list, he was surprised to find that there were very few people he cared to invite. There were acquaintances, people he worked with, drank with, but no close friends. The invitation to his father still lay on the seat in his pickup truck, addressed but never mailed.

At three-thirty, Gloria went out on the front porch and tossed the wedding bouquet over her shoulder. Kandy caught it and all the girls squealed. Kandy's date, Ernie Lazlo, blushed to the roots of his volcanic acne. At six o'clock, when only the hardcore remained, slumped over couches and chairs like discarded coats, boozy from afternoon champagne and Scotch, Gloria went to the bedroom to change.

Soggy cigarettes floated lazily in half-empty glasses, forgotten finger sandwiches rested on crumpled napkins, getting stale in the heat. Bruce Alsop sat stoically in his big brown easy chair, his face red, a lopsided grin on his lips. Eddy Nelson packed his pearl-inlaid accordion in its felt case and prepared to leave. Mrs. Alsop continued to zip around the house, though there was nothing left to do. Bill changed and gave Sluggo his tux to return. Gloria appeared at the bedroom door clad in a tan summer dress, a small yellow suitcase clutched in her hand.

"Oh," moaned Mrs. Alsop, rushing to embrace her daughter.

With considerable effort, Mr. Alsop pushed himself out of his chair.

" 'Bye, Punkin," he said, crushing her with a bear hug.

Bill shook hands with Bruce as Gloria and Kandy fell upon each other and wept. Dawn sat in the corner and glared.

Chapter 14

"Take good care of her," Mr. Alsop said gruffly.

"I will," said Bill.

He gave Mrs. Alsop a peck on the cheek.

"You're such a nice boy," she said, dabbing at a tear with a Kleenex.

" 'Bye everybody," said Gloria, waving like a homeless waif.

They walked two blocks east and a block south to Gloria's new blue Rambler Classic, her graduation present. Despite efforts to hide it, the car had been discovered, a soapy JUST MARRIED written across the back window.

They headed out the Ventura Freeway toward the Blue Jay Hotel in Lake Arrowhead.

"Wasn't it *won*derful?" she said.

"Really nice."

"... Really."

The early evening Saturday traffic was light through the interchange. Sonny and Cher warbled "I Got You, Babe" on the car radio.

> ... Then put your lit-tle hand in mine,
>
> There ain't no hill or mountain
>
> We can't climb ...

"You'll be so-o-o-ory," yelled a man from a passing car.

"Huh," she said. "That's all *he* knows."

They sped through Alhambra.

"Are we going too fast?" she said.

He slowed down.

"Oh, Bill," she said, sliding closer on the vinyl seat. "I love you a lot ..."

"Great," he said. "Me too ... It's gonna be good."

"I really believe that. I really do. This is the happiest day of my whole life."

"Yeh." He wondered why he didn't feel happy.

He coaxed the bulky Nash up the winding road to Lake Arrowhead. At the Blue Jay Hotel, he signed the register as Mr. and Mrs. Mahoney. The clerk directed him to Room 204, overlooking the lake. He lifted her in his arms and carried her over the threshold.

"Well, here we are, Mrs. Mahoney," he said.

She sat on the bed looking very small and fragile.

"Boy, what a day," she said.

"Long ..."

"... Really."

He sat next to her on the bed. She stood up.

"Nice room," she said, walking to the closet, touching the hangars, looking in the bathroom. "Nice bathroom. Really nice ... What time is it?"

"Little after eight-thirty."

"Early, eh?"

"Yeh ..."

"Oh, look honey ... a TV."

"Uhuh."

"Can we watch for a while? ... Before we ... go to bed?"

He nodded his agreement as he turned it on and watched the somewhat greenish face of Victor Mature form on the screen.

"And it's *color*," she squealed.

Bill leaned back against the headboard. The room was warm. He felt dizzy ... *To have and to hold ... till death do you part ... You may kiss the bride the bride the bride ...*

Gloria returned to the other side of the bed, but would not look at him. He unbuttoned the top two buttons on his shirt.

"Look, honey," she said, pointing to the television where a man in a three-pointed hat was extolling the virtues of Pepsodent toothpaste.

"Uhuh ..."

"Could we get a color TV for our place?"

"Sure," he said.

She clapped her hands.

The commercial gave way to the movie where some kind of military action was taking place. There were rifle shots. Victor Mature scurried down an alley in the shadows. The voice of Clark Gable came from a figure in the darkness.

"I guess I'll ... change," said Gloria, getting up from the bed. She opened her suitcase, pulled something out of it and disappeared into the bathroom.

Bill didn't move for a few moments. He was overcome by a strange sense of detachment. On the brink of consummating his marriage, of bedding the lady of his desire, fear as tangible as bone chips pervaded his thoughts.

He forced himself to stand and take off his shirt.

"I am a real person," he said quietly. "I am standing in a room at the Blue Jay Hotel in Arrowhead, California. Glor ... My wife is in the bathroom changing her clothes ... I am not afraid. My name is Bill Mahoney. I am a real fucking person. A real person ..."

He stripped to his shorts. On or off, he thought, thumbs hooked in the elastic waistband of his boxer shorts. He slid them to his thighs, looked at himself, then pulled them back up. Just doing things made him feel better. He sat on the bed and lit a cigarette. The sense of isolation began to recede. He folded the covers back, lay down and drummed his fingers on his chest.

The toilet flushed ... Gloria coughed ...

> ... and now these messages from the
> sponsors of the "NBC Saturday Night
> Movie" ...

He wondered what she was doing. He tried to picture her naked, but he could only see small sections at a time, just flashes of bare skin. She might be inserting a diaphragm, he thought, but it occurred to him that he didn't even know if she used a diaphragm. Or if she could cook. He didn't know much of anything about her. He put his hands behind his head.

> ... and now, we return to the "NBC
> Saturday Night Movie," *Betrayed,*
> starring Clark Gable, Lana Turner and
> Victor Mature ...

Could she cook? Did she sleep in the nude?

The bathroom door opened; she appeared in a sheer blue nightgown that just touched the floor. She turned around slowly.

"Mmmmmmm ..." he said.

She tiptoed to the bed and slid in beside him. He put his arms around her. She shivered slightly.

"Cold?" he said.

"A little."

He pulled her close.

"Shouldn't we ... turn off the lights?" she said.

He got out of bed and turned the lights off.

"The TV?" he said.

"Yes."

He slipped his shorts off in the dark, got back into bed and gathered her into his arms. She nibbled on his ear.

"Scared?" he said.

"... A little."

Would it hurt her? he wondered. The first time? He'd heard stories ... Maybe he should get a towel. Just in case ...

"Maybe I should get a towel," he said.

"A towel?"

"In case you ... In case there's some blood."

"... You think?"

"Maybe ..."

"... Okay."

He groped his way to the bathroom and turned on the light. He glanced in the mirror and made a face.

"I am a real person," he said.

"... Who are you talking to?" she called from the other room.

"Who?"

"You."

"I'm not talking to anybody."

"Oh ..."

He grabbed a towel and returned to the bed. In his absence she had removed her nightgown. She snuggled close.

"Tell me the most terrible thing you've ever done," she whispered.

"What do you mean terrible?"

"You know ... The thing you swore you'd never tell anyone."

"... You first," he said.

She put a finger to her lips.

"Let's see ... Once I stole some money from my mother's purse."

"That doesn't sound so terrible."

"Now you."

"Lemme see ... I ran away from home when I was a kid."

Chapter 14

"You already told me that."

"Did I?"

"Yes."

"Okay ... I ... When I was little I used to steal my mother's underwear and wear it."

"*Really?*"

"Well ... I was real young."

"You really did that?"

"Just once or twice."

"Oh ... I don't think that's so bad. I mean that's more *funny* than terrible."

A vein began to throb in his temple.

"Your turn," he said.

She tapped her index finger against her front teeth.

"I cut school once ... Lied and told them I was sick."

"Huh ..."

His mouth felt dry.

"Your turn," she said.

"... I fucked a chicken once," he said.

"A *chicken?*"

"Yeh ..." Why had he told her that?

"Oh, *honey* ..."

"Well, it was ..."

"What happened?"

"To what?"

"The *chicken* ..."

"Oh, it died. Not right away. Later ... It died later."

"Oh, honey ... A chicken."

The muffled sound from the television in the next room throbbed lightly against the wall. He was glad he hadn't told her about the pig.

"... I was just kiddin'," he said.

"... For true?"

"Yeh."

"I hope so."

She squeezed his hand.

"You suppose we'll always be married?" she said.

"Forever and ever."

"What do you think it'll be like when we're old?"

"It'll be great."

"Will we still be in love?"

"Yeh."

"Even when we're all wrinkled?"

"Yep."

He pulled her close and kissed her. She put her arms around his neck and flicked a tongue in his ear.

"Say the F word," she whispered.

"The what?"

"The F word ..."

"Fuck?"

"Yes ... say it."

"Okay ... Fuck."

"Keep saying it."

He mumbled in her ear while he massaged her buttocks and tried to wedge his erection between her pinched thighs. She breathed heavily, rigid as a stone, a fortress in disguise.

"Do you have any protection?" she asked.

"Yeh ..."

He disengaged himself, fished through his pants pockets, found the packet of condoms and slipped one on. He always felt foolish doing it.

"Did you put it on?"

He eased back into bed.

"Yeh."

She reached down and touched him.

"I can feel it," she said. "Did you bring some Vaseline?"

"... Vaseline?"

"Petroleum jelly."

"Petroleum jelly," he repeated flatly.

"For ... lubrication."

"Oh ... I never use that."

"No?"

"No ... It gets ... lubricated all by itself."

"What does?"

"Your ... vagina."

"It does?"

"... Sure."

"Kandy says you're supposed to use Vaseline. So it won't

hurt."

"Kandy said that?"

"Yes."

"... I don't know," he said. "I never ..."

"You should've brought some," she said reproachfully.

"Well ..."

They lay in the abyss of silence. Finally ...

"Maybe we could try anyway," she said.

"... Yeh?"

"Sure," she said bravely. "Why not?"

She pulled him over on top of her and wiggled seductively.

"Take me," she said, after several minutes of frenzied kissing.

He lifted his hips and probed for an opening. He took her hand and placed it on his erection.

"You help," he said.

She grabbed it firmly and pulled forward.

"Uh," she said.

He could feel no penetration; it seemed to be pressed against a bone.

"Can you get it in?" he said.

She spread her legs and pulled harder.

"Uh," she said.

"Does it hurt?"

"... Uh."

"We can wait," he said. "If it hurts too much."

She strained harder, pushing her hips toward him, shifting from side to side. In desperation she grabbed him with both hands and thrust it in.

"Uhhhhhh," she groaned.

"Jesus," he said, pulling back.

"Uhhhhhhhh ..."

She leaped out of bed, hands to her crotch, and stumbled toward the bathroom.

"... Uhhhhhhh ..."

She flicked the light on and closed the door.

Several crickets chirped. "The Star Spangled Banner" was playing somewhere, perhaps the movie on television. Pearly moonlight filtered through the drapes and cast the room in somber shades of gray. He lay on his back, limp as a noodle. He felt himself drifting away. He wished he had a baseball to hold; that always helped. ... He pictured her trying to stem the flow of blood as he listened for some sound from the bathroom. Was the water running? An eternity passed before the bathroom door opened.

A dim figure drifted slowly through the shadows and sat on the bed.

"You okay?" he said.

"... Yes," she said weakly.

"I'm really sorry."

"Oh ... It's okay." She lay down, dragging the covers to her chin with an effort.

"We'll get some Vaseline next time. If you want."

"... Okay."

"I didn't know ... I mean I never used that stuff."

"... Kandy said ..."

"Oh, Kandy doesn't know everything," he said irritably.

"Well, she *said* ..."

"Huh ..."

"Everybody uses it."

"No, everybody doesn't use it."

"U-*huh*, they do."

"Most women ... *most* women ..."

He stopped.

"Most women what?" she said, sitting up.

"Most women ... don't need it."

"... Are you saying there's something wrong with me?" she said, her voice quivering between tears and anger. "Ohhhhhh ..." The tears won out.

"Oh, Glor," he said, inching toward her. "I didn't mean it that way ... I'm sorry."

"Ohhhh ..."

But she allowed him to put his arm around her.

"I'm sorry," he said. "I didn't mean it like that."

She sniffled noisily.

"Well ..." she said.

"Honest I didn't."

She wiped her nose on the blanket. He pulled her closer. She rubbed her nose on his chest and sniffled again. He rubbed her neck. She stroked his thigh and slid her hand up his leg.

It was over before it began; the stroke, the shudder, the sigh, the slump, the bone that turns to mush at the stroke of five. He got up and went to the bathroom, peeled the squishy condom off and dropped it in the toilet. He rubbed himself with a towel. He noticed that all the other towels were neatly stacked in the metal rack above the toilet. What had she used to stop the bleeding? There was a Kleenex dispenser on the front of the vanity. Maybe that or some toilet paper. Maybe ...

He shrugged and looked in the mirror; seconds later his eyes turned a sudden, fierce red. He squeezed them shut. What does it mean? he thought. He turned off the light and carefully picked his way back to bed.

"Tired?" she said.

"Yeh."

"Me too ... but happy. Tired and happy."

"Yeh."

"Good night, my husband."

"... Good night."

She was asleep in a few minutes. He lay awake, listening to the crickets, to the soft breathing at his side, measuring it against his own. Shadows from the pine trees outside the window played across the bed, moving with the wind; dark, light, a web of intrigue. He spread his hands out and looked at his long, thin fingers. People were always asking him if he played the piano ... *Hands like that, you oughta play the piano ... No, but I crack safes* ... Always got a laugh. And your wife? Oh, great hands. Great ... Light housekeeping and hand jobs.

He reached for his cigarettes on the nightstand. There, under the towel ... the towel, for the bloodbath that never materialized. Was she really a virgin? he wondered. It had not occurred to him to doubt that she was. Until now ... And did it make any difference? His head said, So what? but something else growled unreasonably at the thought.

He tossed the towel on the floor and lit a cigarette with his Zippo lighter. The *clack* as it closed seemed to explode in the silence. Gloria stirred, smacked her lips, but did not awaken.

He looked at her ... Mrs. Mahoney. She was lovely. Then why did he feel so depressed? Jesus ... He just wanted to be alone. Women ... It wasn't that he was insensitive to their needs (at least he didn't think he was); it was just that they often seemed threatening in some way.

There was Gloria next to him; innocent as ice, sweet as a strawberry. Yet he was burdened by her presence. He loved her; he was sure of that. Still, she seemed like an intruder. He stubbed his cigarette out in the ashtray.

He slipped into a troubled sleep, waking several times to find his bride sleeping peacefully at his side. He was up with the morning light, dressed and standing by the window when she woke. A single powerboat with a water-skier in tow carved graceful S's across the smooth blue surface of the lake.

"Hi," she said cheerfully.

"I love you," he said quickly.

"I love you, too," she said, sitting up, drawing the sheet up with her.

He turned from the window.

"Music to my ears," he said.

"This is my first morning as Mrs. Mahoney."

"And they said it wouldn't last."

She giggled.

"Breakfast?" he said.

"Definitely ... I'll get dressed."

She gathered her gown around her, slipped out of bed and sped to the bathroom.

He turned back to the window. Two squirrels scampered through a nearby pine. Sunlight sparkled off the lake. He closed his eyes for a moment. When he opened them, the light and sparkle had been replaced by the frumpy mounds of Oat Mountain. He heard the crackle of gunfire and the pulsating thud of twin hammers. ... He touched his face, tracing a path to his eyes. Were they open? He forced them shut and rubbed them with his knuckles. When the kaleidoscope flashes disappeared, he looked out again on the surface of the lake. He shook his head as if to dislodge something.

After breakfast they walked hand-in-hand along the lake

shore. When they went back to the room to change before going swimming, they had an argument about her yellow polka-dot bikini. Bill said it was too small. She reminded him that he didn't think it was too small before they got married. And besides, it was the only one she brought. Bill said they could buy another one and she said he was just being childish. But Bill wouldn't budge and she finally bought another one in the classy store on the Blue Jay main floor.

Later in the afternoon they played Scrabble. Bill felt he was a better player, but Gloria usually won. She took so much time making decisions about what letters to play that Bill threatened to quit if she didn't hurry. He read her the rules, despite her assurances that she knew the rules very well.

He marched to the local drugstore before dinner and searched the shelves for Vaseline. There were several kinds; some for diaper rash, some that were medicated, some to soften dry skin, others that were anti-bacterial. He settled on the eight-ounce jar that softened dry skin. That seemed appropriate.

But the second night was only slightly more successful than the first. After greasing his upright organ, a small white hand led him to the hidden orifice.

"Uh-h-h-h ..." said Gloria.

"Does it hurt?" he said.

"... Noo-o-o-o," she moaned.

He eased himself in and out in tiny increments, though the aperture did not feel particularly snug. She put a greasy hand on his back and pulled him in.

"Uh-h-h-h. ..."

... in ... out ... in ... out ...

She lay there passive as a pizza, watching his face, trying to match his breathing. Faster and faster, the old Ringmaster, whirlagig, whirlagig, come in a bunch. She shuddered when he shuddered, sighed when he sighed and smiled when it was over.

"You came, eh?" she said.

"Yeh ...you?"

"... I think so."

"Yeh?"

"Uhuh ..."

They left before the week was out, Gloria withering under the onslaught of the menses, clutching her tummy and her bottle of Midol as they retraced their tread down the winding road. Bill had trouble driving; several times he came dangerously close to the edge ... He had the feeling that everyone was real and he wasn't. Gloria didn't appear to notice.

San Jose Municipal Stadium was not the biggest ball park in
the league; 335 feet down the lines, a modest 390 to center.
What made Muni especially difficult for left-handed power
hitters was the fact that center field was not the deepest part of
the field. That was reserved for the right-center-field power
alley, a healthy 406 feet. With the wind blowing in. Hard. Like
Arlington Stadium in Texas, it was a graveyard for lefties with
power. Tremendous shots that left the bat born to be tape
measure home runs died a quiet death on the warning track as
routine fly balls.

Gunner grumped about it as he slipped on his cleats in the
locker room.

"Muni Stadium ... Can you believe it?" he said.

Lanoski checked the lineup card.

"Hey man ... You see this?" he said. "Gunner? ..."

"Here, sir," said Gunner. "What can I do for you?"

"They got you hittin' number four," said Loony.

Gunner looked up from his shoelace.

"Look," said Loony, jabbing a stubby forefinger at the yellow
lineup card. "Ramirez, Tenor, Guttierez ... Gun-der-son ..."

Gunner shuffled across the room, one shoe on, his toe stuck
in the other one, scraping it noisily across the floor. He looked
at the card.

"Well, of course ..." he said.

"Must be a mistake," said Loony.

"Must be," said Tenor.

"Big deal," said Chewy.

"Actually it's *not* a mistake," said Gunner.

"Big fuckin' deal," said Chewy.

Gunner glared at him, then dragged his loose shoe back to the
bench.

"He's got me hittin' cleanup," he said.

"I heard," said Bill.

"Huh ... I wonder why?"

"Why not?"

"... You happen to see my battin' average lately?"

"It's terrible," said Bill.

"Thanks a lot."

"Don't mention it."

"Christ, Mahoney, I ..."

"Gunner, Gunner ... I want you to understand something. You are big league material. You have a real shot at it. You need to know that. Now you can dye your hair orange, or purple ... you can ..."

"Okay, listen up," said Coach Sly, slapping the side of a locker. "Listen up now ... I don't have to tell you that the slide stops here, fellas. Right here." He stamped his foot for emphasis. "We're nine games out. Today. Nine games. And today we start to come back ... You guys are Dodgers. Don't ever forget that. And Dodgers have *pride*. You're part of the best organization in baseball. I expect you to start *actin'* like it. You guys been playin' like a bunch of crumbums. All of you ... Today we turn it around. Today we start playin' like Dodgers." He looked around the quiet room. "You got anything, John?"

J.C. sat on a bench, massaging his chest with his right hand.

"Keep ya heads up," he said.

They finished dressing and went out to warm up. It was nearing twilight. A balmy breeze was blowing in from right field. Gunner plucked a few blades of grass and tossed them in the air; they blew rapidly toward home plate.

"Beautiful," he said. "Just fuckin' beautiful."

Keane began to get loose in the bull pen. Bill, Kaz and Danny did some running in the outfield. J.C. sat in the corner of the dugout looking vacantly out toward left field, his fungo bat resting on his thighs.

"You gonna hit infield, John?" said Sly.

J.C. continued to stare out at the field.

"John?"

"... Uh?"

"You gonna hit infield? ... It's time."

J.C. pondered the question.

"Infield? ... No ... not tonight."

"... You okay?"

"Little tired," he said. He lifted the fungo bat with both hands and offered it to Sly. "You hit," he said.

"You want me to use that?"

"Yeh ..."

"I can use one of the other ..."

"Use dis."

"Okay," said Sly, gently lifting the bat from J.C.'s hands. "You're sure you're okay?"

"Yeh ...

Keane didn't last through the third inning. Two plus and he was gone. The mediocre Missions hit everything that came near the plate. Malducci ran into the right-field fence trying to run down another shot to the outfield. But he made the catch, and after a brief visit from Doc Hardin, decided to stay in the game.

"Holy fuck," said Kaz. "Nick's gonna kill himself out there someday."

"Yeh," said Bill. "But at least he'll go to the big Ballpark in the Sky if he dies during a game."

"Ma-honey," scoffed Kaz.

"You can laugh, but that's what happens. It's like dying in a religious war. The Big Dodger takes care of his own."

"What about the Giants?"

"Be serious," said Bill. "There's no heaven for Giants."

Gunner popped to the shortstop his first time up.

"Major league pop-up," said Loony as Gunner jogged by on his way to the dugout.

"Why don't you show me how it's done?" Gunner snapped.

"No problem," said Loony as he ambled toward the plate. He hung a frozen rope down the third-base line for a double.

"Christ!" said Gunner, slamming his batting helmet down on the dugout bench.

Midway through the second inning, Larry Duffy sprinted to the bull pen.

"Skip wants you to get loose, Buba," he puffed.

"Me?" said Buba Taylor, indicating himself with a long black index finger.

"Not yo mammy, chump."

Buba unfolded his six-feet, six-inch frame.

"Come on, White boy."

Gerry White, third-string catcher and sometimes DH, huddled at the end of the bench. He had been pressed into bull pen service when Nick moved to the outfield.

"Awwww ..." Nobody liked to catch Buba.

"Come *on*, boy. Lightnin' gotta get *loose*."

"Awwww ..." said White, reluctantly picking up his glove and mask. "Take it easy," he grumbled settling in a crouch behind the bull pen plate.

It was 6-0 Missions when Buba got the call. Keane left the mound before his relief arrived. Just dropped the ball and walked off. As a matter of courtesy, J.C. wanted his pitchers to remain on the mound till the relief man came in. It was one of the few things he insisted on. Keane threw his glove in the corner of the dugout and slumped on the bench.

"I never got a fuckin' call," he whined.

"Bush, kid," said J.C.

"... Not one fuckin' call."

"Bush-league stuff."

Their eyes met for several seconds; Keane was the first to look away.

A murmur of appreciation rippled through the stands as Buba Taylor threw his eight warm-ups. Buba heard, and uncorked the mighty Midnight Express on the last pitch.

"Man on first, one out," said Sly, as he departed for the dugout.

Buba manicured the mound with his right foot, then signified that he was ready. The ump pointed to him and assumed his crouch behind Loony. Buba went into a full windup, forgetting the man on first, and delivered a high hard one, two feet over Loony's outstretched mitt. The runner, off with the pitch, jogged easily into third. The Missions whooped it up in the dugout.

"Jesus," said Sly, slinging his cap against the dugout wall. "I just told him, John. Just this minute ... Man on first, Buba. Man on first. And what does he do? He goes into a full windup and throws it all the way to the backstop ... I don't know, John. I just don't know." He cupped his hands and yelled out toward the mound. "Come on, Buba. Suck it up out there. Use your head, for chrissakes."

Buba smiled sheepishly. He got the sign from Loony, came set and delivered a sizzling strike.

"*Now* he goes into a stretch," muttered Sly.

Eleven pitches later Buba jogged off the mound: two strike-outs, runner stranded on third.

"Way to work out of it, Buba," said Sly. "Way to throw the old heat out there."

"I'm just gettin' loose," said Buba. "Wait'll next innin'."

The Dodgers got three back in the fourth on singles by Chewy and Guttierez and a home run by Loony. Gunner popped up again.

"Boy, he hits those things high," said Danny, as the ball threatened to disappear in the night sky.

"'Bout a mile straight up," said Kaz.

"Be a hell of a shot if he got on top of it," said Bill.

"Sure would," said Tenor. "He's due."

"Like the rent," said Kaz.

"I got a feeling he's gonna hit one out tonight," said Bill.

"Not here," said Kaz. "Maybe at Webb or Rohnert. But not here."

"A pizza says he does," said Bill.

"You wanna bet? A pizza? ... That he hits one out tonight?"

"Yeh ..."

"You're on, Mahoney," said Kaz, smacking his lips. "You're on."

Buba continued to blaze away on the mound for the next four innings, surrendering two base hits, issuing only two walks and chalking up seven more strike-outs. The Dodgers scratched for single runs in the fifth and sixth. Gunner popped up again in the seventh. He threw his batting helmet against the fence on his way back to the dugout. Buba tired in the eighth. He gave up a walk and was two balls into his next one when J.C. sent Sly out with the hook. Buba left smiling; it was by far his best outing. Larry Lindell came in and threw hard sliders all over the Missions' rally.

Soprano led off the ninth with a strike-out, his third of the night. Chewy followed with a single and Tenor walked. Guttierez doubled them both home. Gunner stood at the bat rack with a thirty-six ounce Mickey Mantle and a thirty-five ounce Al Kaline. He hefted them both, then decided on the Mickey Mantle and strode to the plate. He worked the count to two-and-two, fouling off the two strikes. He stepped out and rubbed some dirt on his hands. The next pitch was a curveball; he read it all the way. Weight back, hips turned, hands out ...

Steeeeeerike threeeeeeee!

Gunner stood at the plate for a moment, unable to believe what had happened. He watched the catcher throw the ball back to the pitcher.

"That's three, buddy," said the catcher.

He walked away slowly, placed his bat in the bat rack and sat on the bench.

"I'm gonna fuckin' kill myself," he said tightly.

No one spoke.

"Just kill myself ... Don't try to stop me."

No one moved.

Loony strode to the plate and hit the first pitch up the middle for a single. Guttierez scored easily. Malducci and Sosa both struck out, but the one run edge was enough. Lindell shut the Missions down in the home half of the ninth to preserve the Dodger victory.

"I can almost taste that pizza," said Kaz as they walked to the clubhouse.

"How about double or nothin'?" said Bill.

"You sure you can afford this? I mean this is like takin' candy from ..."

"Deal?"

"Double or nothin'? For tomorrow night?"

"Yeh."

"You're on," said Kaz. "You hear that, Newsy?"

Bobby Newsom nodded.

"Perhaps you'd like some of the action?" said Bill.

"Anchovies and sausage?" said Newsy.

"Anything."

"Count me in."

Gunner was unusually somber; he ate only one Double Whopper Cheeseburger at Burger King. At the Lamplighter Motel, he stared blankly at the eleven o'clock news.

"Well?" said Bill.

"Well what?"

"So talk, Gunner Gunderson."

"About what?"

"... About your disastrous night at the plate. Your long running no-hit show. Three pop-ups and a big K."

"Well, I swung, didn't I?" he said angrily. "Like you said. Don't *punch* the ball, Gunner ... Swing the fuckin' bat, Gunner. Well, I did that. And look what happened."

"You want to blame me?" said Bill.

"Awww ..." he grumbled.

"It's okay. Go ahead and blame me."

"Okay. It's your fault."

"Feel better?"

"No ... The thing is, Bill ... the thing is, I'm actually *see*ing the ball better. I mean I really *saw* it tonight. And I *still* couldn't hit it ..."

"I lost a pizza on you tonight."

"How'd you manage that?"

"Oh, I bet Kaz that you were gonna hit one out tonight."

"Here? At Muni? The way I been hittin'? ... You shouldn't take all your medication at the same time. Does something to your judgment."

"Well, I didn't actually lose," said Bill. "I got him double or nothin'. Tomorrow you're gonna hit one out."

"Christ, Mahoney, I can hardly remember when I hit one out of the *in*field."

"I believe," said Bill.

"You believe what?"

"I believe you're gonna hit one out tomorrow."

"... Huh."

Gunner got off the bed, hefted the Carl Yastrzemski bat he'd brought to the room and took a practice swing.

"Nice swing," said Bill. "You ever play baseball?"

"Used to ... You know I got a hitch in my swing."

"I know. So did Ted Williams."

"Yeh?"

"Yeh. Terrible hitch. And he pulled everything."

"Huh ..."

"Maybe you could have an operation," said Bill.

"For what?"

"Have your hitch removed."

"Christ, Mahoney, be serious ... I'm ..."

"Some guys hitch," said Bill. "Let it be ..."

"How come I'm not hittin'?"

"You're just recovering from a long run of that Punch and Judy show. Takes a while to get back in the groove. I figure tomorrow's the day."

"Huh ... You ever hear of pyramid power?" said Gunner.

"Yeh."

"I read somewhere that this guy put his bat under this pyramid thing at night ..."

"... And?"

"He hit better."

"Great ... Did he leave his cleats out so the elves could fix 'em? Maybe you could put your orange hair under the pyramid with your bat and ..."

"Christ, Mahoney, this is ..."

Bill yawned noisily.

"Go to sleep, Gunner. Rest ... Remember the words of one of our great American philosophers."

"Who was that?"

"Tug McGraw. New York Mets ... You gotta believe ... You gotta believe."

"You gotta believe, eh?"

"That's it."

"Funny, Professor Wisdom never mentioned that."

"Wisdom probably never played ball."

Gunner tossed his bat on the bed and took off his shirt.

"Don't worry," said Bill. "I'll believe for both of us tomorrow. But after that you're on your own."

Chapter 15

"I need to find me a chick with big tits and settle down ... Forget all this shit."

"Good luck."

"Easy for you to say. You already found a chick with big tits."

He turned off the television and the lights and got into bed.

"You know, Mahoney, if I had a pussy I'd be a millionaire. Set for life."

"Be okay if you didn't mind a bunch of guys jumpin' up and down on top of you. Besides, you're too ugly. You'd probably have to ball a million guys at a buck a piece. Take forever."

"... You know what has two thousand legs and an I.Q. of seventy?"

"No, Gunner, I don't ... Why don't you tell me?"

"A St. Patrick's Day Parade."

"Good night, Gunner."

"Good night, Ma-ho-ney ..."

Bill always marveled at how quickly Gunner was able to go to sleep. A minute, maybe two, and Gunner was breathing deeply. Gloria was like that. Bill was lucky if he was asleep within the hour. He lit a cigarette ...

Night played tricks on his mind. The voice of his father pitched in the wind, the words garbled, the tone fractious. His mother, the sweet, sainted Dorothy, mindless and addled, screeched like a crone hawking wares at a county fair. Father Murgatroyd stood by, sweating profusely, fingering a rosary made of toad stools and garlic hearts. ... He heard the voices of children, an unfinished symphony. Only Christopher stood apart, watching, a namesake child at his side.

He shook his head and took a drag off the cigarette. It was like that at night sometimes, when it was quiet. He could hear the sound of promises being broken. His own. Others'. See unwelcome memories pass in review, frightening creatures from the Boo Lagoon. He wished it were within his power to banish them, to will them out of existence. But wishing didn't make it so. They were always there, like bursitis, like bone chips, like hemorrhoids, forgotten for a time, triggered by a random movement; just waiting, like naughty children, to leap upon the unsuspecting landscape of his mind ... Behind each sickly bush there lurked a ghoul of Christmas past, hid but not forgot, a haunting bird to foul the nest of Christmas present. He looked back on his life as if it belonged to someone else. Full of wrong turns. Some mercifully unremembered; some not.

He sighed and put out his cigarette. Maybe I'll ask Alice out again, he thought. She seemed to like him. And he certainly liked her. Your favorite warrior at your service, he mused ... He took the baseball from the nightstand, gripped it firmly in his right hand, turned on his side and tried to go to sleep.

Gunner hardly spoke the next day. He watched the "Donahue Show" and failed to comment, though the show was devoted to transvestites, a topic that would normally have drawn some venom from the young Swede. He went to the drugstore but returned empty-handed. Didn't have any orange dye, he said ... It's not real popular, said Bill. Most people end up with orange hair by mistake.

Danny started the second game. There were men on first and third when Gunner came to bat the first time. Bill couldn't see from the bull pen, but he guessed that Gunner was using the Yastrzemski he had at the motel the night before. It took him a long time to get ready; he dug a spot for his left foot at the back of the batter's box. He appeared to point his bat toward left-center.

The book on Gunner was off-speed breaking stuff. Or hard stuff in and tight. Very tight; keep him off the plate. The first pitch sent him sprawling on the seat of his pants. It was the purpose pitch. The face ball. The jam shot ... It said: Look out, hitter. Don't dig in on me ... Gunner got up, calmly brushed off his uniform and got back in the batter's box. Not a word. Not even a dark look at the pitcher.

The next pitch was a change-up, an ecology pitch, a 55 mph fastball. It was almost like Gunner knew it was coming. He didn't lunge at it, didn't try to jump out and beat it to death. He just waited, weight back, then lashed out with that quick, powerful stroke. He got it all, four seams and a sound to gladden a hitter's heart. The center fielder sprinted toward right-center. The right fielder just watched; he knew it was gone. When the center fielder looked up to locate the ball, he stopped too ... It was gone. Round-tripper. Dial eight for long distance. Touch 'em all. Wind blowing in, but it was gone. It landed far beyond the right-center-field fence. Gunner dropped his bat and trotted around the bases. There was a smattering of applause from a few appreciative fans. Gunner slapped all the high fives in the dugout, some twice.

"What a *shot*," said Sly.

"Predijus," said J.C.

"*Jes*us, what a shot," said Sly.

"Predijus."

"Hell of a shot," said Sly.

"... Predijus."

Olde Tymers recalled Tape Measure Home Runs. George Brett in 1972 was mentioned. Harry Heslet with the Visalia Oaks in 1956 was offered. But none could remember seeing one hit any farther. Not at Muni. Not to right-center. Not with the wind blowing in. Before Loony got to the plate, estimates were ranging from five to six hundred feet.

"Holy *fuck*," said Kaz. "Did you *see* that?"

"I don't be*lieve* it," said Newsy.

"One long tayter," said Buba.

"Believe, brothers. Believe," said Bill.

"He hit it off a fucking *change*," said Newsy. "A *change*. ... Unbelievable. And it cost me a pizza."

"What about me?" Kaz protested.

"One gone tayter," chuckled Buba.

"Don't worry," said Bill. "I'm gonna give you guys another chance."

Kaz and Newsy eyed him suspiciously.

"I'll bet you he hits another one," said Bill.

"When?" said Kaz.

"Very clever, Kazmersak," said Bill. "I see I won't be able to pull the wool over your eyes."

"... When?"

"Tonight."

"Tonight?" said Newsy.

"One big tayter," said Buba. "Hehehehe ..."

"You gotta be kiddin'," said Kaz. To*night*? You're gonna bet me he hits another one out to*night*?"

"Us," said Newsy. "He's gonna bet *us*."

"... What's the catch?" said Kaz.

"Catch? Why should there be a catch?"

"... Sounds too good," said Kaz.

"No catch," said Bill. "We are even, Kaz, so I'm going to allow you to bet two pizzas. Newsy, on the other hand, will be out two anyway when Gunner cracks another one."

"Let me get this straight," said Kaz. "You're betting me he hits another one out to*night*?"

"Tonight, brother Kaz."

"... You're on."

"Newsy?" said Bill.

"Count me in." He cupped a hand to his ear. "I can hear the anchovies and the sausages callin' ... Come and get us, Newsy. Mahoney's buyin' ..."

They shook hands on it.

"Hey, Keane," said Kaz. "You want in on this. Mahoney's givin' away free pizzas."

Keane sat sulking on the end of the bench.

"Naw ... Fuck it," he said.

Nesbitt baffled the Missions through the first five innings, holding them scoreless. Bill got the call in the sixth when Danny developed a blister on his pitching hand. He allowed a run in the sixth, but shut them out in the seventh and eighth. Gunner singled in the third and doubled in the seventh, part of a four-run Dodger rally. Newsy warmed up to pitch the ninth. Bill put his jacket on and wandered back down to the bullpen.

"What if he doesn't get up again?" said Kaz, as the Dodgers got ready for their final at-bat.

"Then you win," said Bill.

"He's up fifth ... Soapy, Chewy ..."

"... Sneezy, Grumpy ..."

"... Tenor and Guts are ahead of him."

"Maybe he won't get up," said Bill.

"Yeah," said Kaz. "Sure be a shame. I don't hardly like pizza at all."

"I know ..."

"*Or* ... they may pinch hit for him."

"Get serious, Kaz. They won't pinch hit for him."

Soprano grounded weakly to third. Ramirez was out on a one-hopper to short.

"Tough *luck*," Kaz said brightly. "Poor guy probably won't even get up ... You know what kind of pizza I like?"

"... No."

"Mushroom and sausage. I hate anchovies ... I don't know if I could trust a guy who ate anchovies."

Tenor walked. Guttierez got aboard on an error by the shortstop.

"How could he *miss* that," said Kaz. "A routine ground ball and he *kicks* it."

"Whose side are you on?" said Bill.

"*Our* side, Mahoney. We're nine runs *up* for chrissakes.

"And he-e-e-e-re comes Gunner."

"Holy fuck," said Kaz.

Gunner took the first two pitches, both off-speed and outside. The third one was a fastball right down the pipe. The only question after it left the bat was whether it would stay fair. It was hooking down the right-field line. Kaz took several steps toward the field to get a better look.

"Looks foul," he said hopefully.

"Look again," said Bill, pointing toward home plate where the ump was giving the circular home run signal. Touch 'em all.

"Did he call that *fair*?" said Kaz.

"Pepperoni," said Bill.

"That thing was foul by five *feet*."

"Pepperoni," said Bill. "I love pepperoni."

"Oh ... Fuck your pepperoni, Mahoney."

"Pepperoni Mahoney," said Keane, chuckling for the first time that night. "Dat's good."

Newsy stopped warming up long enough to watch the ball sail over the fence. He shrugged his shoulders and went back to warming up. He gave up only a harmless single in the ninth.

"You know," Gunner said later. "I knew that pitch was gonna be a change. My first time up? ... I *knew* it."

"We won four pizzas on that last home run," said Bill.

"Four pizzas?"

"Yeh."

"... Good things come to he who waits ..."

"... Wisdom?"

"No ... Gunderson."

The Dodgers won the next two in San Jose ... And then they got hot.

Bill and Gloria descended from the mountain and took up residence in his cramped one-bedroom apartment. Gloria brought her yearbook and pompoms and stowed them in the linen closet. She taped her Cougar pennant to the bedroom wall, filled the dollhouse closet with clothes, the tiny bathroom with cosmetics. Bill put his shaving gear on a shelf in the vanity under the sink. She rearranged the furniture several times in the first month and said she wanted to move just as soon as they could afford it.

She bought several cookbooks and studied them diligently. Her first offering was beef stroganoff, the sauce gray and cold, concealing rubbery slices of beef better left undetected. Quiches, casseroles and pâtés followed. She gradually discovered her culinary disasters and shifted to simpler fare.

Gloria hardly stirred when the alarm went off at four-thirty in the morning. Bill pushed the clock to quiet and quickly slipped out of bed. Even on mornings when sleep had been brief, when the intake of tall Oly's and vodka had been excessive, some inner necessity drove him from his bed. It was not that he loved his work; it was a living, something to do. Good money. It did not occur to him that it should be anything else. He pulled his shorts on, went to the kitchen and put the water on to boil. Last night's dirty dishes were piled in the sink. He thought about washing them but didn't. He got a clean set of white work clothes from the linen closet and put them on. The shirt had a Fiesta Pool logo on the back and his name stitched over the front pocket. Bill. Just plain Bill. In blue. Dodger blue.

When the water boiled, he made a cup of instant. He sat at the table, lit a cigarette and coughed fitfully. Oughta quit, he thought. But he never did. He flipped through last night's Sports section. Looked like the Giants and the Dodgers would fight it out for the pennant. Maybe the Pirates. In the American

League it looked like Baltimore or Minnesota. The Yankees were dead; they wouldn't even make a run for it. The mighty Yankees. He hated the Yankees anyway ... He turned to the front page. War in Vietnam. Turmoil in Washington. Social Unrest across the Nation. He folded the paper and drank his coffee.

There was a peaceful quiet to the mornings that he liked. He could hear the ringing in his ears, a soft phlegmy cough, a protesting bed, sounds that were lost in the later noise of the day. He closed his eyes and imagined that he was Captain Marvel. Wouldn't need a truck to get to work. Just *Shazaaaaaam* ... and off he'd fly. Maybe rescue someone in distress on his way ... Look out, Dr. Sivana, it's the Mighty Marvels. .... When he opened his eyes he discovered that he'd crushed his styrofoam cup and spilled coffee all over the kitchen table. He hadn't even felt the hot coffee. He sponged up the mess and made more.

He thought about Gloria while the water boiled. What would she be like pregnant? They had decided; six months and they'd give it a try. We'll practice a lot, he said. She smiled. Practice makes perfect, he said, then felt foolish about saying it ... She was shy. That surprised him. She always put on a robe when she got out of bed; said it made her uncomfortable to be watched. She didn't seem to have much interest in sex. Intercourse became occasional, somewhat reluctant, hand jobs infrequent and hurried. They settled on a Saturday night routine of a movie and a Vaseline slide on the nuptial bed. Sunday she washed the sheets. Bill adapted. He thought perhaps he was doing something wrong, but he never asked. He never asked about anything.

He rarely stopped at Sleeveless John's with the boys any more. Gloria clucked disapprovingly when he drank. Only once in the first few months did he wake with a hangover and scant memory of the night before. Gloria told him all about it the next morning. Said she never wanted to ... to *screw* when he was drunk. Ever. You *hurt* me, she said. ... And I don't want to *do* those things. They're ... they're not ... *nat*ural ... What things? he asked. ... Never mind, she said. Just never mind. ...

She wouldn't tell him. Not until later ...

She'd be pretty pregnant, he decided. A little bowling ball tummy curtained with maternity clothes, hiding a small short-stop eager to go to his right for a hot smash, making the long throw from the hole.

He returned to work, pushing the noisy white pickup along the predawn freeways ... Lushwell asked him if his dick was sore. And did she suck it for him. He lied and said Yes and Yes. Lushwell said Raymond was going to get married soon, too. Yeh? ... Soon as the circus comes to town so's he can find himself another midget. Hahahahah. ...Awwww, growled Raymond, crumpled fishing hat hiding his shifty eyes. They found Toasty asleep in his 1958 Cadillac, roused him and waited while he washed down a handful of pills with a warm beer. *Flaco,* he said, wholly restored in a few minutes. You *beck,* man. Good poosy? ... Yeh, great. ... Lushwell's hands were shaking so badly he had to pour out half his coffee before he could even try to drink it. Al showed up at five forty-five, lunch pail in hand.

A cruel summer sun appeared on the horizon, coolly hiding its intent. Raymond put on his sunglasses, squashed his hat down, climbed aboard the two pillows in the cab of the blue deuce-and-a-half and bumped out of the yard. The two pickups followed. Lushwell, riding with Bill, had to stop and get his morning half pint of Jim Beam. Bill declined his usual Oly. Your old lady won't let you drink? said Lushwell, twisting off the cap and tossing it out the window ... No, I just don't feel like it ... She give good head? ... Great, said Bill ... Lushwell squeezed down a drink, shuddered, opened the door of the pickup and threw up in the parking lot. Smo-o-o-o-oth, he said. I had an old lady didn't want me to drink, he said. A religious fanatic. ... My old lady's not religious, said Bill ... Good, said Lushwell. Mine ended up runnin' off with a Jewish banker. The Jesus freak and the Jew. Wonder how they made out? Hope they fuckin' died. Both of 'em. Long, painful deaths. Cancer maybe ... Cancer of the snatch. That's what she deserves ... He took another drink as Bill pulled out of the parking lot.

Early morning cars began to creep eagerly up the on-ramps, a harbinger of the freeway flood to follow. A few minutes after six and Bill was heading north on the Long Beach Freeway. If everything went well, they would be finished with the first pool by ten or ten-thirty, the second by midafternoon, before the crush of cars returned to swamp the roads. Lushwell whistled "Mack the Knife." Bill hummed along. The radio in the truck didn't work.

Sometime between the winter solstice and New Year's Day, Gloria got pregnant. January came and went without the dreaded menses. Bill grew paternal. Gloria shopped for maternity clothes. Bruce Alsop couldn't decide whether he wanted to be a grandfather or not. Mrs. Alsop zipped around like Daffy Duck, gathering bits and pieces of yarn and clothing for the nest. In March they moved to a two-bedroom house on Cohasset Street. (Oh, I'm glad you moved from that ... that slum, dear, said Daffy.) It was a rental, but it had a small frontyard and backyard with a single blighted tree. They bought a baby bed, crib mobiles, blankets (Get blue, said Bill. It's a boy), diapers, tiny shirts no bigger than Bill's hand (How do you know? said Gloria), teddy bears, potty chairs (Trust me, said Bill. I know), and a small plastic bat.

Bill got drunk on St. Patrick's Day. He and Lushwell went to Sleeveless John's and drank green beer till they couldn't stand up. Bill got home at midnight, shook off his clothes in the living room, announced loudly that he was Captain Marvel with a cock of iron, got into bed and tried to get Gloria to perform an unnatural act. When he wouldn't let her alone, she locked herself in the bathroom and wouldn't come out till he promised to behave. By one o'clock he had settled for a hand job. But he felt contrite the next morning and volunteered to do the dishes for a whole week. She graciously agreed.

They went to the Alsop's for dinner once a month. Gloria chatted with her mother about baby things. Dawn just schlepped around the house looking bored, though she favored Bill and often stayed close to him. Mr. Alsop (just call me Bruce ... son) seemed as uncomfortable as Bill. An occasional golfer, he didn't follow the sports scene; Bill was unacquainted with politics, bond issues or engineering problems. They were warily tolerant of one another. The only thing they had in common was Gloria, and that more a barrier than a bond ... Bill had a brandy or two. Even smoked a cigar.

The winter months sauntered into spring, traceable only by the calendar. Gloria's tummy began to bulge noticeably. She was not afflicted with morning sickness and appeared to be the picture of health, though entering her second trimester she began to protest that even occasional intercourse was painful. Doctor says, she said. He agreed to refrain, choosing motherhood over whatever was in second place. He dreamed of tiny Nurse Nora, her moonlit buns like sunnyside eggs. Once he awoke with an erection wedged between Gloria's unwilling thighs. Oh Bill, she said, her annoyance apparent. Ohhhhhhhh, said Bill, still dreaming.

Gloria and Kandy talked daily, went movieing and shopping and listened to Gloria's "Peter, Paul & Mary In Concert" album by the hour. Kandy began to act like the theater arts major she was. She dumped Ernie, a Philistine prick, she said unkindly. She discovered Arthur Miller and Tennessee Williams. And Eugene O'Neill. God, he's so *power*ful, Glo ... Summer brought the beach back. Gloria went clothed in maternal billows. Kandy read O'Neill's plays to her.

September was the cruelest month. Gloria, wide-eyed and frightened, took on the look of one perpetually startled. She tottered around holding her protruding tummy, groaning to sit or rise, applying a soothing balm to her screaming hemorrhoids, counting the days with a stubby red crayon. Bill fussed and cooked and washed the dishes, overzealously scrubbed all the No Stick off the good frying pan one evening after he scorched the scrambled eggs. He fought with the voice in his head that chanted *dead baby dead baby dead baby* ... He sang "Oh, What a Beautiful Morning" each morning on his way to work and struggled to stay focused on the world around him. Kandy came to visit and read the last three pages of *The Great God Brown*. Margaret Alsop entered like a humming bird in distress, a mere blur with her cleaning cloth, gone before the air could settle.

It was one hundred three degrees at three o'clock in the afternoon that September Monday. The contractions began at three o'clock the following morning, Bill asleep, Gloria not. Slowly at first, the minutes dragging in between. Bill the Timer kept falling asleep, losing count of the precious seconds. They left for the hospital just after four-thirty. Bill roared through the empty streets, afraid the baby would arrive en route. Gloria clutched her distended stomach and pressed an imaginary brake pedal on the passenger side.

At the hospital, bored and yawny nurses, complaining about food prices and worthless husbands, propelled her away in a wheelchair. Bill went to a phone to call the Alsops. Bruce answered.

"... 'Lo?" His voice gummy with sleep.

"Mr. Alsop?" He still had trouble calling him Bruce.

"Yes?"

"This is Bill."

"... Who?"

"Bill Mahoney."

Bill held the phone and waited for a few moments.

"... Your daughter's husband," he said finally.

"Oh. Of course ... It's five in the morning, eh ... Bill." He could not hide the irritation in his voice.

"I know. We're at the hospital."

"... What's wrong?"

"The baby ... It's coming."

"Oh, the *baby* ..."

The next voice he heard was the staccato trill of Mrs. Alsop.

"... The ba-by?" she said.

"Yeh."

"You're at the hospital?"

"Memorial," he said, anticipating the next question.

"She's in labor?"

"Yeh."

"We'll be right there," she said, and hung up before he could answer.

They arrived thirty minutes later, Bruce rubbing sleep from his eyes, Mrs. Alsop looking like she'd been up for hours. Bruce begged off after a brief stay, pleading a heavy office schedule. He pecked Margaret dutifully on the cheek and lumbered out the door like a disheveled bear.

Bill and Margaret were allowed a short visit in the labor room to see Gloria. She lay on the bed, all tummy, twisting in pain with each contraction. She squeezed Bill's hand till her knuckles went white. Margaret said *There, there* and patted her forehead with a washcloth. Bill squirmed uneasily and hoped the nurse would return soon and tell them they had to leave.

He hated hospitals. He recalled his own brief stay, the indelicate pain of his sutured elbow, his mother's irreversible decay. He wondered if Christopher had died in a hospital. No one ever spoke about it—how he died, how it all happened. Maybe nobody knew. Bill hoped that he had gone in a blaze of gunfire; heroically, painlessly, his body riddled with neat, round, comic-strip holes. But not in a hospital.

"Did you call Kandy?" Gloria said between contractions.

"... Forgot," said Bill, simulating regret.

"Better call now," she admonished.

He went down to the waiting room and called.

"I'll be right down," she said.

"No," he said. "Don't come."

"What do you mean, no?" she sputtered.

"No," he said. "N-o." Why did he detest her so?

"You don't own the hospital, buster."

"Smart girl," he said, "but don't come down ... If I see you here, I'll stick you in a trash can."

"Why you arrogant assh ..."

He severed the connection. She didn't come to the hospital, but she never forgot.

Margaret arrived in the waiting room soon after and announced that things were proceeding normally. She took a seat on one of the couches, pulled out her knitting and began to work furiously on a small white blanket.

Bill read the *Sports Illustrated* article on Sandy Koufax for the second time. Cortisone shots before the game. Constant pain. Bill flexed his right elbow. Oddly enough, it didn't hurt when he was working. He smoked and watched the elevator for Dr. Westbrook.

At eleven o'clock, he and Margaret went to the cafeteria where he had a tuna sandwich that tasted like cardboard and a cup of coffee that snapped at his tongue. Margaret had a cup of tea and related the story of Gloria's very difficult birth. When he returned to the waiting room, "Guiding Light" followed "Search for Tomorrow" on the elevated television ... He wondered what people in love really thought about. He worried that he didn't know what love was; hadn't ever known.

"Your first?" said a man with flecks of gray at his temples.
"Yeh," said Bill.
"My sixth."
"Huh ..."
"Been here long?"
"... Since this morning."
"Don't worry. First one always takes a long time." He leaned over and lowered his voice. "Tough gettin' out of that little hole ... First time." He chuckled.

Bill picked up the same *Sports Illustrated* and opened it at random ... He wondered if something had gone wrong. What if the baby was deformed? No fingers. No toes. A basket case. Jesus ... Margaret attended to her knitting as if it were the only thing in the world.

A perspiring doctor in pale green O.R. garb stepped out of the elevator, shook hands with Flecks and announced that it was a boy. Flecks took it calmly enough, gave Bill a cigar and advised him to hang in there. Bill mumbled thanks and watched as he got into the elevator with the doctor.

"You take a couple of stitches for old Fred?" said Flecks as the elevator door began to close.

The doctor smiled noncommittally.

Bill dozed off.

"Mr. Mahoney?"

He was startled awake by Dr. Westbrook's hand on his shoulder.

"Oh ... Hi, Doc ..."
"Congratulations. It's a boy."

Margaret appeared like an apparition.

"Oh," she said. "I'm the mother. Mrs. Alsop."

They exchanged smiles.

Chapter 16

"Mother and baby are fine," he said. "Quite a struggle, but they're fine." He wiped his forehead to indicate the depth of the struggle. "You can see your wife in a few minutes. She's in recovery. First we'd like you to look at the baby and sign the form."

He and Margaret went to the third floor and viewed the boy through the long glass window; a dark, squirming infant with a shock of black hair and an oversize Band-Aid spanning his stomach. He looked like a tiny Eskimo. Bill counted all the fingers and toes, then signed a form stating that all appendages were present. Margaret insisted that he be the first to go into the recovery room to see Gloria.

"Hi," he said.

She opened her eyes and blinked slowly.

"Oh ..."

"How you doin'?"

"Okay," she said, still groggy from the anesthetic. She ran her tongue around her lips.

"You see my baby?"

"Yeh. He's beautiful ..."

"... It was awful ... awful ..."

"Yeh ... Well, it's over. You did real good ..."

"Yeh ..."

"Your mom'll be in in a minute," he said. "Get some rest. I'll be back later." He kissed her lightly on the forehead and left.

He went back to the nursery and searched the rows of infants till he found "Mahoney" printed in black on the three-by-five card. It didn't seem possible. His son ... Christopher Mahoney. Jesus ... Bill bit his lower lip and blinked away the tears. The boy had his fists clenched; his arms were moving as if he were trying to tread water. He didn't look particularly happy, but he wasn't crying. He just seemed to be struggling. Bill hoped he would be tall; at least six feet. Certainly there were tall genes in the family. Thomas was six, two; Chris must have been at least six feet, three. Only Bill was short. Well, not really short ... And Dorothy. She couldn't have been much over five feet ... He wondered what kind of a fastball he would have had if he'd been six feet, four or five.

He tapped on the glass. "Christopher?" he whispered. "It's me." Two nurses turned toward the tapping. He smiled sheepishly, walked to the elevator and went down to the first floor.

He thought about calling his father, but found a number of reasons not to. Something would be wrong and he'd have to comment on it. That's the way he was. The baby would be too small. Or too pink. Or too something ... Bill remembered a game in his senior year when he'd struck out fourteen and given up only three hits. But he had allowed a home run in the sixth inning, and that's all Thomas talked about.

> ... Shoulda pitched him outside. And
> up. You could tell by his stance that
> the guy had good power inside. You
> could tell by lookin'. Hell's bells ... If
> you watch. If you got your head in
> the game ...

No, Bill decided not to call. Maybe later, when the boy was older ... The thought of calling Kandy drifted briefly through his mind, but he dismissed it. Fuck her, he thought. She had to call the hospital herself to find out. But she had the last laugh. It took years, but she had the last laugh.

He drove home in the blistering heat, slept for a few hours before he returned. Margaret was still there, attending her deflated daughter like a Sister of Mercy. She stopped long enough to say hello to Bill and excuse herself to get a cup of tea.

"We're gonna name him Christopher, eh?" said Bill, as soon as Mrs. Alsop had gone.

Gloria extended her lower lip in a pout.

"I thought Bruce," she said.

"Christopher," said Bill.

Gloria shut her eyes. Twin tears trickled down her cheeks.

"Oh, Glor," he said, sitting on the side of the bed. "I wouldn't ask if it wasn't important. You know that ... I know I said that maybe Bruce would be okay, but when I saw him ..."

She nibbled her lower lip.

"Christopher's my only brother," he said.

"And Bruce is my only dad."

"... But Christopher's dead. He died in the war."

"I practically *told* Daddy."

"... How about Bruce for a middle name?" he said.

She cocked her head to one side and listened to the interior sound of Christopher Bruce Mahoney.

"Oh ... you," she said, but she smiled through the wad of Kleenex she held under her nose.

He stopped at the nursery again before he left the hospital. Christopher was asleep, his mouth open, his breathing shallow. Bill decided that Bruce for a middle name wouldn't be all that bad, though some contrary part of his soul had toyed with the idea of Thomas for a middle name. Besides, nobody used middle names anyway ... Big Chris ... But the boy was so tiny. Maybe everyone started out that size. Seven pounds; not much bigger than a couple of good size baseball bats. He wondered if there was a way to tell how big he'd be from how much he weighed at birth. Probably not, he decided.

Christopher yawned, clenched his fists and began to cry. Bill smiled.

"I love you," he said quietly.

The Dodger ship, becalmed through the better part of June and July, set sail in the early days of August and began to overtake the Giants. It wasn't that the Giants were playing badly, it was just that the Dodgers suddenly seemed unbeatable. Everything worked. The suicide squeeze in the bottom of the ninth worked like a textbook example of How To Score The Winning Run. The Hit and Run was elevated to high art, the well-struck ball invariably bouncing through the side of the infield just vacated by the defender sprinting to cover second base. Successful steals and double steals proliferated like fleas on a stray dog, the runner always safe by the smallest of margins, the defender dropping a ball lodged securely in the webbing of his glove. J.C. became the Master of Moves, an eloquent heir to Miller Huggins, John McGraw and Joe McCarthy, a Colossus of Intuition, gently lifting a pitcher at the right time, putting a play in the works when time-honored percentages would seem to belie its success.

Coach Sly, the signalman, stood on the bridge and silently relayed messages to his accomplished crew, his body a ballet of information. Chewy, Tenor, Guts, Gunner and Loony stroked the ball like eager schoolboys. Malducci, though not yet a gazelle, began to field his position with reasonable skill, no longer running into fences with murderous intensity, maintaining a fair consistency at the plate. The DH spot was alternately filled by Gerry (White boy) White and Tom Coleman. Larry Duffy was stealing bases with the impunity of a man who had just turned state's evidence, his presence a threat to opposing pitchers and catchers, producing a certain shyness in fielders who didn't relish the prospect of avoiding thigh-high spikes ... *Don't bother me to cut no muthafuckah, man,* he said blithely ... Manny Sosa learned a little English (Suck my deek, lady?) taught to him by helpful teammates and covered ground in left field like a frisky mustang. Charley Soprano still sparkled in the field, but was becoming even more anemic at the plate. He took on the look of a saintly ascetic. J.C. guessed that his fielding would soon be affected.

The pitching was somewhat spotty, one excellent outing followed by one equally poor. Starters became relievers and relievers starters in an effort to find the right combination. Relief is just a pitcher away, said Bill. Maybe two ... three at the most ... Mississippi Buba Taylor got in a groove, a glossy ebony machine mowing down hitters like a Colorado combine.

The huffnpuff bus sped north on 99, the short sixty-odd miles from Modesto to Lodi following a Sunday afternoon game that the Dodgers won 15 to 1. Gunner was four-for-four. Loony stole a base, his first of the season. ... Chumley had trouble seeing in the twilight.

The major league baseball strike which began June 12 was finally settled on July 31.

"Says here," said Gunner, squinting at the Modesto Bee, "that the strike cost Dave Winfield three hundred and eighty-five thousand dollars."

"Holy fuck," said Kaz.

"Makes your hemorrhoids hurt, don't it," said Tenor, "just thinkin' about it."

"When they gonna start playin' again?" said Loony.

"Uh ... August ninth," said Gunner. "The All-Star Game. Regular season starts the eleventh."

"August ninth," said Chewy. "Isn't that when Mahoney said the strike would be over?"

"It was over July thirty-first," said Gunner.

"Gunner just wants to welsh on his bet," said Bill.

"Can't blame the guy for not wantin' to kiss your ass," said Tenor.

"That's not true," Gunner said calmly. "The strike was over on the thirty-first. All that is well documented in the newspaper."

"It's not really over till you start playin'," said Loony.

"That's not true, either," said Gunner. "It's over when they settle it ... July thirty-first."

"Funny," said Bill. "You don't look like a welsher."

"I am not a goddam welsher. Christ, Mahoney."

"It's okay ... I understand."

"Christ ..."

"You see me steal second today?" Loony said brightly.

"We were there, Loon," said Gunner.

"See how I got that great jump? ... Safe by a mile." ·

"Catcher dropped the ball," said Chewy.

"... Awwww ..."

"Honest to Christ," said Tenor. "Catcher dropped the ball."
Loony appealed to Bill.

"Is that true? Did he really drop the ball?"

"Well, he didn't actually drop it," said Bill. "He just couldn't get
it out of his glove. I don't think he ever actually dropped it ...
You had it beat anyway."

"See?" said Loony.

"He dropped it," said Chewy.

"You fuckin' guys ..." said Loony.

"You know," said Tenor, " I been thinkin' ..."

"Careful," said Gunner. "Don't hurt yourself."

"Wouldn't it be funny if some of us ended up playin' *for* the
Giants."

"You strained somethin'," said Gunner. "A mental groin pull.
Call Doc ..."

"Your mother and father married?" said Bill.

"... Yeh," said Tenor. "Why? ..."

"Can't play for the Giants if your folks are married."

"Why's that?" said Loony.

"Christ, Loon," said Gunner. "Wake up, willya?"

"I'm awake, Gunner. I'm plenty awake."

"Hey, Chewy, you know what?" said Gunner.

"Yeh, I know," said Chewy. "Don't tell me. Please."

"This guy told me that Mexicans are living proof that the
Indians used to fuck the buffaloes."

"Jesus," said Chewy, shaking his head.

"Is that true?" said Gunner.

"Get fucked, willya?"

Gunner went back to the paper.

"Says that the Dodger juggernaut continues to roll ... Do
juggernauts roll, Mahoney?"

"If they're round."

"And ... it also says that the A's were foiled ... foiled yet ... in the last three innings by the mystifying offerings of Bill Mahoney ... or is that *mis*erable offerings. Says you're a reclamation project ... How's it feel to be a reclamation project?"

"Okay," said Bill. "Except in the mornings. My reclamation hurts in the mornings."

"No wonder," said Gunner. "At your age ..."

The Dodgers would be in Lodi for a ten-game home stand, on the road for eight and then back home for the final week of the season. The Giants were due in for two games during the present home stand. They would return for the final four games of the season. There were twenty-four games left; the Dodgers were four games off the pace. The surprising Stockton Pilots, nobody's favorite to even stay close, were nestled a cozy two games back of the Giants. The Dodgers picked up a full game when they swept their first home series with the Pioneers. The Giants juggled their pitching rotation so that the two aces, Simpson and Macefield, would start against the Dodgers. Sly pressed for a change in the Dodger rotation. J.C. declined.

Bill took Alice out to dinner after the final game with the Pioneers. He was well into his third beer when the spaghetti arrived.

"The Giants tomorrow, eh?" said Alice.

"Yeh ... the big bad Giants."

"You guys'll do great," she said, reaching across the table to touch his hand.

He smiled weakly. Yeh, he said, not knowing if he said it out loud. He was thinking about the end of the season; only a few more games. The Giants, the Oaks, the Pilots, the Missions, the A's ... Three weeks. Then what? Handshakes ... Goodbyes ... See-ya-next-year's ... No. Not Bill. He wouldn't be back next year. In December he'd be forty years old; a chill, wintry reminder. Forty miles of hard road. He pictured himself alone on the mound, a cold wind blowing, the sun going down, the stands empty except for the old man in the white Panama hat leaning on the curved handle of a hickory cane. And the Dance would begin ... First the music, faintly. ... The old man had eyes like a fox. He never said *I told you so*, but Bill could read the words in the hooded smile and knew he had a powerful need to be right about things. First the music ... Bill wanted to be free of it, yet he took to the floor each time the music began. The Dance of Death. Maybe it was habit. He had something to prove, though he couldn't tell what ... *We are all in the dumps, for diamonds are trumps* ... Yeh. Diamonds are trumps, he thought. Always have been. I wonder how she knew?

"You okay?" said Alice.
"Oh ... yeh." He picked at his dinner.

For diamonds are trumps. The Ace was gone, played long ago. The King, the Queen, the Jack—artless tricks lost to the hand of Fate. Dreams ... The torment of his unskilled labors in life's tangled thickets. How does it happen? he wondered. Let the dance begin ... Now there was Alice, as pretty as tomorrow, as juicy as a secret.

"You sure you're okay?"
"Yeh. Just a little ... scattered."
"... Anything special?"
"... Just thinking ..." He twirled the beer bottle between his palms.
"... About?"
"Things ... life ..." He shook his head.
She touched his hand.
"It's been a mess," he said. "My life. I don't think I ever learned how to *do* life. That was the trouble. I never learned that ... I'm almost forty years old, Alice. Almost forty. And I'm still playin' baseball. A kid's game. At forty ..."
"I'm thirty-two," she offered.
"... It's like I made a wrong turn somewhere. You ever think about that? About what would've happened if you turned right instead of left?"
"Yeh."
"How your life might have been completely different?"
She nodded.
"I think about that sometimes," he said. "About how things might have been different."

He signaled the waitress for another beer.

"Twenty years ago. There I was. Bill Mahoney, star material. Twenty years ... I had something; a big league arm. Funny ... Muscle and bone. An arm." He held his right arm out. "Some arms are worth a million dollars. Did you know that? Some arms. Mine's worth about a dollar-and-a-half. But twenty years ago? Not a million dollars maybe. But something." He took a drink from the bottle. "Then the arm went bad. It wasn't worth anything; not even a dollar-and-a-half. Then the marriage went bad. Jesus ... Then me ... Defective. You ever feel that way? Defective? Like there's something basically wrong that can't be fixed?"

"... Yeh."

"Really?"

"Really ... I felt like I was the bad seed when I was little. You remember that movie? *The Bad Seed?*"

"Yeh."

"I felt that way ... like I was evil."

"Why?"

"... I don't know."

"Isn't it weird that sometimes you feel a certain way and there's no reason for it? For feeling that way?"

"Yeh."

"Huh ... Sometimes I think I'd like to start over. You ever think that?"

"Yeh ..." she said.

"You think it's possible? To just start over? Maybe not make so many mistakes this time. Just forget about all the bad stuff and start over."

She blotted her mouth with a paper napkin and looked at the imprint.

"I do," she said carefully. "I really do."

"How do you suppose you could do that?"

"... I think you just say, I'm starting over. I'm forgetting the past and starting over ... I think that would work."

He picked at the label on his beer bottle.

"Sounds simple, doesn't it?" he said.

She shrugged.

"Trouble is," he said, "I don't know how to *do* anything. If I started over I wouldn't know what to do ... Oh, a little construction maybe. Pump gas ... All I really know how to do is play baseball."

"That's something."

"Yeh ... But I don't think there's a big market out there for old relief pitchers. If I'm gonna start over I should know how to do something. Don't you think?" He spilled some beer as he poured it into his glass.

"Oh, maybe not," she said, "Maybe it's not all that important."

"You know," he said, leaning forward, "sometimes I have this feeling that I'm only twelve or thirteen years old and I've been *play*ing at being grown up all this time."

"... Me too."

"Yeh?"

"... And I'm afraid somebody's going to find out."

"Right." He jabbed the air with his forefinger.

"I always thought my mother *knew* that I felt like a ten-year-old, so she always treated me like one. Even after I was grown. After I had a baby of my own."

"Huh."

"I finally had to *tell* her that it made me crazy. Her treating me that way. Like a little kid. I yelled at her. At my own mother. And I never yelled at my mother. Never ..."

"What happened?"

"Oh ... it turned out better than I expected. I was terrified. She said that she was *sor*-ry that I felt that way. She was just trying to help. Very hurt." Alice nibbled on her spaghetti. "You'd have to know my mother. She's so ... treacherous. Yeh. Treacherous ... But we get along okay now. Better than before. She still treats me like a ten-year-old sometimes, but it's okay."

"... Huh."

He ate two pieces of garlic toast but hardly touched his spaghetti.

When he drove her home, she asked if he wanted to come in. He shook his head.

"Carla's at my neighbor's," she said.

He shook his head again, afraid to trust his voice. She squeezed his hand.

"I think you're a really beautiful person," she said. "And I'll be here ... when you're ready." She kissed him on the cheek.

"Ciao." A little wave and she was gone.

Opportunities. They came ... and they passed him by. He stood paralyzed by the track and watched the train go by ... Something stirred inside, faintly reminiscent of other times. Could he afford another failure? He recalled a woman with a face like chiseled pine who tried to beg him to bed. ... You don't understand, he said. That's what he always said. You don't understand.

"Did you fuck her?" said Gunner.

"No."

"I just lost the farm."

"Double-up next time," said Bill. "Then you'll have two farms."

"Just what I need," said Gunner. "Two farms."

"I don't have to tell you guys how important this game is," said Coach Sly at the pregame meeting. "This is a ve-ry important game. We win this one and the one tomorrow night and we're only a game out. One game ... with twenty-some left to play. We lose, we're out by five." He held up his left hand to indicate what five looked like. "Five. Now I don't have to tell you the difference between one and five ... All I ..."

"Is it four, Coach?" said Gunner.

"That's close enough," said Tenor.

"You mind if I finish, Gunderson?" said Sly.

"No, go ahead, Coach."

"Thank you," said Sly.

Sly flashed the left hand again.

"Now I expect you guys to suck it up out there. It's okay to be loose. But not *too* loose. Too loose and you lose it ... Keep your head in the game. Know what to *do* when the ball comes your way. Check the signs before *every* pitch. I am not down there at third base for my health. Play heads up. I don't have to tell you guys. Now, Kaz is startin' tonight ..."

J.C. sat quietly on one of the benches, hands on his knees, rocking slowly back and forth. In recent weeks he had turned over most of the managerial duties to Sly. He seldom hit pregame infield anymore; just didn't feel up to it. The chest pains came and went; he told no one. He went home alone after the games, figured the averages, read a page or two of *This Time It's Love* (it usually took him a whole season to finish a book), watched the late news, often fell asleep in his easy chair, Waldo and the two remaining kitties curled up in his lap. He'd pretty much decided that this would be his last year. He'd maybe move to Oregon. Fish some. He'd always liked Oregon, though he'd never been there. And fishing .... well, he'd never fished either, but he liked to picture himself sitting by a small stream with a fishing rod in his hands, battered old hat full of fishing lures. He could learn. Hell, he thought, couldn't be all that hard to learn how to fish. Little kids did it.

"... with the usual lineup," said Sly. "Duffy, you're gonna DH tonight. We need some speed out there. You got the green light. Go when you think you can make it. Don't wait for a sign. Might put Simpson off his feed."

Duffy muttered something about puttin' one of his muthafuckin' kicks in somebody's nuts ... man ...

"Now," said Sly, "we got 'em where we want 'em ... Let's go get 'em." He slammed a fist into his open palm. "*Bam*-o! ... You got anything, John?"

J.C. shook his head.

"Bam-o?" said Gunner.

Kaz pitched like he had never thrown a baseball before. The Giants got four in the first. Soapy made two errors on routine ground balls. He hung his head and kicked at the dirt.

"Suck it up out there," yelled Sly.

"*Bam*-o," said Gunner.

Harry and Dean called loudly for relief from the stands. Bill warmed up between innings. The Giants got two more in the second without surrendering an out when Bill got the call.

"Holy fuck," said Kaz, handing Bill the ball and walking off the mound.

Bill took his warm-ups. Though it was hot, he couldn't seem to get loose. He could see the snack bar in the gap between the stands on the first-base side, a golden head bobbing behind the counter. Loony trotted out to the mound after his eighth warm-up.

"Okay, Pops." he said. "Mystify them fuckers."

But he didn't. The curveball was as flat as a Kansas cornfield, the hummer as slow as molasses in March, the knuckler as straight as a yo-yo string. Nothing worked. The jolly Giants teed off. Newsy was warming up in the bull pen before he got the first out.

"Come on, Mahoney ... suck it up out there."

He finished the inning amid a barrage of singles and doubles. The Giants scored three more. It was a rout; they went on to win 18-4. Duffy was out trying to steal when they were twelve runs down. *Jesus*, Duffy, said Sly. ... He *gim*me the muthafuckin' green *light*, man. ... According to Gunner, Sly threw his hat against the dugout wall thirteen times for a new record.

Alice waved to Bill as he passed the snack bar after the game. He waved back, a weak effort. He did not stop.

The Friday game was close, but the Giants won it 5-3 and left town a full five games ahead of the Dodgers. Sly had them out early Saturday morning for infield drills and batting practice. He prowled the field like a battlefield sergeant. J.C. sat in a folding chair outside the dugout, reading.

> ... "There are no words to describe anything that really matters," said Rex sweepingly, "just as there are no words to express love or hatred, happiness or sorrow. One can only feel such things."

He looked up from his book to see a grass-cutter skip through Soapy's legs. He shook his head.

> ... "This is mad," she protested. "The others will miss us."
>
> ... "Does it matter?" he asked. "Does anything matter except this?"
>
> ... He kissed her and she felt a flame run searingly through her. She trembled. She could not withstand him.

She's in for trouble, he thought. Dat Rex. Huh ... An' what about Nicholas? ... She'd be better off with Nicholas, he decided.

Chewy let a high bouncer get under his glove.
"Keep ya glove down," said J.C., but nobody heard him.

The Dodgers won four of the next five games. They left Lodi on August 14 for an eight-game road trip, four games behind the Giants. Only fourteen games left; eight on the road and six at home. Any combination of Giant wins and Dodger losses that totaled eleven would automatically eliminate the Dodgers.
"I don't have to tell you guys," said Sly. "We got our work cut out for us."
"No problem," said Loony.
On the morning they left, Bill found a letter addressed to him in the mailbox outside the apartment.

> Dearest Bill:
> The Spirit in me would like to speak
> to the Spirit in you. You are very dear
> to me.
>
> Alice

"Who's it from?" said Gunner.
"The police."
"Yeh?"
"A bench warrant ... Failure to appear ..."
"For what?"
"... Life."
Gunner thought about that for a moment.
"I like that," he said. "It's ... insightful."
"Does have a certain ring to it, doesn't it?"
"Yeh. I like it. Sounds like something Professor Wisdom might have come up with."
"Or Tug McGraw."
"... Maybe."

They left at noon Friday for the short ride to Billy Herbert Field in Stockton. Gunner was trying to explain to Loony how to figure out when they would be mathematically eliminated.

"We're four games out, right?"

"Right," said Loony.

"With fourteen games left, right?"

"Uh ... right," said Loony.

"So ... if you look at the standings ..." He spread the paper on Loony's lap and pointed to the standings. "Here. We've got four more losses and four fewer wins than the Giants."

"That's eight," Loony said quickly.

"Well ... yes and no," said Gunner.

"Four and four is eight, Gunner," said Loony.

"Don't get ahead of yourself," said Gunner. "Each win only counts half a game. Same with the losses. So it takes one win and one loss to make a whole game."

Loony looked puzzled.

"Let me put it another way," said Gunner. "You take the number of games that you've won. Then you take the number of losses that you have *more* than the team ahead of you."

"Better start over," said Bill.

"Okay ... Say the Giants won twenty games and we ..."

"They won more'n that," said Loony, jabbing his finger at the paper.

"I know that," said Gunner. "But we'll just *say* that. For purposes of ... illustration."

Loony nodded but looked doubtful.

"Say the Giants have twenty wins and we've got sixteen. That puts us four back in the win column, right?"

"... Right."

"Okay. Now say the Giants got ten losses and we've got four*teen*. That's four *more* losses. Which puts us four *up* in the loss column. So now we got four back and four up for a ..."

"May I have this dance?" said Tenor.

"Do you do the four-up-and-four-back?" said Bill.

"Is that the minuet, dahling?"

"... for a total of eight games. Now we divide the eight by two ... since each game is really only worth half a game. What's eight divided by two?"

"Four?" said Loony.

"Right," said Gunner. "Now we're gettin' someplace. The next thing is ..."

"... Is this the way to Stockton?" said Sly.

The road-sign read GALT.

J.C. looked up from his book.

"Galt? ... No ... wrong way ..."

"Chumley?" Doc Hardin said timidly.

"What?" he snarled.

"Are we going the wrong way?"

Chumley pulled onto the gravel divider and slid to a stop.

"Who's drivin'?" he said without turning around.

"... *You* are, Chum," said Doc. "I was just ..."

"Don't forget it," he snapped. He slammed the bus into low gear, made a U-turn, and headed south.

"What was *that* all about?" said Chewy.

"Maneuvering to avoid the Klingons," said Bill.

"The who?" said Loony.

"Just pay attention," said Gunner. "I've only got about an hour to explain this. Now we have established that we are four games out of first place. With fourteen left to play. Which means ... that any combination of Giant wins and Dodger losses that total eleven will put us out of it. You got a pencil? I need a pencil to explain this."

"I got a calculator," said Loony.

"You do?"

"In my bag." He pointed to the floor of the bus. "It's with the gear."

"A calculator, eh? ... What do you use it for?"

"I figure my average."

"... I'm impressed," said Gunner. "What kind is it?"

"A Bomar Brain."

"Is it programmable?"

"Is it what?"

"Does it have a memory?"

"Tell him you don't remember," said Tenor.

"... I just figure my average," said Loony.

"Never mind," said Gunner. "Why do I get involved in conversations like this?"

"Because you're a dummy," said Bill.

"... I need a pencil for this. Anybody got a pencil?"

"I can't figure with a pencil," said Loony.

"Can't figure what?"

"My average."

"You figure it on a calculator ... but you can't figure it with a pencil?"

"Yeh."

"... They have *schools* in Trenton, Loony?"

"Sure they got schools."

"Did you *go* to one?"

"Awww ... get fucked, willya?"

"Christ ... We ever have a power shortage you'll be lost."

"... Why?"

"Your *tele*vision won't work. And your Bomar *Brain* won't work ... and you won't know *what* the ..."

Loony crumpled the paper with both hands and shoved it at Gunner.

"Here ... Take your fuckin' paper ... I know all I need to know."

"Well said," said Bill.

"Beautiful," said Gunner. "Just beautiful ... America's future ..."

The Dodgers roared into Stockton and swept the four-game series. Bill got one of the wins, an extra-inning relief job in the second game of Sunday's doubleheader.

"Good job," said J.C.

"Way to go, Pops," said Loony.

"Thanks," said Bill. He took off his cap and toweled the sweat from his forehead.

"Your hair's gettin' thin," said Gunner.

"Good," said Bill. "It's on a diet. Nobody wants fat hair."

Gunner pretended that he didn't hear.

They picked up a game on the Giants. Ten games left, three games out.

... huffnpuff ... huffnpuff ... huffnpuff ...

J.C. read his book on the way to Visalia.

"... Don't take any notice of me tonight,
Nick," she pleaded. "I've got what Nannie
used to call an 'imp on my shoulder.' "

He put out his hand toward her and then checked himself, as if he was half afraid that she would resent the gesture.

"... Shall I tell you what I think?" he asked.

"... Yes, do."

"... There are people in this world," he said, "who flow through other people's lives like a wide, steady river. There are others who come bursting in like a sudden shower of rain. One notices the rain; it's unexpected, it has an immediate effect on one, but the river is always there. You're like a river, Fenella; those who know you will always want and need you however much they may be taken up for the moment by the showers."

Nicholas had spoken with only a slight hesitancy, but Fenella knew that every word had been difficult for him to utter and yet it came straight from his heart.

She felt a sudden impulse of tenderness toward him.

J.C. closed the book and smiled ... Now dat's better ...

huffnpuff ......

huffnpuff ....

huffnpuff ....

On July 26th, 1967, nearly ten months after he was born, Christopher took his first step. Bill watched for some evidence of hand preference, but could find none; the boy simply accepted what was offered with either hand and stuffed it in his mouth. Bill hoped he was left-handed. He bought another plastic bat, a large leather mitt and white whiffle ball. Chris banged on the side of the playpen with the bat, chewed on the leather mitt and ignored the whiffle ball once he found out that it wouldn't fit in his mouth. Bill read aloud from the Sports section which was then lamenting the sad state of the Dodger offense. Christopher made bubbly sounds, swaying as he held on to Bill's knee, swinging his bat at the paper for attention. Bill measured him every month, marking his growth with penciled lines on the closet door.

Gloria toiled at the Whirlpool with the diapers, watched the daytime soaps and generally felt weary. Chris never wanted to take a nap; she had to lock him in his room. He banged on the door and screamed until he was exhausted; he often fell asleep on the floor.

She talked to Kandy every day; it was the one thing she looked forward to. She went shopping, tried on a few mini-skirts, fussed over the budget and sniped at Bill about his drinking. She endured. Kandy came over on the days she had no school, bursting with enthusiasm, often dressed in government surplus coats and pants. She talked about the Movement and the play she was writing. Gloria listened eagerly.

The first heavy rains came in October that year, soon after Christopher's third birthday.

Bill got to work at five-thirty, the usual time. There were a few clouds in the sky. They drank coffee from the Roach Coach and watched the clouds quickly darken the dawn. Then the rains came. Heavy. Dismal. Someone suggested Sleeveless John's for a beer. He couldn't remember who said it. Just a voice. Nor could he remember who had the pills. Whites. Reds. They played shuffleboard. And peg pool. He didn't remember if it ever stopped raining; no one went outside to look. He vaguely recalled holding the eight ball and showing Lushwell how to grip it to throw a curve. Was it Lushwell who threw it against the back wall?

It was night when he went home; he remembered the headlights being on. And Gloria at the front door.

He awoke the next morning with a throbbing headache. He rolled over in bed. He was alone. He opened his mouth to groan, but no sound came out. He listened intently. It was raining. Nothing else. He got up slowly, pulled on his shorts and pants and walked into the kitchen. Gloria was seated at the kitchen table holding an ice pack to her cheek.

"You son of a bitch," she hissed.

A cigarette was burning in the ashtray.

Christopher toddled through the door in his one-piece Dodger-blue jammies. He looped an arm around Bill's leg and knuckled the sleep out of his eyes. He surveyed the scene for a few moments before he spoke.

"Mommy hurt?" he said finally.

She nodded and held out her arms. He ran across the floor and crawled up on her lap.

"Wanna kiss?" he said.

"U-huh." She began to cry.

He kissed her and tenderly explored her cheek with his fingertips.

"Here?"

"U-huh. Mommy fall down ... go boom."

He smiled knowingly.

"Ohhh," he said. "Don' cry." He looked at Bill. "Daddy hurt?"

Bill shook his head.

Chris squirmed off her lap and padded over to the kitchen counter. He pointed up at the cabinet.

"Trix?" he said, grinning. "Kids like Trix ..."

Bill took a deep breath and tried to steady himself. Christopher started to pull out the bottom drawer beneath the cabinet.

He had already discovered that by pulling out the two lower drawers, he could climb up on the counter top and get his own Trix.

"No," said Bill. "Daddy'll get it."

Chris pushed the drawer back in, stuck his thumb in his mouth and waited.

Bill dumped some Trix in a bowl, poured the milk and brought it to the table. He put the telephone book on the chair and lifted Chris up on it.

"Spoon?" said Chris.

Bill got him a spoon.

"*Big* spoon," said Chris.

Bill got him a bigger spoon.

"Sugar?" said Chris.

"It's got sugar on it," said Bill.

Gloria got up and left the room.

A small frown creased Christopher's forehead.

"Sugar?" he repeated.

"It's got plenty on it. Sugar's not good for you anyway."

Chris stared at him.

"See?" said Bill, pointing to the cereal. "It comes with sugar on it. You can see it."

"Sugar?" said Chris.

"God*damit*, Chris. It's got sugar *on* it."

The boy's face dissolved into a rubbery mask of tears. He opened his mouth, choked in some air and wailed loudly.

"Don't take it out on the baby," Gloria shouted from the living room.

"Jesus," he snapped. "Jesus fuckin' Christ."

"Don't *say* that in front of him."

Chris gripped the spoon in his left hand and threw it on the floor. Bill felt nauseated. He closed his eyes and tried to shut out the noise. Gradually, it subsided. When he opened his eyes, Chris was looking at him.

"Spoon?" he said.

Bill opened the silverware drawer, found another big spoon and handed it to him.

"Sugar?" said Chris.

Bill got the sugar and sprinkled some on the cereal.

"Me," said Chris, reaching for the sugar.

"No," said Bill. He sprinkled a little more.

"Daddy?"

"Yeh."

"I'm a big boy, eh?"

"Yeh." He mussed his hair. "Real big."

Chris made a sound like a motor boat, rapidly piloting his spoon through the bowl of Trix.

Bill put the sugar away and walked into the living room. Gloria sat at the end of the couch, her legs tucked under her, one hand holding the robe at her throat, the other holding the ice pack to her cheek. Bill sat at the other end of the couch.

"... You," she said contemptuously.

He cleared his throat.

"What happened?" he said.

"You hit me ... You know that? You hit me."

Bill took a Winston from the pack on the coffee table, put it to his lips but didn't light it.

"God," said Gloria.

Bill fixed his gaze on the swan-shaped lighter on the coffee table. Pier I Imports. From India. He had taken it apart several times and tried to fix it, but it never worked for more than a day.

"... There's something wrong with you, Bill. You know that? Something very wrong ... People don't *do* the things you do. Normal people. I mean there's something *wrong* with people who go around ... beating up their wives. Screwing chickens. Wearing women's underwear. Drinking like you do. Normal people don't *do* those kinds of things. I'm taking the baby and ..."

His head felt like ice; he couldn't seem to think. He picked up the copper lighter and tried to light his cigarette. He flicked it several times, then set it back down on the coffee table. He dug into his pants pocket, found his Zippo and lit the cigarette.

"... I'm sorry," he said.

"I'm sorry I'm sorry. Is that all you can say?"

He shrugged.

"I'm sorry and everything's okay? Just like that?" She snapped her fingers. *"God* ... When I think about it."

A sliver of ice worked its way to the base of his skull and started down his spine. *Take the baby and leave* ... Is that what she said? He put his hands on the couch to steady himself.

"Don't go," he heard himself say.

She adjusted the ice pack.

"... It won't happen again," he said.

"Huh ..." She cinched the robe at her throat. "Will you see someone?"

"... About what?"

"Your ... problems."

He blinked several times. She watched him closely.

"Get some help," she said.

"Help," he said quietly, as if the word had no meaning.

"Counseling. Therapy ... Group therapy. Kandy says the Community Center has ..."

... *Kandy says Kandy says Kandy says* ... Why did he hate her so? Gloria was talking; he could see her lips move. He nodded, though he couldn't hear the words. He looked toward the kitchen. His older brother was standing in the doorway dressed in Marine fatigues, his upper body perforated by small round holes. The kitchen light shined through them and made a pattern on the floor. He was smiling.

"... will you?" she said.

He turned toward her.

"Help?" he said.

"Yes."

"Okay ..." When he looked back at the door, his brother was gone. He heard Piglet talking to Pooh:

> "Tigger is all right, *really*," said Piglet.
> "Everybody is *really*," said Pooh.

"I'll get the number," she said.

"... Of what?"

"The ... Community Center." She purposely avoided saying Community Mental Health Center.

"... Okay."

They briefly touched hands. Bill went to the kitchen.

"Alllll gone," said Chris, holding the empty bowl over his head with both hands.

"All gone," said Bill. "That's my big boy."

"Big boy," Chris said proudly.

Kandy, though she was busy rehearsing for the male lead in *Love Is a Woman* with the Twelfth Street Players, found time to visit when Bill was at work.

"He's getting very strange," said Gloria.

"Men," said Kandy, shaking her head. "They think they *own* you."

"I mean really strange."

"... Men."

She put her arms around her best friend and embraced her warmly.

"Maybe you'll have to dump him," she said.

Bill was surprised and dismayed by his reported behavior. He didn't think of himself as the kind of person who would do something like that, hit a woman or force himself on her. Of course, he only had her word for it. He had been drinking all day and didn't remember anything after he got home. And he hadn't actually seen any swelling on her cheek. Maybe he didn't hit her at all. Maybe she made the whole thing up. But why?

The marriage, though not yet openly adversarial, sank in the quicksands of resignation. Gloria kept a catalog of certain events hidden in the folds of her memory, wielding it like a hatchet in moments of crisis. There were times when she parted his tattered shorts, encircled him with her deft right hand and slowly pumped some life into his flaccid manhood. Even times when the Vaseline was removed from the medicine cabinet. But they were rare. ... Later, he would picture her smiling maliciously behind his back, tepid hand to the tiller, steering him toward the shoals.

It was during one of those infrequent encounters that a hardy sperm fought its way through defective latex, Vaseline, and spermicide to unite with a wandering egg. Bill was informed of the pregnancy two months later. He had not guessed; he was no longer privy to the ebb and flow of sexual cycles.

Chapter 18

Gloria sent him off to Planned Parenthood to have his future parenthood plans severed. He went with some trepidation, grimacing as the chatty doctor and nurse exchanged pleasantries over his exposed genitalia. He imagined them whispering about the size of his peewee pud.

The second child, a girl, was born that fall. Margaret Mahoney. Maggie. She was beautiful. She had her mother's brown eyes.

For a time, Bill became a regular member of the Thursday Night Group at the Community Mental Health Center. He and seven others turned up every Thursday night in various stages of derangement to express their discontent. Moderator Mayfield, a huge black man who sucked on an unlit pipe during the sessions, smiled benignly as the group traded insults. He seemed most pleased when they were on the verge of physical violence. After six months, Bill quietly left the group, though he continued to leave the house each Thursday on the pretext of attending.

The following year the headaches started. Aspirin didn't even make a dent. Drinking was the only thing that seemed to help.

As the 1972 Dodgers were preparing to depart for Florida, the Mahoney backyard took on the look of a baseball training camp, with batting tees, toss-backs, Nerf balls, whiffle balls, baseballs and bats. Bill had to dig up the blighted tree so they would have enough room. It was the year Chris would be allowed to play T-Ball. He wasn't quite old enough; you had to be six before August 1. But he was a husky youngster, bigger than most six-year-olds. Bill lied about his age.

Maggie, then eighteen months old, sped around the yard like a windup toy, screeching *ball ball ball* at the top of her lungs, holding both hands over her head as if she expected a ball to drop from the sky. She wrapped herself around Bill's leg with both her arms and legs and would not let go until he pried her loose.

Chris sometimes lobbed a Nerf ball to her, but it invariably hit her in the face before she could get her hands together. He was not above tossing a hardball at her when he was angry with her. She was averaging one bloody nose a week during spring training that year. She tried to throw the balls back, but they never went where she aimed them.

Chris was an apt pupil, eagerly following Bill's instructions. He had a smooth swing and a strong arm. Bill didn't realize how good he was till he saw him out on the diamond with the other kids.

He hurried home from work each day to practice with him. He guarded their moments together; they were times filled with uncomplicated joy. He marveled at how happy he could be just playing catch.

"You're gonna be good," he told Chris. "Real good."

"Better'n you?" he said with an impish grin.

"Well ... maybe."

"*Lots* better," said Chris, burning one in.

"Ouch! ... Take it easy on an old man."

"Lots better."

"... Maybe."

"Were you good?" said Chris.

"Yep. Real good."

"I'll be better," he said, burning another one in.

"Just might be," said Bill.

Many nights the three of them sat together on the couch watching the new color television, the two younger ones sucking their thumbs, Bill drinking his beer. He read to them from his favorite Pooh book:

> "Well," said Roo, "can Tiggers jump as far as Kangas?"
>
> "Yes," said Tigger. "When they want to."
>
> "I *love* jumping," said Roo. "Let's see who can jump the farthest, you or me."
>
> "*I* can," said Tigger. "But we mustn't stop now or we shall be late."
>
> "Late for what?"
>
> "For whatever we want to be on time for," said Tigger, hurrying on.

They stole his beer and hid it. Maggie tried to flush a can down the toilet.

"Come on, gang ... Where's Daddy's beer?"

He found the tall cans of Oly under Christopher's mattress, stuffed in Maggie's pillow, in the oven, under the couch cushions, nearly everywhere.

"Come on, gang ..."

They were his delight, their presence a balm to his soul. Still, some nights he drank himself to sleep; he didn't know why. He couldn't seem to stop.

Gloria was being drawn into a life in the theater. Under Kandy's able guidance, she was learning about scenery, lights, make-up. She was at rehearsals three or four nights a week.

The Twelfth Street Players held forth at a tiny theater on Santa Monica Boulevard, sandwiched between the gay bars and sleazy bookstores that mushroomed in West Hollywood. It was devoted to presenting fresh new plays by fresh new authors, performed by fresh new talent unable to find paying jobs. Bill attended only once, commenting that it was located in a lousy part of town. She let that pass, but did react when he mentioned that the place seemed to be full of queers. She told him that that was really a pro*vin*cial remark and that people's sexual preference didn't have anything to do with talent. He was not invited again.

His father called that summer; they had not spoken in some years.

"It's me," said Thomas.

"Who?"

"It's me."

"Dad? ..."

"Yeh. How are you?" The tone was gruff, unmistakable.

"Okay. I'm okay. How are you?"

"Okay. I retired last year ... From the Co-op. I don't work anymore."

"I didn't know ... Sounds good. Real good."

A familiar gulf of silence separated them.

"... How's the boy?"

"Great. Doin' great ... Growin' like a weed. You know kids."

"Christopher, eh?"

"Yeh," said Bill. "Chris ... We have another one. A girl."

"... Oh?"

"Yeh ... Maggie."

"... I was thinkin'," said Thomas, "maybe we could go to a ball game sometime. You and me ... Maybe the boy."

"... Maybe."

"I don't work now. I'm retired."

"Lucky you."

"Yeh."

"Why don't you give me your number," said Bill. "I'll call when I get some time."

Thomas gave him his number.

"How's the arm?" he said.

"... It's okay. Doesn't hurt much."

"Crazy about your arm, eh. How things worked out. Coulda been different."

Bill bit his lower lip.

"Maybe ... maybe not."

"Oh, it coulda been different ..." He sounded very sure about it.

Bill was silent.

"I know some things," said Thomas. "I'm not so old I don't know things anymore ... If you'd *lis*tened instead of being so *bull*headed ... things would be ..."

Bill broke the connection with his finger and then cradled the phone. He went to the refrigerator and got a tall can of Oly.

Chris was dazzling in T-Ball that first year. He was one of the few kids in the league who could catch. He developed a nice level swing that sent line drives spraying to all parts of the field. Opposing infielders recognized him and began to back up when he came to the plate ... *Oh oh, it's lefty ...*

Bill and Maggie attended all the games. Gloria stayed home to do the laundry and clean the house. Sometimes Kandy came to visit.

Two years of T-Ball, a year on a Farm Team and Chris was ready for the Little League Majors. Greedy managers vied for the first-round draft pick. If they could get him now, they'd be allowed to keep him until he was twelve. Four whole years. Derek Stoddard, long-time manager of the Indians, always one of the top teams, called him The Franchise. Other managers said ... Christ, don't let that bastard Stoddard get him. In midwinter, while Santa was out distributing toys to all the good little boys in Van Nuys, Derek Stoddard was busily devising ways to rig the draft.

No one could remember a nine-year-old who was good enough to play in the majors. Most spent two or three years on one of the farm teams. Some never made it at all. But Chris was an exception; no one doubted that.

"You ready for the majors?" said Bill.

"Yep," said Chris.

"*Yay yay yay,*" said Maggie. "Where's Mommy?"

"She'll be home soon."

"*Yay yay yay ...*"

At tryouts that spring, the eleven- and twelve-year-olds scoffed at the little kid who was trying out for the majors. The majors, man. Looka that shrimp. Jeeeeezzz. ... They stopped scoffing when they saw him play.

"Number fourteen, Chris Mahoney," said the announcer.

"Okay, Mahoney," said Stoddard who was running the tryouts as he did every year. "Take three in the outfield, three at shortstop, then come in and we'll time you down to first base."

Chris nodded without speaking and jogged to the outfield, Dodger cap pulled low over his eyes. He fielded the first fly ball in his tracks and fired it to the plate.

"Keep it down, Mahoney," said Stoddard. "Gimme a bounce for the cutoff man."

He went to his left for the next one, gloved it easily and drilled it to the plate on one bounce. Duane Stoddard, Derek's twelve-year-old son, nonchalantly swiped at it. It skimmed off the grass and hit him squarely in the groin. He doubled over in pain.

"You wearin' a cup?" said Derek.

"Arghhhhhhhhhhh ..." said Duane.

"What'd I tell you about always wearin' a cup? Even at practice."

"Aghhhhh ..."

"Next time you'll remember."

Chris went back for the next one, took a step in, gloved it and fired another strike. His three in the infield were equally impressive. Derek clocked him to first base.

"Four point eight," he barked.

The managers and coaches in the stands looked bewildered; seemed like the kid was a lot faster than that. But they wrote it down. A definite minus to be that slow. Derek checked his stopwatch again before he reset it; three point seven. He allowed himself a little grin. Bill checked his own watch and smiled, too. Chris' five swings at the plate were all line drives.

At the draft two weeks later he ended up on Derek's team. Through a semilegal maneuver the year before, Derek had the second pick in the first round. His only worry was that Ted Moon, the man with the first pick, might be smart enough to take Chris. He needn't have worried; old Moony had promised his neighbor that he'd pick his son first. Several managers groaned. That's all that fucker Stoddard needs. A kid like Chris for four years.

On the 23d of May, the Indians were scheduled to play the Astros.

"You know what we call the Astros, Dad?" said Chris.

"Yeh."

"You do?"

"Yeh."

"... How do you know?"

"You'd be amazed at the things parents know."

They went early to watch the nine o'clock game. Ten minutes before Chris' game, Bill realized that he had forgotten to bring his scorebook.

"Come on, Mag," he said. "I gotta run home and get the scorebook."

"I'll stay," she said.

"No. Come on."

"I'll have some Red Hots."

"No. Come with me."

"We'll be late," she said.

"Come on, Mag."

He dragged her away and they sped home.

"Can I have some Red Hots when we get back?"

"Yeh."

"Promise?"

"Yeh, I promise."

"... Can I have *two* Red Hots?"

He stopped in front of the house.

"Stay here," he said.

"I'll watch the car," she said.

"Good."

He jumped out of the pickup, left the door open and ran to the house.

He nearly didn't see them. He rushed through the living room toward the bedroom where he kept the scorebook. Gloria looked up, startled. She wiped her mouth with the back of her hand and put her other arm across her breasts. Kandy just lay on the couch.

"Gotta get my scorebook," he said, almost apologetically. But his mind was already spinning. For a moment he forgot what he was looking for. "Scorebook," he said. He found it next to the bed, picked it up and hurried through the living room. Gloria was pulling on her jeans. All he remembered of Kandy was the great black thatch between her legs.

It was all he could think of during the game. Chris made a great catch in left field. Went two-for-four at the plate. For two whole innings he didn't keep score at all. Maggie wanted him to get her some Red Hots. He gave her a dollar. "You go," he said. "I'm too *little*," she said. And she was. She couldn't reach the snack-bar counter to get anybody's attention. He trooped numbly to the snack bar and bought the Red Hots ... He didn't take them to McDonald's after the game. They complained loudly that they *al*ways went, but he just took them home and dropped them off.

He stopped and bought a half pint of vodka on his way to South Gate, opened it and tossed the cap out the window before he left the liquor store parking lot.

Sleeveless John greeted him warmly.

"Hey kid, how ya doin'?"

"Okay," said Bill. He had already finished the half pint.

"Gimme them mothafuckers," said Mambo, reaching for the dice cup.

"How about a beer?" said Bill.

"Comin' up," said John. "Don't cheat, Mambo," he said over his shoulder.

Mambo smiled wickedly and began rearranging the dice.

"Hey, Lushwell," said John. "Look who's here."

Lushwell looked up from his pool game.

"About time," he said.

Bill drank quickly. He tried to harness the racetrack notions that sped through his mind. Why had he just walked out of the house. Why hadn't he ... done something? Anything? Except walk out.

He pointed to his blurred image in the back-bar mirror. No balls, Mahoney. No balls. You shoulda *done* somethin'. Somethin' ... meaningful. He had to laugh at that. Gloria always talked about that—doing something meaningful. Was going down on Kandy meaningful? He'd have to ask her. If he ever saw her again.

Maybe I should just kill her, he said.

"Great idea," said Lushwell, seated next to him.

Bill didn't hear him.

... Bury her somewhere up on Oat Mountain. Up by the Nike base. No one would ever find her.

He had another beer.

Divorce is really the answer, he said.

"Just kill her and get it over with," said Lushwell. "Believe me, you'll be better off."

... Wasn't a judge in the world wouldn't give him custody of the kids. Not one. Not when he explained what happened.

> ... Gloria Alsop Mahoney was discov-
> ered face down on the nude form of
> one Kandy Karol, admitted lesbian. The
> court judges her to be an Unfit Mother.
> Custody of the children is hereby
> awarded to Just plain Bill ...

Voices and music seemed to come from a distance. The

shadows that moved belonged to friends; he was grateful for that ... His surroundings melted. It was quiet for a time. Was he sleeping? ... Someone said, Let's go to work. That you, Lushwell? You say that? ... Can't make it right now, old buddy. Maybe later. Gotta finish up my finish up. Hahahaha ... Catch this beer, willya? Whoooops! ... Oly-olay-eee-oooooo ...

The public phone outside the door wouldn't stop ringing. Everybody thought it was a big *joke* that the phone was ringing. Bill couldn't figure out what was so funny about it. He finally had to answer it himself.

"Sleeveless John's," he yelled into the mouthpiece.

"... Jesus died for our sins," said an old scratchy voice. "Jesus died for our sins ... And you got no balls."

He stared at the receiver. They laughed when he went back inside. Asked who it was on the telephone. How could he tell them?

He had no way to judge the passage of time.

He pulled out of the parking lot in his pickup and turned the radio on ...

...KABC, the "Ken and Bob Show" on
a beautiful Wednesday morning ...

Wednesday? He shook his head but the fuzz remained. That didn't seem right. Still ... He touched his face and felt the stubble. What had happened to ... to the other days? He had trouble driving; he couldn't seem to stay in any one lane.

The door to the house was locked. He fished for the key and opened it. Inside it was dark, the drapes drawn. He flicked the hallway light on and went to the kitchen to get a beer. First thing he noticed was that the refrigerator was gone. He looked for a chair but there were none. And no table.

A sheet of notepaper was pinned to the front drapes. He pulled it off and read it.

> Bill:
> I have taken the kids and left. While
> there is still time. You are on a collision
> course. So I am leaving to make a life

for ourselves. There is no meaning in my life today. You have destroyed it.

Do not come looking for us. I have gone to another state. Besides, I will have you arrested.

Gloria

P.S. You are not really a bad person. Not really. You are just sick.

Nothing about Kandy. Nothing about what happened last ... Saturday? Sunday? Nothing about that. He could have *her* arrested. For what she did.

He looked for something to break, but there was nothing left. He crumpled the paper and threw it across the room so hard that he hurt his arm.

"You son of a bitch," he shouted, holding his elbow. "Goddam worthless son of a bitch."

He went through his closet, gathered some clothes, his baseball glove, and stuffed them into a green lawn bag he located under the kitchen sink. He tossed his shaving gear in after them and hurried out of the house.

He drove to South Gate, closed the bar and slept in his car that night.

Heat waves shimmered off the surface of Highway 99 on the drive south to Recreation Park in Visalia.

"*Christ*, it's hot," said Gunner.

"You can say that again," said Bill.

" … Christ, it's hot."

Modesto ... Merced ... huffnpuff ... huffnpuff ... Chowchilla ...

Gunner smiled. He was on a roll, riding the crest of an incredible hitting streak. He had hit safely in twenty-six games, closing in on the record of thirty-four set by Max Macon in 1949. His thirty-one home runs led the league, though there was no chance he could top the fifty-one hit by Harry Heslet in 1956.

... Madera ... huffnpuff huffnpuff ... Fresno, home of the hated Giants.

"We're comin' to getcha," Loony yelled out the window as they passed under the sign that read:

> FRESNO
>
> NEXT 6 EXITS.

"Don't bother," said Gunner. "They're not home. They're in Modesto this week."

"No problem," said Loony.

"It was in the paper ... the *news*paper."

"We'll get 'em wherever they are."

"Okay, Bomar ..."

Bill closed his eyes and tried to remember what it was like to be cool ... He had called Alice from Stockton the night before. Collect. He didn't have any change ... Collect call from a Mr. Mahoney. Will you accept? ... Yes, of course, she said, her voice like summer wind chimes.

"I got your note," he said.

"... I'm glad."

"It was ... nice. I liked it."

"Good."

"I never thought of it like that ... the Spirit in me and the Spirit in you."

"U-huh ..."

"It just made me ... feel good. I don't know ... I wanted to tell you that."

"Maybe the Spirit in you ... misses me," she said.

"... Yeh. I thought of that. The thing is ... the Spirit in me is not always ... well. Sometimes it's ... not well at all."

"Yes," she said softly. "... I understand."

"Do you?"

"Yes."

"And that doesn't bother you?"

"No."

"... Huh ..."

"I'm really glad you called," she said. "Will I see you when you get back to town?"

"Yeh. I'll call."

"Good ... Take care of yourself."

"You too."

"... And Bill?"

"Yeh?"

"I'm very good at starting over."

He grinned.

"... 'Bye, Alice."

"Ciao."

"Christ it's hot," said Gunner.

"You said that," said Bill.

"Just wanted to be sure you were payin' attention."

J.C. massaged his chest and tried to keep his mind on what he was reading ...

> ...She said nothing. Nick looked at her
> but did not speak and she knew that
> he was neither glad nor surprised to
> see her; he was past any feeling save

numbness and despair ...

He thumbed to the end of the book. Only three more pages. He closed it and tried to take a deep breath.

"Is it possible," said Bill, "that women know more than men?"
"About what?" said Gunner.
"... Everything."
"Hardly ... about babies maybe ..."
"Huh ... I think that sometimes. That they just know more."
"Probably the heat, Mahoney."
"Yeh ..."

They tore the Oaks apart. Gunner kept his streak alive. Nesbitt threw a no-hitter, the first by a Dodger in over four years. They headed home in high spirits. Six games to play and they were only two back of the faltering Giants.

The hapless Pioneers were mere fodder for the Big Blue Machine. Gunner was six-for-nine in the short series. Bill got a start in the second game and pitched seven complete before he tired. He didn't overpower anyone; he knew those days were gone. His arm still hurt, but in the middle innings he had a sense of how it used to be: the feel of his body as he pushed off the rubber, the arm whipping forward, the ball spinning away, a feeling as clean and pure as summer rain. He tired in the late innings and began to struggle with his control.

Lindell came in to pitch the eighth and ninth. Bill sat next to J.C. to watch the rest of the game.
"Good job, kid," said J.C.
"Thanks."
"Good year."
"Yeh ... it was okay," said Bill.
J.C. leaned forward and spit on the dugout floor. He rolled the fungo bat slowly back and forth along his thighs.
"What now?" he said.
"Oh ... I don't know, Skip."
"Baseball?"
"No ... too old."
J.C. smiled.
"You don' know old."

"Too old to play, anyway," said Bill. "I'm thirty-nine years old, Skip."

"I know."

"... Yeh?"

"Yeh. Ain't no secrets in baseball."

"Huh ..."

"Me? ... It's my las' year," said J.C.

"You'll be around forever."

"Time to quit, kid. Maybe go fishin'."

"Fishin', eh? I'll believe it when I see it."

"You'll see it." He took a deep breath. "Ya ever fish?"

"No ... Always wanted to, but I never did."

"Me ne'der. You suppose it's hard?"

"No. I don't think so."

"Little kids fish," said J.C. "I seen 'em."

"Yeh. Can't be too hard. You know, Skip ... baseball ... won't be the same without you."

"Ahhhh, baseball ... It'll be de same ..."

They both coughed.

J.C. took another deep breath and rubbed his chest.

"You okay?" said Bill.

"Yeh ... Ya ever t'ink a coachin'?"

"... No."

"Be a spot nex' year. Sly's movin' up. Ya'd be good, kid. T'ink about it."

They left it at that.

He stopped by the snack bar to see Alice.

"Oh, you were good tonight," she said. "I watched ... when I could."

"Thanks."

"It's a pleasure to watch a pitcher with ... what would you call it? ... Class?"

"You could call it that. Or luck."

"I like class."

"Me too."

"Are you ... busy tonight?" she asked.

He hesitated.

"... Sort of ..."

"Don't tell me," she said, placing an index finger to her lips. "You've got a dragon to slay ..."

"... Or a Giant."

"Will you come back ... even if the dragon gets away?"

"Yeh ... I think so."

"It's doesn't matter," she said.

"What doesn't?"

"If the dragon gets away."

"... No?"

"No."

"How do you know?"

"... Women know," she said, wiping the Sno Cone dispenser, smiling mysteriously.

"Yeh ... I suppose they do."

J.C. stayed till everyone was gone.

"Wanna ride, John?" said Sly as he left.

J.C. waved him away without speaking ... In the silence that followed he could hear the sound of good dry ash meeting an inside fastball, pulling it hard down the line, see it kick up some chalk just in back of the bag. Extra bases sure. He could hear the crowd ... Oh, the crowd. They were standing, cheering ... Oh ... Oh. .. ..

"You okay, John?" said Fred as he dragged the water hose by the dugout. "John? .... John? ...."

John Christianson was slumped in the corner of the dugout, his old fungo bat across his knees. It took Fred awhile to unlock the snack bar and get to a phone. John was dead when they got him to the hospital.

Most of the players already knew about it before the team meeting the following day.

"I don't have to tell you guys," said Sly, "that the Skipper died last night." He took off his cap and placed it over his heart. "... May he rest in peace. Amen."

He put his cap back on.

"Now we got a big series with the Giants. John wanted this one. Bad. We need a sweep here. Three only gives us a tie. We sweep, we're in the play-offs ... I don't have to tell you guys that ..."

Loony raised his hand.

"Coach?"

"Yeh."

"Should we wear ... black armbands maybe? For the Skipper? Sly rubbed the back of his neck.

"... No. Just suck it up and play some ball out there. That's the way John woulda wanted it. He'll know ... Play 'em one at a time. Watch the signs. Know what the count is. Keep your head in the game ... Suck it up and play some ball."

Lawrence Stadium was nearly filled that day, only a few of twenty-five hundred seats were empty. A minute of silence was observed to honor the passing of John Orville Christianson. The flag was flown at half-mast.

"You know," said Kaz, seated next to Bill on the bull pen bench, "I keep thinkin' about what you said ... about the Big Dodger in the Sky."

"Yeh?"

"I have this weird feeling that he's *watchin'*."

"... The Skipper?"

"Yeh. Like he's somewhere ... like maybe there really *is* a Big Dodger in the Sky."

"Maybe there is."

"And a field. A diamond. Lots of 'em. Like at Vero Beach. Only bigger ..."

"Yeh ... diamonds are trumps."

"... You know I cried," said Kaz. "When I heard."

"Me too."

"And Tenor ... he cried, too."

"Yeh ... He told me this was gonna be his last year. He wanted to go to Oregon. To fish ... old J.C. .... Jesus."

The Giant center fielder went all the way to the warning track to snag a drive by Gunner in the third inning. Snake Simpson sent Loony sprawling with an inside fastball just because Loony happened to be the next batter. He brushed himself off and glared out at Simpson.

"Don't do that no more, Two Six," he growled.

Simpson did it again on the next pitch. The umpire stepped

out from behind the plate and warned him. Loony got up and stared at the top of the backstop with his hands on his hips. He picked up his bat and got back into the batter's box. Simpson came in with a sizzling fastball. But Loony got around, hips open, quick hands. He took it downtown. The fans erupted from the sea of blue. Simpson walked off the mound, picked up the resin bag, and threw it down in disgust.

The one run held up. Danny Nesbitt, with ninth-inning help from Newsy, threw a shutout. Gunner kept his streak alive by legging out a late-inning Baltimore Worm Killer that bounced high off the rock-hard dirt in front of the plate.

The mortal remains of John Christianson were flown home to Philadelphia the next day. His old fungo bat remained propped against the wall in the corner of the dugout. Sly never used it again.

The next three weren't as close. It seemed to take the wind out of the Giants' sails when the Dodgers beat their ace in the first game. They looked like they might be saving their best stuff for the play-offs. Gunner eclipsed the old consecutive-game hitting record by hitting safely in the next two. He drew the collar in the last game, but it didn't seem to bother him. Bill got some work in the Sunday finale, an inning-and-a-half of scoreless ball.

"Hey, Mahoney," said Gunner, poring over the Sunday Sports page at the motel, "here's another Mahoney just threw a no-hitter in the senior Little League semi-finals in San Bernardino. ... You don't happen to have any stray kids running around, do you?"

Bill looked up from his book.

"I look old enough to have a kid in Little League?"

"Maybe you were a child bride."

"... What's his first name?"

"Christopher ... Christopher Mahoney."

Bill didn't speak for a few moments.

"... Who's he play for?"

Gunner scanned the article.

"The Reseda Indians. Struck out fourteen. Maybe we could

use him in the play-offs."

Bill put his book down.

"Christopher. I had a brother named Christopher."

"He have any kids?"

"... No."

Gunner turned the page.

"Valenzuela strikes again," he said. "Shut out the Cards on four hits."

"Let me see the paper when you're done," said Bill.

"You're next. Just leave your fifty cents on the table."

Bill smiled and went back to his book.

The play-offs were to start Tuesday. The best of three. The first game would be in Lodi, the second in Fresno, then back to Lodi if a third game were necessary.

They had a light workout on Monday. Sly talked about momentum. He had them practice a new pick-off play and changed the bunt coverage with a man on second. He stayed late and threw batting practice for Soapy. His arm was sore for a week.

"Where would you go if you were runnin' away with two kids?" said Bill.

"Montana," said Lushwell without hesitation. "Nobody'd think to look there."

"Montana ... Never find 'em in Montana."

"Gone forever."

"Montana ... Huh."

"Bozeman," said Lushwell. "You ever been to Bozeman?"

"No."

"Indians and sheepherders."

"... Bozeman."

"You shoulda killed her when you had the chance. Woulda been easier."

"Yeh ..."

"Next time you'll listen."

He took up residence in the Sherman Arms Hotel, a twenty-eight dollar a week flop only a year removed from the wrecker's ball. The night lady was a round mound of Swedish bile who sniffed him contemptuously each time he entered, and charged him an extra two dollars every time he wet the bed. He hated her.

"You could hire a private eye to find 'em," said Lushwell.

"You think?"

"Sure. People do it all the time. Remember that show? 'Mr. Keene, Tracer of Lost Persons?' "

"... No."

"Radio ... He was a private eye. Found lost people. That was his job."

"... Huh."

"I know a guy," said Lushwell.

"Yeh?"

"Mike Radovich ... Tomato."

"Tomato?"

"Yeh. That's what everyone called him. Had a big red face. Like a tomato. Useta drink with him. I hired him once to find a guy owed me money."

"He find him?"

"No ... Tomato couldn't find his asshole if he was sittin' on it."

The days droned on into weeks. His drinking got worse. He had to take uppers to get out of bed in the morning. Throwing up was routine.

He drove by the house from time to time, but there was no one there. (He never even thought to drive by her parents' house, though it wasn't far away.) The lawn turned brown and died in the summer heat. One night he threw a rock through the front window, but it didn't make him feel any better.

He hired Tomato to find Gloria, suggesting Montana as a possible location. Tomato sent him a bill every other week for one hundred dollars plus expenses. He never left the office. It didn't make any difference; Bill never paid him.

He drifted up a few doors on Atlantic Boulevard and started hanging around Rudy's Bar & Grill; he was burned out on Sleeveless John's. Rudy even gave him a job cleaning up the bar and the restrooms in the morning. The days and nights blended together in a seamless robe of rushes and valleys. Summer passed like a lingering illness.

For Christmas that year, Rudy bought a little plastic tree and set it on the back bar. Kalkan Oberon waxed poetic about Christmas in New York and the halcyon days when he wrote movie reviews for *The Village Voice*.

Floyd moved like a shadow, his face tattooed with paranoia, his pockets full of pharmaceutical hope. He was careful; every stranger at the bar was a potential bust.

Pamela wept for her lost children, her face ravaged by acne and despair, sharp enough to cut a dream, her body a gracious gift that Time had left untouched.

"Three boys," she told Bill. "Benny, Barney ... and Billy. *Your* name," as if she had just discovered the similarity. "All three ... gone."

Bill grunted. Talk of children made him uncomfortable.

"You know where they went?" She continued without encouragement. "With their father ... that cocksucker. You should excuse my French. They *gave* them to him. My kids. They gave them to that prick. The courts. The fuckerola courts." She spilled some beer on her sequined blouse.

Floyd drifted toward Bucky who was reading aloud from his favorite Doctor Seuss book:

> He likes to drink, and drink, and drink,
> The thing he likes to drink
> Is ink.
> The ink he likes to drink is pink.

Bucky, a tiny replica of a man, chuckled to himself and bought a roll of whites from Floyd.

Kalkan called loudly for a pickled pig's foot. Rudy brought the jar reluctantly and allowed Kalkan to make his choice. He didn't like to watch him eat. Nobody did. Kalkan could make a foot last an hour, snorting noisily, the lower half of his face one large grease stain.

"You got kids?" said Pam.

"Yeh," said Bill.

"You married?"

"No more."

A smile exposed her tiny cat's teeth. She touched his arm and leaned closer.

"You know, we could go home to my place some night, Bill. You and me ..."

He felt a cold surge in his bowels.

"Ah yes," said Kalkan, expounding through the pig's foot. "Life is not always kind ... Even on Christmas, when our dear Savior was born, there is sadness in the land." His eyes became misty. "*Sic transit gloria pussy* ... It goes, my boy. It all goes." He gazed at the gristly foot. "The dew is off the red, red rose. The women's thighs have lost their clutch. That's Steinbeck ... And miles to go before I sleep ... And miles to go ..." He returned to the pig's foot.

"I useta love Christmas when I was a kid," said Pam.

"Yeh," said Bill.

"Did you?"

"I ... I don't know. I guess. It's hard to remember ... We listened to Lionel Barrymore on the radio. I remember that. I had a brother. Chris ... Great big guy. I don't know ..."

"... My mother baked ..."

"We lived near a mountain," said Bill. "Oat Mountain. I hiked to the top once. It was seven miles. Exactly. There were rabbits. Squirrels ... I fucked a chicken once. Jesus ..."

"... cookies for us. Christmas cookies. Star-shaped. You remember those kind? With the red and green speckly things?"

Bucky continued to read:

> ... My shoe is off
>
> My feet are cold ...

"The quintessential pig," said Kalkan, toweling his mouth with both sleeves.

> ... My hat is old
>
> My teeth are gold
>
> I have a bird
>
> I like to hold ...

"... and we went to church," said Pam. "I always loved the crib scene. With baby Jesus and the shepherds. And Mary ... You suppose Mary really was a virgin?"

"... Maybe."

"... I wanted to be a dancer when I was little. I took ballet. Two years. Two years ..." The rest was lost in a sigh.

"I was a ballplayer," said Bill, feeling the amphetamine rush. "Baseball. A pitcher. I could throw, Pam. Really bring it. I had a contract ... for the big leagues."

"Pro*fess*ional?"

"Yeh. I was good. Really good."

"What happened?"

"Oh ... Arm trouble." He flexed his arm. "Bone chips."

"Ohhhh ... I'm sorry," she said.

" 'S okay," he said. "Not your fault."

... My hat is old
My teeth are gold
And now
My story
Is all told ...

"Come on," whispered Pam. "Let's go to my place."
Bill studied his beer. The thought frightened him. Still ...
Someone played the juke box. They left to the strains of
"American Pie."

She lived in a squat little bungalow overgrown with foliage.
The outside smelled like rotting leaves, the inside reeked of
cats. They rushed to greet her from every corner of the house
when she opened the door. The cover on the bed turned out
to be calico cats. They surged across the room like a psyche-
delic surf, brushing against his legs, *meow*-ing unpleasantly.
Two stuffed chairs bookended a coffee table made from an
old splintered door. A small television cowered on a cardboard
box next to the bed, its antenna a twisted metal coat hanger.
She returned from the kitchen with a bottle of wine and two
plastic cups. She handed him a cup and drew him to the bed.
He breathed in shallow gasps, suffocated by the smell. The sea
of cats washed up on the shore of the bed and watched. He
finished the wine in two long gulps. She refilled his cup.
"First we better do the I-Ching," she said.
She led him to the coffee table and lit the candles. The cats
followed, tails high in the flickering light, casting shadows like
long willow reeds on the yellow walls. She produced the three
coins. He tossed them the required six times.
She read the coins and referred to the book.
"... Too bad," she said, shaking her head. "You got Po
hexagram. Collapse." She read from the *Oracle Book*:

> ... Your spiritual path is overgrown with
> bad karma. All your rituals, sacrifices,
> meditations and revelations are infused
> with non-spiritual desires ...

She lit an incense stick and returned to the reading.

> ... You will cross the water and talk to
> the Great Man ...

"Well, that's good anyway," she said. "Let's look at the moving lines ... Hmmmm ..."

> ... Ominous. Guilt. Calamities. A turn for
> the better has come and gone. You have
> let it pass you by. Conservative and
> fearful, you have stuck to old, decayed
> ideas, a stagnant way of life, an outdated,
> outmoded routine. You believe you
> display backbone by resisting change;
> you mistake your fear for stubbornness.
> This attitude is disastrous. It denies the
> inevitable flow of change in the Universe
> — a flow that will carry you along, if not
> buoyant and upright, then tumbled head-
> long and willy-nilly. You must patiently
> wait for things to resolve themselves.

"At least you're gonna cross the water and see the Great Man," she said, closing the book. "That's something ..."

He drank another glass of wine. He almost fell as he walked back to the bed. She undressed with her back to him, her vertebrae like fleshy rivets. He undid the top button on his pants. His heart raced. He lay back and closed his eyes. She removed his shoes, unzipped his pants and pulled them off. He felt a moist tongue on his shoulder. He opened his eyes and looked into the furry face of a one-eyed cat. The cat stopped licking and stared back at him with its one good eye; the other socket was an open wound. He had trouble breathing. He looked down at Pam; she was kneeling between his legs pulling on a small appendage that he didn't recognize. He couldn't feel anything; he wondered if he was dying. He opened his mouth to call for help ... He tried again. Pam looked up.

"You okay, Chuck?" she said.

Chuck? ... Chuck? ...

"Oh, Chucky," she said, throwing herself on top of him.

"Ohhhhh Chucky ..."

The one-eyed cat placed a tentative paw on his shoulder. The ceiling began to fade.

He was next conscious of being shoved out the door, standing on the walkway. A few seconds later, two shoes *thunked* out after him. The door closed and a bolt slid home. He stood with his pants clutched to his chest until a chill wind reminded him to put them on. He had to sit down to do it; he was too unsteady on his feet. He took deep breaths and tried to get his bearings. It took him a long time to find his way home.

Bill's grip on reality was tenuous at times. Lushwell started calling him Space Cadet.

A voice in his head suggested that everything was hopeless. Everything. Life was a bad deal. He had suspected as much for some time.

Bruises appeared in unlikely places. He picked at a scab that suddenly materialized on his lower lip. He couldn't seem to leave it alone.

"Been out kissin' the sidewalk?" said Lushwell.

"... Brakes on my space ship gave out and I ran into a planet," said Bill.

"Yeh? ... Which one?"

Bill frowned.

"Can't remember," he said.

Lushwell shook his head.

"Jesus ... Gimme a beer, Rudy."

"... I'm in charge of the planetary fleet," said Bill.

"Make that two, Rudy," said Lushwell.

"Thanks," said Bill.

"Anytime ... Captain." Lushwell took his beer over to the shuffleboard.

Bill stared at the back-bar mirror until his face began to dissolve. Life became an effort.

Though the Sherman Arms Hotel was only two blocks from Rudy's, he sometimes got lost coming and going. Rudy fired him twice for being late, but hired him back again each time. Bill informed Lushwell that he was Walter "Big Train" Johnson, famed hurler from Humboldt, Kansas. Lushwell continued to refer to him as Space Cadet.

One night he went to his room, pulled out the middle dresser drawer and counted the money he had taped beneath it: $320. He had some money from the sale of his truck, but he wasn't sure how much. Rudy sold it to a friend. He dug in his pocket and pulled out a crumpled wad of bills, another $67. He sat on the bed and held his head in his hands.

The knocking at the door went on for some time before he answered it. An elderly lady with wavy blue hair appeared on the other side of a fly-specked screen door. She was holding a tray covered with a white cloth.

"I thought you might like something to eat," she said.

Behind her he could see a lawn, some trees, part of a white picket fence. He held on to the door.

"Shall I bring it in?" she said.

He managed a weak yes.

She opened the screen door, came in and set the tray on a coffee table.

"Your favorite," she said. "Peanut butter sandwiches ... And you know, Booby, I found the flower we were looking for." Her powdery face looked like a close-up of the moon.

"... Oh? .."

"You remember. The state flower of Alaska?" She smiled.

"Oh ..."

"Forget-me-not," she said triumphantly. She tapped her temple with an index finger. "Forget-me-not ... They can't fool old Hazel for long." She whipped the cloth off the tray with a flourish. "Ta-da. ..."

All he could do was nod.

"My pleasure." She gently touched his arm, walked out the door and disappeared around the side of a white house.

He looked at his clothing; flannel shirt, faded blue cords. He walked through the living room, into the bathroom, flicked on the light and looked at himself in the mirror. It was him. Clean shaven, hair combed. When his eyes began to glow, he looked away and turned out the light.

On the kitchen table there was a typewriter with a piece of paper scrolled out the top, beside it a small stack of typed pages. He read a few lines from the paper in the typewriter ...

... Santa Claus brought Billy a book that
Christmas, though he couldn't read yet.
He put it on the desk in his room alongside the praying mantis that was struggling
for life in a large Mason jar ...

He picked up the stack of typed pages, thumbed to the bottom and read the first page ...

...The sign outside the ball park was blue
and white ...

He walked to the living room, sat on the couch and tried to take stock of what was happening. There were only questions. He looked at the newspaper on the coffee table.

HERALD EXAMINER
Tuesday, July 17, 1979

That didn't seem right. He searched his mind for the last remembered date, but was unable to come up with anything better. Only bits and pieces, isolated episodes, fragments. A deep sense of anxiety enveloped him. It took him several minutes to realize that the voice that was screaming was his own. He put his hands over his mouth to stifle the sound.

"Oh, Tex honey, you wanna dance?"

She nibbled on the edge of the styrofoam cup with small yellow teeth. Her face was the color of a faded sunflower, her eyes two dark seeds on the weathered surface.

"... Who?" said Bill.

She reached for his hand, but he pulled it away.

"It's *me*, honey. Ma*til*da. You remember."

"Leave him alone, Matty," said Commander Sperry, cleaning his half-moon glasses with a soiled handkerchief. "He's on suicide watch. You're liable to drive him right over the edge."

"Oh, shush," said Matilda, fiddling with her straw hat. "You don't know diddly."

The Commander bristled.

"Hardly," he huffed.

Bill Mahoney looked around, struggling to make sense of his surroundings. The bed he was on seemed to be the only one in the room. The room was large, abundantly windowed, though there were bars on them. A few brown Naugahyde chairs were scattered at odd angles. He blinked several times and tried to focus on the sign over the door at the end of the room:

WARD 206

Two people were seated at a large redwood table just to the left of the door.

"You play like *piss!*" yelled Jello Jarvis, throwing the checkerboard to the floor, getting up from the table and stomping away.

"Poor sport, poor sport, poor sport," taunted Mad Mary, her narrow face a wedge of contempt.

At the near end of the room was the nurse's station, enclosed in glass from the wooden counter to the ceiling. There were two round holes in the glass.

"Thirs'y," said Bill. His tongue felt thick and fuzzy.

"I'll get water," said Matilda.

"No, Matty," said the Commander. "You can't get water for him."

"I *will*," she said stubbornly.

"No. The nurse has to get it for him. You know that. He's on *su*icide watch ... He may have holes in his stomach or something."

"God," she muttered. "Holes in his stomach ..."

They both stood at the foot of the bed, the Commander much shorter than Matilda. They carried on the conversation without once looking at him. It wasn't till he glanced up and saw the television over his bed that he knew what they were looking at.

"Nurse Paula," called the Commander, without averting his gaze.

"Paula," said Matilda.

A tall nurse with a red Afro walked across the room.

"Yes, my dears?" she said.

"He needs a drink," said the Commander, pointing at Bill.

"A drink," said Matilda.

Paula rubbed the top of the Commander's bald head.

"Don't *do* that," he said.

"Okay," she said. "Shall we get him some whiskey?"

"Just water," said the Commander, shaking his head. "... Nurses."

Paula returned in a few minutes with a cup of water. Bill reached for it, but his hands were shaking so badly he couldn't hold it.

"Let me," she said, placing the cup to his lips.

He managed a few swallows.

"More?"

He shook his head. She picked up the clipboard and scribbled out the fifteen minute suicide report.

A slender young man with severe acne hurried to his bed.

"Ah, you've come around I see. Have you seen Doctor Eva?" he asked. "I'm Doctor Dilsee. Two e's. I'm fit as a fiddle, skinny as a rail. I've seen Doctor Eva and Doctor Horvath and Attila the Hun." He spoke rapidly, pulling at one ear, shifting his weight from one foot to the other. "I saw them in Camarillo. Have you been to Camarillo yet? You look like Doctor Pell. How are you, Doctor? I'm Doctor Dilsee. Two e's ..." He became more agitated as he spoke, shifting his weight back and forth so rapidly that he was almost running in place. "Pell mell, what a smell. Pell mell, can you tell?" He began to pull at both ears and jump up and down.

"Come on, Doc," said Paula, gently leading him away.

"... Me-di-*ca*-tion!"

The patients lined up at the nurse's station. Bill sank into a brownout.

He remained on suicide watch for several days. A number of people came to see him, but he couldn't remember any names. Twice (or was it three times?) he was led into a small room and given an injection of some kind. He had trouble walking; all he could do was shuffle. His hands shook so badly he could hardly eat.

"Mistah Bill doin' his *walk*in'," said old black Theodore. "Dat's it, Mistah Bill. Be walkin' now ..." He imitated Bill's strange shuffle. "Look like de Kansas City Shuffle, boy. He he he ... You been to Kansas City?"

Sometime later he went to see Doctor Eva. She had short black hair and eyes like flint. She asked how he felt. He said he didn't know. She said they had reduced his dosage of Thorazine now that he was no longer on suicide watch. She spoke so softly he had to lean forward to hear.

"What?" he said.

"... Is there a buzzing in your ears?"

He listened for a moment.

"Yeh."

She wrote something on her pad.

"That happens sometimes with the drugs. Any dizziness? Constipation?"

He nodded, though he had no idea if he was constipated or not.

She outlined his therapy in her soft monotone. He would see her three times a week. There would be some continued medication. He would be transferred to Ward 215 when his ...

condition improved. She made it sound like a good deal—Ward 215.

"We'll talk," she said. "In the weeks to come. Would you like that?"

He shrugged. It didn't seem particularly important.

"We'll talk about how you *feel*. About your disa*ppoint*ments. Life is sometimes full of disappointments, isn't it?"

"... I guess."

Her features blurred. All he could see was the sparkle of light from the yellow metal frame on her glasses. She tapped the pencil eraser on the desk ... *Pah ... Pah ... Pah* ... Like the sound of a hammer slamming eight penny nails into tongue and groove siding.

There was a witch there, on the mountain. He remembered her name was Gilbin. Black cone hat and a wart on her nose; she could fly like the wind. But he remembered the rabbits and chickens, horses, too. His mother sang in her shaky vibrato ... *We are all in the dumps, for diamonds are trumps* ... sang until she lay abed and died on that harmless summer day.

He felt himself get tense. Firm hands helped him out of the chair and back to the Ward.

He shaved with the harmless plastic razor and learned the routine, rising and falling with the others, his emotional barometer chemically controlled. He checked his appearance in the mirror each morning and noted that his hair was turning gray at the temples, his eyes were darker than he remembered.

The colors and shapes of his medication changed from time to time; Thorazine and Haldol gave way to Elavil and Tofranil. The Commander informed him that Thorazine also came in suppositories.

He was given a questionnaire to fill out:

> ... You sometimes can't help wondering if anything is worthwhile?
>
> ... Do you feel somewhat apart or alone even among friends?
>
> Do you have trouble going to the bathroom?

Chapter 21

Doctor Eva asked him if his father had a large penis? He just shrugged. How would he know that? But she wrote something in her notebook anyway.

He slept in one of the small cubicles in the men's dorm. Number eleven. Lucky number eleven. Commander Sperry told him that the last man who slept there died of a bleeding ulcer. Perforated, he said. Right there; in that same bed. The Commander saw it all. Blood pouring from his mouth and nose and ... everywhere. Help was on the way, he said, but it was too late. He ventured a guess that perhaps help always came too late. Bill nodded that he understood. Tragic, the Commander concluded. But then, that's war ... *Children of the fatherland, we wander aimlessly like lost orphans* ... von Clausewitz, he said with a twinkle.

Bill woke with the others to breakfast on hard-boiled eggs and cold cereal. Theodore always went immediately to the bathroom to sing his morning blues ...

> ... Oh, rock me mama, till you can't
> rock no moh ... Ohhhh, rock me
> mama, till ...

Checkers and parcheesi were the games of the Ward. Cards occasionally. Jello Jarvis never finished a game of checkers. Whenever anyone jumped one of his checkers, he threw the board on the floor and yelled, You play like *piss!* His opponent, usually Mad Mary because nobody else would play with him, chanted, Poor sport, poor sport, poor sport, until he retreated to the other end of the Ward. Mary smiled pleasantly, picked up the board and finished the game without him. Oh, I won a*gain*, she said in her sweet sad voice.

Bill usually spent the mornings slumped in one of the brown Naugahyde chairs near the television, his mind far away, searching the past for some thread of memory. The Commander and Worker often joined him for a round of Popeye, Bugs Bunny and the Road Runner.

"They're in Baltimore now," said the Commander.

"... Who is?" said Bill.

"The Russkies. It's Idaho next. Pocatella by nightfall."

"... Where's Pocatoca?" said Worker.

Stella wandered the Ward like a drooping magnolia, talking into her translucent hands. Worker swaggered around like a pirate in his black muscle shirt and his porkpie hat tilted to one side. Theodore really wanted that hat; had one just like it when he lived in Kansas City ...

> ... Oh rock me mama, till you can't
> rock no moh ... Ohhhhh ...

He had a rich baritone voice. Theodore could sing the blues.

Bill played checkers with the Commander and always lost. The Commander was in the habit of jumping checkers forward and backward and sideways, sometimes over several squares, not above removing checkers from the board when he thought Bill wasn't looking. He said that chess was really his game. Chess was a military game. A game for strategists. Like himself. And von Clausewitz.

Bill thumbed through the tattered magazines and paperbacks that were strewn around the Ward. When his vision cleared he read a little, though he couldn't make much sense of it. He sat for hours with a book open in his hands, drifting through realms that had no order, no substance.

At ten, two and four, Dr. Pepper time, the small Ward store was open. Patients could purchase candy, cigarettes and soft drinks. Round plastic chips were the medium of exchange. Green chips were worth ten cents apiece. (Little Julie would take off her dress for a greenie, all of her clothes for two. Jello was her primary patron.) Those who had money in the system could draw on it at the office, ten chips at a time. Bill evidently did because they handed him ten chips each time he asked.

White chips were dispensed by Ward personnel for good behavior. Attaboy chips. One white chip could purchase two cigarettes, five white ones a soft drink or a small candy bar. All other essentials were furnished by the state. No matches were allowed. Ward personnel furnished lights for smokers, who were only allowed to smoke near the office. Worker and Mad Mary tried unsuccessfully to counterfeit the green plastic chips and were denied Ward privileges for a week. Worker complained bitterly and bummed cigarettes from Bill. Mad Mary affixed her most beatific smile and continued to torment Jello at every opportunity.

Stella almost died the day she choked on a white chip, thinking it was a communion wafer. If it hadn't been for Paula, she wouldn't have made it. Father Pogo just held her hand and watched her turn blue. All he could say was that he just wanted to be a good priest. It didn't seem too much to ask.

Fragments of the past filtered slowly into Bill's hazy reality; random tiles in a cracked mosaic. He remembered the house; Hazel with the wavy blue hair doing those crossword puzzles ...

> What's the state flower of Alaska,
> Booby?
> Forget-me-not ... Oh, forget-me-not ...

He had taken to writing notes to himself so he wouldn't lose track of things. But he often found notes that he didn't remember writing, though the handwriting was similar to his own. Time seemed to skip erratically, leaving long blank spaces.

He remembered the Day. The Pills; they were red. He lay on his bed wearing his old Levis, gray sweatshirt and his Dodger cap. The radio was on ...

> ... beautiful day at Holman Stadium
> here in Vero Beach. This is Ross
> Porter along with Jerry Doggett and
> Vin Scully bringing you Dodger base-
> ball. Today it's an early game ...

He didn't remember how many pills he took, nor could he remember why he took them.

He did remember walking to the front door and looking out at the yard. His brother was standing on the lawn some twenty feet away; the small round bullet holes in his torso formed a question mark. Christopher smiled and said something, but Bill could not recall the words — only that they were important. That was all he remembered. Other clues were rendered lifeless by salvos of chemical welfare.

His sessions with Doctor Eva droned on. She tried to draw him out. She repeated that she would move him to Ward 215 when he became more ... responsive. She talked about taking risks, communicating, being open. She resorted to Ritalin, but it did not produce the desired results.

The trees turned gray and lost their leaves. Father Pogo said Mass every morning at the redwood table. Stella attended religiously. People left the Ward. Some returned. Others were new. Bill had no desire to leave. One night he dreamed of a surgical saw slicing through his chest. A large hand reached inside and crushed everything.

Paula taught him how to play gin rummy.
"Gin," she said, laying down the rest of her cards.
Bill labored to add up the points in his hand.
"... nine, ten, eleven ... and a six of hearts."
"Seventeen," she said. "The hearts don't count."
"No?"
"Not in rummy."
She gathered the cards and shuffled them.
"You know what suicide is?" she asked, staring at him with those wide, saucer eyes that never blinked.
"... No."
"A permanent solution to a temporary problem."
"... Huh."
"You tired of this place?"
"... No."
"Too bad. These kinds of places get to be habits. Bad for your health." She set the cards down and got up from the table.
"You wanna play some more?" said Bill.
"Nope."
The Commander whispered that she was an ex-hooker, doing penance for her sins at Metro State Hospital.

One day, as Bill was staring out a window on the north side of the Ward, his gaze was drawn to a small white ball that rolled into view. An ungainly figure lumbered after it, picked it up and threw it straight up in the air. A second attempt propelled it out of Bill's line of vision. It looked a little like Jello Jarvis, but he couldn't be sure at that distance. Bill crossed the room to look out the south side (the east end had no windows). He could see a few people seated on a bench, several baseball bats on the ground. He heard the klinky sound of a metal bat hitting a softball, walked quickly to the other side of the room but waited in vain for the ball to appear. Paula watched as he crossed the room each time he heard the sound of the bat. The ball only appeared once more in the next half hour. When a woman finally appeared to retrieve it, she was only walking. She picked it up, turned around and walked slowly out of sight. Shortly after, the people on the bench left and Bill went to join the Commander and Worker for the finish of the Road Runner.

"I could get that Road Runner," said Worker.

"You have to be smarter than the Road Runner to catch him," the Commander said dryly.

"Hey, I'm smarter," said Worker.

The Commander looked doubtful. Worker chuckled.

"He's only a cartoon, man. A car*toon*. I'm smarter'n a car*toon*. Jeez ..."

"They're playing baseball out there," said Bill.

"... Where?" said the Commander.

Bill waved toward the east end of the Ward.

"Out there," he said.

"Baseball?"

"... Softball."

The Commander arched one eyebrow.

"Not likely," he said. "Not likely."

Bill saw Jello Jarvis later in the day.

"Were you outside today?" he asked.

"Me?" said Jello.

"Yeh."

"... You got a smoke?"

Bill produced a pack of cigarettes. Jello took two. Matilda pulled on Bill's sleeve and asked if he wanted to dance.

"Were you?" said Bill.

"... Was I what?"

"Outside today."

Jello pinched his lower lip and frowned.

"I don't think I'm allowed," he said.

"You sure?"

"... Sure about what?" said Jello.

"Me-di-*ca*-tion! ..."

Bill didn't pursue it any further, but he was back at the window the next day.

"They won't play today," said Paula.

"... Play what?"

"Softball. They won't play today. It's Saturday. They only play during the week."

"Huh ..." He turned to walk away.

"You like baseball?" she said.

"... Yeh."

"You wanna play?" She nodded toward the window.

"Can I? ..."

"Depends."

"On what?"

"Well, we can't let just *any*body play," she said.

"Oh? ..."

"The really disturbed ones can't play ... You know ..." She stuck her tongue out and made a face. "Those kind."

"... How do you know which ones are ..."

"You're not," she said.

"No?"

"Nope ... Some people hide, Bill, in places like these. They get to like it in here. Play crazy long enough and you *get* crazy. Don't ever get to like it in here."

"... No?"

"No." She tapped on his chest with a bright red fingernail. "Stop hiding and stop feeling sorry for yourself."

"... I tried to kill myse ..."

"Boo-hoo poor baby," she said.

"I tried to ..."

"Bullshit," she snapped. "Self-pity, Mahoney."

He pushed her hand away.

"How's it feel to be pissed?" she said.

"I'm not pissed," he said angrily.

"Stay in touch." She smiled and walked away.

Bill wandered over to the table where the Commander and Worker were playing checkers.

"She's a hooker," said the Commander. "Tried to grab my dong one night."

"Wish she'd try me," said Worker.

"Our battle plans do not include camp followers," said the Commander.

"Mine do," said Worker, giggling excitedly.

The Commander informed Bill that a device designed to emit brain-softening waves had been concealed in the wall.

"Over there," he said, pointing toward the east wall.

"I feel okay," said Bill.

"Just wait ..."

"Bring on them hookers," said Worker. "Time to go to war with a whore."

Bill wouldn't look at Paula when he received his medication. He tossed the pills in his mouth and washed them down; his initial interest in their size and color had long since vanished. He couldn't tell the difference between Librium and Tylenol ... though he did have trouble sleeping for a while.

The next day he was fidgety and nervous. He stared at Paula. She smiled pleasantly. He made a conciliatory gesture of asking her to play cards.

"I'm not allowed to play with really disturbed people," she said.

He watched the ballgame on Monday, what he could see of it. Paula wasn't there. When it was over, he sat in one of the brown chairs for the rest of the day. On Tuesday Paula asked him if he wanted to play. He said he did.

"I had a cousin played for the Mets," she said.

"Yeh?"

"U-huh ... You ever play?"

"Yeh. Some ..."

"You good?"

"Not bad ... Played in the minors for a couple of years."

"What happened?"

"Oh ..." He flexed his right arm at the elbow. "Bone chips. Bad elbow ..."

"That why you gave up?"

He looked at her but didn't answer.

"How old are you?" she said.

"Thirty ... six. Seven maybe." He felt a moment of panic; he couldn't remember how old he was.

"Maybe we can fix it so's you can play."

"Okay."

"... If you're not too disturbed."

She waited for a response. He looked at the floor and mumbled. She lifted his chin with her index finger.

"I can't hear you," she said.

"... No."

"No what?"

"No I'm not too ... disturbed ..."

"You sure? I mean I don't want to let you outside and have you try to *kill* yourself." She stuck her tongue out and made that funny face. "Looks bad on my record."

He smiled weakly.

The next day she took him outside at ten o'clock.

"This is against the rules," she said, as she unlocked the door.

It was the first time he'd been outside since he'd arrived. He had no idea how long that had been. They walked across the lawn to the makeshift diamond. White towels marked the three bases; home plate was an inverted bedpan. He played that day, running and throwing with some difficulty. They lobbed the ball up to the plate, but he couldn't hit it. He was tired when he got back to the Ward, but eager to play again.

"How'd I do?" he said.

"Not bad for a rookie. You'll get better ... You gotta believe."

"... Believe what?"

"That you'll get better. That's a Tug McGraw line ... The sixty-nine Mets."

"Oh ..."

His fingers gradually stopped fighting with themselves. The faint sounds of familiar voices began to fade. A timely hemorrhage seemed to cleanse his mind. He began to feel better. He started exercising; the first day he could do only two push-ups.

"What are you doing?" said the Commander.

"... Push-ups."

"Huh ... Not likely. You can't do push-ups."

"Watch me ... I can do anything."

"My head hurts," said the Commander.

"Stay away from the wall," said Bill.

Paula took him out to play every day, talking to him as they walked to the field and back.

"It works all by itself," she said.

He looked puzzled.

"... What does?"

"Life ... The trick is, you gotta show up every day. For life. You stop showin' up, Billy boy. Bad news ... Bad news."

She tapped her finger on his chest. He hated that.

"Get yourself a ticket and join the dance. You deserve to live. Remember that. You've got a chance, Bill. Most of these don't." She gestured toward the Ward. "Get out while you can. If you stay, you'll join the Recycling Program. We send 'em out with a bottle full of pills and wait at the door till they come back. It's a joke."

"How come you ... do this then?"

"Every once in a while somebody makes it. It's worth the wait."

Some weeks later he slid hard into second base and got into a shoving match with King Kong Keller, the grouchy giant from Ward 304. Paula watched from the sidelines, nodding her approval.

"Nice slide," she said, unlocking the Ward door.

"Took him right out, eh?"

"Yep. Big league play."

The next day she handed him the *Patient's Rights Handbook*, opened to page six:

> ... You cannot be held for treatment
> unless you have been informed of
> this in advance and have been told of
> your right to remain as a voluntary
> patient and of your right to go to
> court if you think you ought to be
> released. Staff must assist you in
> requesting a Writ of Habeus Corpus

from the Superior Court if you think
you should be released.

He read it slowly.

"... What's it mean?"

"It means you can go."

"... Where?" he said.

"Out. Away from here. Back into the world from whence you
came ... Back to life."

"I'm not ready," he said.

"Do it anyway ... You can get ready later. I've got a brother
owns a gas station. He's a baseball nut. You can start there."

She helped him request the Writ from Superior Court.

Doctor Eva noted that he appeared to be making satisfactory
progress. She was encouraged. The Commander complained
that his head often felt mushy.

The following Wednesday Bill hit a home run over the ten-
foot fence at the end of the yard.

"Nice hit," growled Keller.

"Routine," said Bill.

Stella died on Thursday, a white plastic chip wedged in her
throat. Father Pogo gave her the Last Rites, what he could
remember of them. His Latin was never very good anyway.
Matilda wept and tore at her blouse where the surgeon's
murderous scythe had removed her breast.

Soon after the Writ arrived, Paula helped him process it. He
packed his few belongings and waited.

"Time to go," she said, walking him to the door. There were
tears in her eyes. "Walk tall." She embraced him and unlocked
the door.

"My pills?" he said.

"You haven't had anything stronger than aspirin for weeks."

The Commander squeezed his head with both hands.

"Bring on them hookers," said Worker.

"I ... I'm afraid," said Bill.

"Welcome to the human race," said Paula. "Everybody's
afraid." She pushed him outside and closed the door.

"Oh, Tex honey," said Matilda. "Oh, Tex ..."

The Commander stood at the window and cried.

Bill had butterflies in his stomach all day. It wasn't just the game; he'd been thinking about Chris and Maggie. Of course Gloria hadn't run off to Montana. She'd taken the kids and gone to her parents' house. Why hadn't he thought of that? The Reseda Indians. God ... it seemed so obvious. He resisted the impulse to try to contact them immediately. He had waited a long time; he could wait a little longer.

He got up early and drove to Lawrence Park, sat in the stands near the announcer's booth and looked at the ads on the outfield fence. One of the bull pen pastimes was trying to memorize them.

"*Close* your eyes, Kaz. The purpose of this is to see how many things you can remember with*out* looking ..."

"They're closed, Mahoney. I swear, man."

"Your eyelids flutter."

"I got nervous eyelids."

"I *seen* ya peekin'," said Keane.

"Turn your head the other way," said Bill.

"I'll look down," said Kaz.

"Turn your head."

"Don't you trust me?"

"... Of course not."

"I don't wanna play if you don't trust me, Bill."

"Okay ... look down."

"... Jameson Plumbing, Moss and Craig, North American Van Lines ... eh ... gimme a hint."

"Honk-honk."

"... Baldwin Buick."

"Ya peekin'," said Keane.

"I don't have eyes in the top of my *head*, Vin. Jesus ..."

No one managed to memorize them all. Buba came closest; he only missed True Value Hardware.

Bill walked out to the mound and looked in toward the plate. The batting cage was off to one side, ready to be rolled out for batting practice. Out of the corner of his eye he thought he saw a tall figure in Marine fatigues, standing near the dugout, but when he looked there was no one. He smiled and looked back at the sea of empty blue seats. By early evening the stands would be teeming with fans.

The man in the white Panama hat would be there; he was at all the home games, faithful as a terrier. Bill knew it was unfinished business. More unfinished business. Some day he'd have to deal with it.

Thomas arrived in Lodi shortly after Bill did. Just took a seat in the stands and dealt with the missing years by ignoring them. That was his way. Never said how he found out or how he got there.

He called from time to time, conducted mostly one-sided conversations laced with prewar bromides and thinly disguised advice. Each time he mentioned his age: *I'm seventy-five years old.* A play for sympathy? Bill didn't think so; that wasn't like Thomas. There was something else.

He smoothed the dirt in front of the rubber with the toe of his loafer. Habit. A game of habits. Superstitions. Gunner always tapped the outside edge of the plate with his bat. Pedro made the sign of the cross on his heart with his thumb; he didn't think anyone noticed. Loony had a Miraculous Medal taped on the inside of his shin guard. Tenor carried his bat to the plate holding the barrel end. Ever since that good outing in Visalia, Kaz always ate chicken the day he was due to start. Bill spent a lot of time manicuring the mound, filling in the divots created by opposing pitchers. He got into the habit of bouncing the resin bag in the palm of his hand. Twice. Always twice. Under the guise of picking stray rocks off the field, Chewy traced a small M on the ground in front of his fielding position. You could always find J.C. in the same spot near the dugout steps when things were going good.

Baseball ... Jesus ... He loved the game. Always had. He could feel in its rhythms a sense of grace and joy he found nowhere else. Blessed is the Game, he thought. Blessed is the Game that

brings joy to so many ... But what was it? The nine men? Was
nine a magic number? The ball? The diamond? Or was the game
itself simply a celebration, a commemoration of some ancient
truth long forgotten, a ritual of life? Its roots were sunk in his
soul, nourished by the hot dogs and rhubarbs of summer,
watered by boisterous fans. Baseball ... It had saved his life; he
knew that ...

They were at the ball park at five o'clock. Sly didn't have
much to say in the locker room. Soprano would start at
shortstop. He went over the signs and the new bunt coverage.
"Let's win one for the Skipper," he said.
"... I don't believe he said that," said Gunner.
"Believe, Gunner. Believe," said Bill.

It was standing room only; the overflow crowd lined the
fences down the right- and left-field lines. Priscilla Penwick
pumped out the National Anthem with more than the usual
number of klinkers. Perhaps she was nervous, too. At least the
Dodgers had live music. The Giants had the Mormon Taber-
nacle Choir. On record.
Danny couldn't seem to settle down and find the plate with
any consistency. He gave up five walks in the first four innings.
The Dodgers were lucky to be down only two-zip starting the
fifth. Simpson looked like he'd been saving his best stuff for the
play-offs. He retired the first nine Dodgers he faced. He gave
up a walk and a scratch single in the fourth, but the Dodgers
couldn't score.
Sosa was aboard on an error in the fifth. Coleman rapped a
clean single to left, but a good throw from the outfield forced
Sosa to stop at second. Soapy checked the signs before he
stepped into the batter's box. Simpson came inside with a
fastball that sounded like a pistol shot when it popped the
catcher's mitt. Soapy didn't move a muscle, though the pitch
couldn't have been more than a few inches from his nose.
"Holy fuck," said Kaz. "Did you *see* that?"
"Close," said Bill. "Very close."
Loony yelled something at Simpson from the dugout. Soapy
stepped out and checked the signs again. The next pitch was
a low fastball. Soapy slid his hands up the bat and pushed the

ball down the first-base line. The Giants had rotated their bunt coverage to the left, giving Simpson the right-side responsibility. Soapy, Simpson and the ball all got halfway down the first-base line at the same time. Simpson reached for the ball, still moving just inside the chalk, just as Soapy's foot came down. Right on his hand. Soapy turned his ankle and went sprawling. Simpson grabbed his hand and howled. The Giant catcher sped down the line, picked up the ball and tagged Soapy. He turned to see if there was another play. Sosa had already crossed the plate; Coleman was streaking home. The catcher raced for the plate and dove just as Coleman slid ...

Safe! barked the ump, barely visible in a mushroom cloud of dust.

The Dodger dugout emptied as Simpson went after Soapy. Then came the Giants, closely followed by the Dodger bull pen. Bill jumped on the first Giant uniform he came to and wrestled a muscular young man to the ground. They rolled around for several seconds before either could get up. Then they stood glaring at each other. Sly and Milo Kinsolving, the Giant manager, rushed around trying to break it up. Harry got so excited he sprayed everyone around him with popcorn.

It was over in a few minutes, the way most baseball fights are, the pushing and shoving replaced by pointed fingers and similar threats. Soapy and Simpson had to leave the game; Soapy with a sprained ankle, Simpson with a gash on his pitching hand.

Doc Hardin snapped a Cold Pac open and wrapped it around Soapy's ankle.

"All *right*," said Tenor, pounding Soapy on the back. "Way to go down the *line*."

"No problem, eh?" said Loony.

No one asked if he did it on purpose. Soapy wasn't even sure. But he knew he was through being shy at the plate.

The man in the white Panama hat was standing, waving his cane. Without thinking, Bill waved back.

"Holy fuck," said Kaz, brushing off his uniform. "A guy could get *killed* out there. Some of those guys were serious."

Possum Darville got the relief call for the Giants. Due to the injury to Simpson, he'd have as much time as he needed to warm up. Fans lined up at the snack bar. Alice could have used three more hands. The stands buzzed with excitement. Olde Tymers judged the fight in relation to others they had seen. Sly sent word for Buba to get loose. Buba put on his meanest scowl and started to warm up.

Darville dusted Chewy with the first pitch. The home plate umpire called a conference with both managers. Milo went out to talk to his pitcher. Sly told the Dodgers he didn't need to tell 'em to cool down. Just suck it up and play some ball.

"Blow the charge," shouted Dean.

Harry got up and tootled through his fist.

"Doodle da doot a dooooooooooo ..."

The stands rocked with *CHARGE!*

The Dodgers scored no more that inning. By the time Nesbitt got back on the mound, he had lost what little stuff he had. He walked the first batter on four straight pitches. The second hitter slapped a single up the middle. Sly came out with the hook. Buba lumbered in like a black semi and hurried through his eight warm-ups. Then struck out the next three Giants.

It was still tied going into the ninth. Lindell relieved Buba with two out in the eighth. His hard sliders set the Giants down in order in the top of the ninth.

Coleman led off the Dodger half with a strike-out. Malducci beat out a high bouncer over the mound. Duffy went in to run for him. Harry punched out the bottom of his popcorn bucket and used it as a megaphone:

"Doodle da dooot a dooooo ..."

CHARGE!

Duffy tried to steal on the first pitch. The Giants figured he'd be going and pitched out. The throw beat him to second, but Duffy gave the shortstop a high left leg, then took it away and caught the corner of the bag with his right toe.

Safe! was the call.

Milo charged onto the field and jawed with the ump, but the decision stood. Then the Giants walked Klinger to set up the double play.

"Bad move," said Harry.

Dean indicated maybe.

Chewy took the first two pitches, both balls. He looked down at Sly, expecting the take sign. ... Tweak, pull, rub, touch ... Hit away ... Possum, also expecting the take to be on, came with a fat pitch. Chewy drilled it between third and short. Sly was windmilling his right arm and jumping up and down as Duffy sped by, pushing hard off the inside of the bag and heading home. The Giant catcher moved a few feet up the line and got ready to block the plate. Duffy arrived a fraction of a second before the ball. He lowered his shoulder, hit the Giant catcher and bounced back. But the collision was enough to allow the ball to skip through to the backstop. Duffy crawled to the plate and gave it five. The Dodgers poured onto the field. Duffy tried to protect his dislocated shoulder from the mob of backslappers. Bill and Kaz did a little dance in the bull pen. Priscilla played "Give My Regards to Broadway" on the Lawrence Park portable organ. It was one of her favorites.

Bill answered the phone when it rang later that night. He thought it might be Alice.

"Good game," said a familiar voice.

"Yeh ..." said Bill. He felt his throat muscles tighten.

"You looked good," said Thomas.

"Me? .... I didn't do anything."

"The way you went after 'em."

"The fight?" said Bill.

"Yeh."

Bill fumbled a cigarette out of the pack and lit it. His hands were shaking.

"... The fight," he said.

"It was somethin'," said Thomas.

"Jesus ..."

"You were right in it," said Thomas.

"That was it, eh? The fight? ... Me in the middle sluggin' it out. That mean I got balls now? I'm okay now? ... Finally?"

Bill clenched the fist that held his cigarette and sent a shower of sparks to the rug. Gunner gingerly extinguished them with the toe of his slipper.

"... I didn't say anything about havin' ba ..."

"Yes, you did. You don't hear yourself. You been sayin' it for thirty goddam years."

"What I said was ..."

"I *heard you*," Bill snapped. "I always heard you ... I'm tired of listenin'. Tired."

Neither spoke for a few moments.

"Hell's bells," said Thomas.

Bill could hear himself breathing into the mouthpiece. He felt sick inside. He looked at the crushed cigarette in his hand and leaned back against the headboard.

"... You want me to hang up?" said Thomas. The voice was dry, reedy, an old man's voice.

Bill bit his lower lip and shook his head.

"Do you?" said Thomas.

"No," said Bill. His heart was racing. He did not notice the tears on his face. "... You know what I want?"

"No."

Bill took a deep breath.

"... I want you to love me."

The few seconds silence seemed much longer.

"You think I came to Lodi for the scenery? ... You looked outside lately?" He chuckled softly, as if he had just remembered something.

Bill gripped the receiver so tightly that it squeaked.

"Say it," he said.

"... You know that."

"Say it," said Bill.

"... I love you," he said quietly. "I always loved you."

Bill ran his fingertips over his face. He felt the tears and discovered that he was smiling. He lit another cigarette.

"Jesus ..." he said. "Like pullin' teeth."

Thomas cleared his throat.

"Season's almost over," he offered.

"Yeh," said Bill. "But there's always next season."

"You gonna take the Giants?"

"You can bet the farm on it."

"... You know I'm seventy-five years old."

"I know."

"That's old. Not many more seasons left."

"Take care of yourself and you'll probably last another twenty."

"Huh ... Who needs it?"

"Yeh," said Bill, but the thought saddened him.

"... Maybe we could get together for dinner sometime."

"Very possible," said Bill.

"On me," said Thomas.

"Bring lotsa money. I'm a big eater."

"Baloney. I know you. You eat like a bird ... Well, I guess I ...."

"Dad?"

"Yeh?"

"... I love you. Whatever happened before is ... is over. Done."

Thomas coughed noisily and mumbled something Bill could not hear. Then he said good-bye quickly and hung up. Bill listened to the buzz in his ears for a few seconds.

"So long, Dad," he said, before he hung up.

John Euless Park in Fresno had the same seating capacity and outfield dimensions as the Dodger home field in Lodi. There was a WELCOME sign over the ticket-taker turnstile, but that was for the fans. Dodger haters turned out in droves, fueled by tales of treachery detailed at great length in the Fresno papers.

Keane got the start for the Dodgers, but he wasn't sharp. The Giants got a run in the first when Malducci ran into the right-field fence and knocked himself out. By the time Pedro could run the ball down, the Giants had their first inside-the-park home run of the year. Coleman went in to replace him.

Mike Macefield, the Giant starter, baffled the Dodgers with his junky assortment of forkballs, palmballs and slow curves. Despite repeated admonitions from Sly to suck it up and be patient at the plate, the Dodger hitters showed little inclination to wait for a decent pitch. In the fourth inning, Gunner swung at a pitch that bounced a foot in front of the plate.

"Read the spin," yelled Sly, throwing his hat against the dugout wall.

Keane made it to the fifth inning before he gave up back-to-back home runs and got an early trip to the showers. Newsy toiled for a lackluster inning and gave up two more runs.

"I'm ready," said Bill fidgeting in the bull pen.

"They're savin' you," said Kaz.

"For what?"

"Tomorrow."

"Yeh?"

"Yep. You and me. Beauty and the Beast ..."

"I won't ask which is which," said Bill.

"That's because you already know the answer, you ugly sucker."

Lindell lasted an inning. Buba got the last of the shelling. Hostility in the stands reached a fever pitch in the late innings. The final disgrace was 11-0.

"Lucky eleven," said Bill.

The Giants were still stealing bases in the eighth inning. Sly stopped throwing his cap sometime after the sixth. He sat in the corner of the dugout and simmered for the rest of the game.

"Just like the Giants to rub it in," said Kaz.

"God will punish them," said Bill.

"The only thing I hate worse than a Giant is two Giants ... Giants are no good, worthless, prick, asshole, cocksuckers ..."

"Amen ..." said Bill.

The silent Dodgers piled aboard the old huffnpuff and prepared to head north. Sly stood up in the front of the bus to say a few words.

"Forget it," he said. "It's done. We got it out of our system ... Now we're headin' home and I don't have to tell you guys ..."

Chumley blasted out of the parking lot in midsentence. Sly stumbled toward the back of the bus and almost fell down.

"God*damit*," he sputtered.

Chumley continued through the gears, heading along North Blackstone toward the freeway as if he had not heard. Doc Hardin tittered nervously. Chumley could hardly see at night; the lights all looked like Fourth of July sparklers.

Gunner answered the phone at noon the next day.

"It's Tits," he whispered, holding his hand over the receiver. Bill took the phone.

"It's your friendly snack bar person," she said brightly.

"Hi, friendly person."
"How are you?"
"Eh .... good. You?"
"Nervous," she said.
"Yeh?"
"Big game tonight."
"I heard," he said. "We're gonna win."
"I know ... but it's so *busy*. I hardly get to watch."
"Listen."
"To what?"
"Us. We'll play real loud."
She giggled.
"Will you be busy ... after the game?" he said.
"Not for long."
"How about some pie and coffee. Peach pie ..."
"Ummmmm ... my favorite. I'll be ready."
"Yeh," he said. "I'll be ready, too."
"Ciao."
Gunner rubbed his hands together.
"I'm bettin' both farms on some action tonight," he said.
"And the tractors," said Bill. "Don't forget the tractors."

Doc Hardin taped Soapy's ankle before the game.
"What do you think?" said Sly.
Soapy tested it.
"Feels good," he said.
"Can you play?"
Soapy grinned and did a few jumping jacks.
"Never felt better," he said.
Sly filled in the rest of the lineup card, then banged on the side of a locker.
"Okay, listen up," he said. "I don't have to tell you guys how important this game is. There's no tomorrow. A hundred and thirty-two games and it comes down to this. One game ... I want you to suck it up and play some ball out there tonight. Kaz will start. Mahoney, you got a few days rest. If we need you, I expect you to come in and do a job for us ... Coleman, you're gonna start in right ..."
"Aww, Coach," said Malducci.

"You'll pinch-hit," said Sly. "I don't want you tearin' up any walls tonight ... Now the Skipper wanted this one real bad. Real bad ..." He glanced reverently at the ceiling. "Let's go kill them goddam Giants."

The Dodgers exploded with cheers and tumbled out onto the field.

It looked like the whole town had turned out for the final game. The stands were swarming with kids wearing blue Dodger caps. Harry was wearing his usual bright Hawaiian shirt. The man in the white Panama hat had exchanged his khaki windbreaker for a blue warm-up jacket. He waved his cane as Bill did his jogging in the outfield. Bill waved back. He stopped to watch Kaz warm up.

"Piece of cake," said Bill.

"Ducks on a pond," said Kaz. "Just mow 'em down."

"Our National Anthem," boomed the P.A. announcer, "played on the Lawrence Park organ by Miss Priscilla Penwick."

Ooo say can you seeee, by ...

Some three thousand voices drifted up in the warm twilight air.

Bill felt a tingle at the back of his neck. This was it. There was no tomorrow. Maybe that was the secret ... Maybe it was just a series of todays that stretched from that two-story house in Chatsworth to a baseball diamond in Lodi. Yeh, diamonds are trumps. Hallowed ground ... the hits, the runs, the errors of Time. All part of the Game. Bill shook his head and smiled.

Play ball!

Kaz purred along like a well-oiled machine through the first six; two scratch hits, a walk, four strike-outs. He looked like he could go on forever. Gunner tripled in the second, but they couldn't get him home.

It was a seventh-inning line drive off his ankle that took Kaz out of the game. Bill got the call. Kaz was still rubbing his ankle when he got to the mound.

"Holy fuck," said Kaz.

"You done good," said Bill.

"Fucker hurts."

"Pain's part of the deal," said Bill.

"Easy for you to say."

Kaz handed him the ball and limped off the field. The fans rose in unison and gave him a standing ovation. He tipped his cap.

Bill began the slow process of getting loose. The Giants got on him right away.

"It's the old *man*."

"Hey, Pops, ain't it past your bedtime?"

"Bring in the wheelchair."

What surprised Bill was that his arm didn't hurt. Even the first few pitches, which always hurt, were fluid and painless. He took only a few minutes and indicated that he was ready. Sly came out to the mound.

"You sure you're ready?"

"Yeh."

"You can take as long as you want."

"I know. I'm ready."

"Okay ... You got a man on first. No outs. Go at 'em, kid."

He straddled the rubber and looked in to get the sign. Loony went through the normal sequence with a man on base. Bill came set, glanced at first, looked to the plate, then fired to Gunner with his best pick-off move. The Giant runner was caught flat-footed. Gunner slapped him with a high tag that almost knocked him down.

"Watch it," growled the runner.

"You're out, speedy," said Gunner. "Take a seat."

The fans loved it.

"Ah, shades of Gotham," said Harry.

"Forget Gotham," said Dean.

Harry tootled his makeshift bugle.

CHARGE!

Bill got the sign, went into his windup and came with a fastball. He knew it wasn't going to be low and away as soon as he released it. It looked too fat, belt high. But by the time it got to the batter, it was shoulder high and still rising. The batter swung late, a foot under it, badly misjudging the speed and location. It popped like a firecracker in Loony's mitt. He took it out of his glove, looked at it and fired it back to Bill.

"All *right*," said Tenor. "Show 'em some *heat*."

The second pitch was a duplicate. The batter looked bewildered. Loony showed him the ball before he tossed it back to Bill.

"Here it is," he said. "Case you didn't see it."

"Fuck off," snapped the batter.

Bill was as surprised as anyone. It was all there again. The Heater. The Hummer. The Dark One. The high-rising fastball, red cotton stitches in the wind, taking off as it approached the plate. He didn't seem to be doing anything special. Just a normal windup. Normal delivery ... And sheer, overpowering speed. Throwin' BBs, the Olde Tymers said. Asp'rins ... Energy from some unseen source seemed to speed the ball on its way, as if generations of pitchers gathered in spirit at the mound to add their substantial talents to the dwindling skills of one of their own ... Bill felt so good he wanted to laugh out loud.

"Holy *fuck*," said Kaz. "Did you *see* that? Mahoney can't *throw* that hard."

"I know," said Sly, not taking his eyes off the mound.

The third pitch was in Loony's mitt before the batter could react.

"Oh, my God," said Harry, wiping the top of his head with a large white handkerchief. "Oh, my God."

"We're *in*," yelled Dean.

"Two more innings," said Harry.

"Forget it ... Light the cigar. We're home free."

The last Giant batter in the inning waved weakly at three blazing fastballs and the side was retired. Loony took off his glove and looked at his swollen hand.

"No problem, eh?" said Gunner.

"No problem," said Loony, rolling his eyes. "You just been savin' it for the big one, eh Pops?"

"Yeh," said Bill. "Why waste it." He could hardly wait to get back out on the mound.

Though the Dodgers got two hits, they failed to score. Bill jogged out to the mound and gave a repeat performance. He seemed to get stronger with each pitch. He spotted the ball at the knees, inside, outside, anywhere he wanted. He just had to think it and it was done.

Coleman led off the home half of the eighth with a pop-up to the catcher. Soapy got a base hit down the line. He didn't even slow down rounding first. The Giant left fielder hesitated for a split second before he threw. That was enough for Soapy to make it into second with a hard slide. Chewy struck out. Tenor lashed a single to left. Soapy ran through Sly's stop sign at third and headed home. Pedro was on the first-base side of home plate frantically giving him the slide sign. He slid hard. The throw was high, the tag late. The catcher landed on top of him and split his lip with a well-aimed elbow. Soapy got to his feet, jogged to the dugout and received high fives from his jubilant teammates.

Priscilla played "You Must Have Been a Beautiful Baby." She loved the old tunes.

The one run was all the Dodgers could manage.

"Okay, let's hold 'em," said Sly. He stood near the dugout steps where J.C. used to stand when things were going good. "Suck it up out there."

Bill lingered through his eight warm-ups. Loony shuffled out to the mound.

"This is it, Pops." He handed Bill the ball and headed back to the plate.

Bill nodded. This was it.

The crowd was quiet as he went into his windup. He kicked his leg high, stepped forward and unwound like a coiled spring. ... *Pah!* ... The echo was smothered in the crowd noise. Everyone was standing and cheering. The ball was a blur as he flicked it home. This was it. He knew it. It was just for tonight. He knew that, too, but it didn't make any difference. ... He curled his fingers around the ball and felt the red cotton stitches on his fingertips. He smiled. He knew he had a chance. Somehow. He knew it.

ACKNOWLEDGMENTS

He likes to drink, and drink, and drink, / The thing he likes to drink / Is ink. The ink he likes to drink is pink.

... My shoe is off / My feet are cold ...

... My hat is old / My teeth are gold / I have a bird / I like to hold ...

... My hat is old / My teeth are gold / And now / My story / Is all told ...

From *THE SNEETCHES AND OTHER STORIES* by Dr. Seuss. Copyright 1953, 1954, 1961 by Dr. Seuss. Reprinted by permission of Random House, Inc.

This Time It's Love ... Barbara Cartland. He remembered someone who read Barbara Cartland novels. ... The words burst from Rex, deep and low as if they were spoken in the extremity of pain. "Do understand," Fenella pleaded. "You've got to understand." "And if I don't?" He spoke the words harshly, then suddenly his hands went out towards her, taking her by the shoulders, drawing her nearer to him. "I loved you," he said. "I loved you more than I believed it possible to love any woman—and now this has happened. It isn't your fault and it isn't mine; Fate has been too strong for us ..." ... "Time has never counted in love," Rex answered seriously, as if a million men had not voiced the same sentiment before him. "Love either happens or it doesn't; you can't force it, you can't create it. Heaven knows what it is in reality!" "Isn't it wanting to give oneself completely to someone else?" Rex caught her in his arms. "Will you give yourself to me?" "I am yours." Their lips met and time for both of them stood still ...... She gripped her fingers together and knew already that Rex's power over her was strong. She ached now for the touch of his lips and the strength of his arms holding her. She longed to hear his voice, low and broken, calling her name. She gave a little sigh and realized that the kettle was boiling. As she made the tea she found herself whispering his name aloud: "Rex! Rex!" ...He spoke the last words in such a lover-like way that Fenella glanced up apprehensively. Elaine, fortunately, was not in the room, having gone upstairs after dinner. Sir Nicholas and Moo were in the corner playing Corinthian bagatelle which Rex had brought back that afternoon from his home and not yet taken down to camp. This intimacy with Rex was too dangerous, she was afraid it would betray them. And yet she found it hard to ignore him even for a moment when he was in the room with her. ... "There are no words to describe anything that really matters," said Rex sweepingly, "just as there are no words to express love or hatred, happiness or sorrow. One can only feel such things." ... "This is mad," she protested. "The others will miss us." ... "Does it matter?" he asked. "Does anything matter except this?" ... He kissed her and she felt a flame run searingly through her. She trembled. She could not withstand him. ... She said nothing. Nick looked at her but did not speak and she knew that he was neither glad nor surprised to see her; he was past any feeling save numbness and despair ...

From *THIS TIME IT'S LOVE* by Barbara Cartland with permission of Berkley Publishing. Copyright 1977 by Barbara Cartland.